Rule Of Thumb

Theodosia Palmer

The Pentland Press Limited
Edinburgh • Cambridge • Durham • USA

© Theodosia Palmer 1998

First published in 1998 by
The Pentland Press Ltd.
1 Hutton Close
South Church
Bishop Auckland
Durham

All rights reserved.
Unauthorised duplication
contravenes existing laws.

British Library Cataloguing in Publication Data.
A Catalogue record for this book is available
from the British Library.

ISBN 1 85821 595 1

07618929

Typeset by CBS, Felixstowe, Suffolk
Printed and bound by Antony Rowe Ltd., Chippenham

To my husband
for his support
in this venture

CHAPTER ONE

Doctor Bernard Dawes stretched his thin, long legs out in front of him, as he sat before a roaring fire in his parlour. He rested his stockinged feet upon the brass fender. In the grate the glowing sea coal spluttered and cracked, filling the room with a pungent warmth. He sipped his whisky and water and then putting his glass upon the table, took up a book on medicine that he had been consulting for the last half an hour. It had been a busy day for him with three out of the way visits made, and a few cases in surgery with obscure ailments that he had decided to read up on. He was not yet thirty years old and this was his first lone practice. He was aware of the dangers of returning seamen from foreign lands but as yet he had found nothing to alarm him unduly. It was a small port though, and he knew that inexperience in medicine could prove a pitfall. That was why he now diligently applied himself to the text before him, not to ascertain diseases he had seen, but to eliminate the possibility of them being similar, though more serious, afflictions. He had found the majority of the men from the town hard working, hard drinking, and rough, but he liked them, recognising their other qualities. Open-faced honesty, tenacity, and comradeship in adversity. He settled himself down more comfortably into the deep cushions of the chair and let the heat of the room wrap him in its cosiness after the cold of the day. A few moments later the knocker banged. The thunderous tones penetrated his sleepy frame with a vibrant shock and his feet fell off the fender onto the fur rug on the hearth. Seconds later his housekeeper Miss Haddon entered the room.

'What is it?' he asked, putting his book upon the table and slipping his feet back into his stout shoes.

'It's Marie Deane, Doctor. She's in labour and things are not well. They have called on Mother Booth,' Miss Haddon went on apologetically. 'Mother Booth says to tell you that the baby is the "wrong road about" and born too soon. She is afraid it will be stillborn and asks will you shift yourself and come and give a hand with the delivery.'

Rule Of Thumb

Doctor Dawes gave a little smile as he heard this. He knew Mother Booth meant no disrespect. It was the way here to give no frills to everyday conversation, but his heart lurched with sickening alarm as he searched about for his outside boots which he had flung under the sideboard. Having found and laced them he went into his surgery for his instrument case and checked over the contents. Miss Haddon helped him into his heavy overcoat and opened the door. He stepped out of the door into the little forecourt of cobbles and shells and shivered. It was a little after ten o'clock on February 3rd 1808. Already anxiety was gnawing at him. He knew why the baby had come too soon! It was all the lifting she had to do at the Cat and Garter, the tavern which she kept down by the quayside. Marie Deane was a wide-hipped woman who could have had a dozen children without any difficulty at all, and a breech birth was the last sort of delivery he had expected.

'Just my luck,' he said grimly to himself, as he hurried down the narrow cobbled street that led into a dark and foul-smelling alley. As he picked his way amongst decaying garbage and rag-litter, he went over in his mind all he knew of complicated births. He knew from the talk he had heard amongst his patients, that Mother Booth was a competent midwife. She only called on a doctor's services when delivery was less than straightforward and beyond her skills. A woman of Mother Booth's age and experience was sure to have met up with a breech birth before, so what had made her call for him this night? Was the child already dead? Was he being brought in for consultation to share the burden of a stillborn child? Was the mother dying? Was the cord around the baby's neck? Well, he thought to himself, he would soon know.

He reached the end of the alley and saw the Cat and Garter. The front of the tavern was on the harbour walk facing a low and monotonous dockyard wall, slippery with green weed and slime. As the doctor approached he could see by the lights of the tavern the oily sheen of the sea and the black shapes of the wharves, slips, and bulwarks, by the shore. There was still a crowd of sea-men and locals in the tavern when the doctor entered. They were laughing and joking amongst themselves, taking the opportunity to wet the baby's head when it arrived, for they had been expecting to hear its cry for over two hours. A roar went up from them as the young doctor stepped through the doors and into the wainscotted room. Doctor Dawes was somewhat surprised by the look of the tavern. It was reasonably clean and the wooden walls and low oaken beams, together with the long tables and benches and settles, gave the room a warm and friendly atmosphere. It had not always been a tavern. Originally, it had been a private house owned by a merchant of means, hence it was more solidly built than some taverns and with interesting additions, wooden postings and carvings at the door archings and ornate fastenings of the heavy studded doors. The doctor took all this in at a glance as the customers crowded forward, slapping him on the back and wishing him all haste.

'Here's the babby's father!' crowed one, pushing Everard Deane into the limelight. 'See, he's a full-blown Dadda afore we leave here tonight.'

Doctor Dawes took hold of Everard Deane's proffered hand. 'I thought you were still away.'

'I came back yesterday. What do I find? My son can't wait to be born.'

'Good God, man,' groaned the doctor. 'Don't tell me your wife has been in labour since yesterday?'

'She has that! And making heavy weather of it too!'

'I should have been sent for before this,' replied Doctor Dawes, now somewhat annoyed and anxious to make it clear in front of the men present that if something did go amiss it had been intensified by their neglect to send for him sooner.

'Well, you go on through to the kitchen,' urged Everard Deane. 'Mother Booth will show you up to Marie's room.'

Mother Booth was indeed busy in the kitchen. 'She's bad, doctor,' she warned as she set a huge copper kettle down onto the hot, glowing coals, pushing the embers close with the coalrake.

'So I believe,' he answered sternly as he eyed her critically.

She was an elderly woman, heavy in the hips, flat-chested, her face a muddy-grey as was her hair. A screw of curl-paper bobbed at each side of her head which made him think that she too had been preparing for her bed when brought to Marie's side.

'It's a breech, Doctor. And that awkward . . .' She shook her head sadly. The doctor did not answer but looked about him with a preoccupied air.

'Well, get along up to her, sir!' Mother Booth cried out impatiently, the lighted lamp in her hand. The light revealed a narrow passage terminating in a narrow staircase. No carpet covered the floor and the grey and red tiles were cracked with age. The doctor fumbled his way up the rickety back stairs and entered the room where his patient lay. The bedstead was heavily carved and had once graced a Captain's cabin, but now spoke of neglect, the heavy drapes around it, almost of the thickness of carpeting, appeared laden with dust. Not the best of hangings for a birth couch, he thought grimly as he approached his pale and sweating patient.

'How long have you been like this?' he asked her as he examined her gently.

'A long time. Too long,' she whispered faintly.

'You should have had help before,' he chided as Mother Booth came into the room. She had lit the landing with the lamp and had carried up water and cloths and towels. 'The baby is in a very bad position. Take hold of her whilst I try to manipulate the baby to a better position. If you wish to scream, do so, you will not hinder me, and may help yourself.'

Mother Booth held Marie tight as she watched the doctor deftly turn the child still within its mother. Sweat poured from his head and she wiped it with one of the cloths. Then she patted Marie's head with a cold cloth and placed it over her eyes.

'Is it time?'

'It is.' He slipped his fingers round the baby's head and pulled down sharply. The shoulders came almost immediately as the mother slipped into a deep faint.

'There now,' crowed Mother Booth, as the mother began to arrive at a level of consciousness again. 'It is all over my pet. You have a lovely boy!'

Doctor Dawes felt rather anxious as he lifted the baby free from his mother and began to tie the umbilical cord. The baby was very still and white and he feared that he might be dead.

'He'll be alright now,' assured Mother Booth. 'Give him to me.' She stretched out her hands to receive the small, still baby. 'He'll stir soon enough. Warm and cold water dipping till he yells. Always done the same with breeches. Never fails! Makes 'em crammed, but wakes the blood.'

Doctor Dawes let her get on with her cure. Surely, the child could fare no worse and some good may come of it. He turned his attention to the mother only to find that she was bleeding heavily, large clots emerging freely from the vagina onto the cloths on the bed. He cleared the clots away and the flow eased. He tried packing the vagina with a clean cloth and massaging her abdomen to get the uterus to contract. The blood still continued to flow. He took out the packing, washed his hands with a solution, then thrust one hand into the enlarged vagina and massaged the uterus internally. The blood ran over his wrist and dripped down into the chamberpot ensconced in the flocks of the mattress. 'God,' he thought in despair. 'Suppose the child lives and the mother dies!' Then, to his relief, he felt the first weak contraction, then another and another. The blood began to ease and he withdrew his hand but continued kneading the abdomen until the uterus felt firm and the bleeding had stopped.

Marie Deane was bathed in sweat and so was the doctor. He didn't care for himself, only for his patient to survive. He looked at the clock on the stone mantlepiece. It was thirty minutes after one o'clock. He washed his hands in the basin of cold water and dried them. He wrote the birth time in his booklet, then he approached the bed and tidied Marie as best he could knowing that Mother Booth would be back to make Marie comfortable. Marie stirred on the crumpled bed and breathed a deep sigh.

'Is it all over?' she asked, looking into his face.

'It is. Your son and heir is born. I hope there will be no others, for your sake,' he added tersely.

'Aye, indeed, sir. He's been a thorn in my side for the past month or two. I'm heartily glad to have him kicking on the outside at last.'

The doctor felt a twinge of alarm and he thought, 'I wonder if he is kicking?' He prayed fervently and silently as he heard the slow and laboured footsteps on the stair. Mother Booth entered the room. In her arms was the newborn baby, oiled and wrapped tightly in his first swaddlings, the baby born, born three weeks before his time, the boy Marie and Everard Deane were to call Alexander. As Mother Booth laid the bundle into the cradle beside the bed, for Marie was far too weak to take him into her arms, he began to howl.

'That howl is like music to my ears,' said the doctor smiling broadly.

'I'll bet he's disapproving of being brought in the chill of a February morn,' replied Mother Booth. 'I've honeyed him Doctor,' she went on, 'honey and water will feed him till the morrow.' She offered a sly and knowing wink towards the bed where Marie lay. The doctor said nothing. He was still inexperienced in the folklore medicines of the poor.

'I will see she gets plenty of goats cheese and eggs and milk. I doubt there will be a need of a wet nurse. There, what did I tell you?' she crowed as the child howled again. 'I told you he'd be crammed! There, there, didum!' she crooned, rocking the cradle gently with the toe of her shoe.

Marie opened her eyes and held out her arms. 'Give him to me,' she asked pleadingly. Mother Booth picked up the baby and lay him in the arms of his exhausted mother. He lay quiet and comfortable in her warmth and love. Mother Booth wiped her nose on the back of her thumb as she finished tucking in the bedclothes.

'Now, Mother Booth,' said the doctor, as he took a small bottle out of his case, 'three drops every three hours in a small amount of water. Can I depend on you to do that?'

'Indeed you can!' Her reply was full of indignation that she should fail in her duty. He put up his hand and placed the bottle on a small table by the window.

Rule Of Thumb

'I shall call again later today. Ask for your drops, Marie, if they are not given. Is it possible for her to be given clean clothing and bedding?'

'Certainly, sir. I will see to all that myself. I will indeed!'

'Things have turned out better than expected. Thank you for your help, Mother Booth and you, Marie, you were a brave lady.'

The brave lady permitted a large tear to trickle out of her left eye and down her cheek where it hung tremulously on her jawline. The doctor beat a hasty retreat, gathering up his things, and going downstairs two at a time now that Mother Booth had hung a lantern in the passage.

When he pushed his way through the door to the bar he found Everard Deane, alone, deliriously drunk, and rolling coins along the bar counter to the other side where they fell off with a clatter.

'You have a son,' said the doctor, laying a hand on the reeling man's shoulder.

'Aye, I've seen the boy.' He raised his tankard into the doctor's face. 'Thanks to you. I'll not forget you.'

'Or my fee, I hope,' replied the doctor with a drawn smile. He had heard from others of this carefree drifter who, only by chance, had been present for his son's entry into the world. 'Your wife needs sleep now. See that she gets it,' said the doctor as he lifted the latch of the door. 'Mind me now,' he admonished. 'Don't disturb your wife. I'll be back tomorrow.' He stepped out into the chilly air and heard the church clock strike twice. 'Two o'clock,' he groaned, gripping his bag and cane tightly and stretching out his legs as he walked swiftly towards his own home and his own clean and comfortable bed.

CHAPTER TWO

As Doctor Dawes made his way down the passage from Bellinger's Wharfe in the starlit nip of a February morn, Everard Deane, in the dim confines of the Cat and Garter, sank his head on his hands and wept bitterly. Sober, he had the soul of a bold adventurer but his frame was sparse, his energies intermittent. Sometimes he left Marie alone at the tavern for weeks at a time, wandering the country, loafing, tinkering, harvesting. Then suddenly he would be back again at any hour of the day, his face bearded, his pockets and belly empty. It was well that Marie had been a strong and healthy Irishwoman when he married her, with her eyes and hair as dark as a Spaniard and the fine features of a noble race. Everard Deane would have sorely tried the patience of a weaker woman, but she would take him in, fuss over him, and scoff at his lack of funds and clothing in need of repair or renewal. She would listen patiently to all his mis-happenstances, and the whys and wherefores as to how he did not come home with a fortune because he had been waylaid by brutes, tricked by sly acquaintances or been sorry for others less fortunate than himself.

Marie would just say, 'You'll do better next time, my love, you mark my words. I shouldn't wonder if you don't come home with a mule laden with money one day!' Then they would laugh, self-consciously, knowing in their own hearts that it was all a game. All Everard Deane ever brought back from his travels besides extra sewing and cleaning were the tales of his travels. These tales were retold in the firelight hours or under the mellow glow of the oil-lamps which swung from the blackened rafters of the tavern bar. He would sit for hours amongst the drinking wharfmen and sailors, his soft, lilting voice charming them to quiet, quicker than the sharp, bitter-sweet, tongue of Marie calling for less noise. When the men complained to Everard of Marie he would say, 'Well now, isn't that just why I married her? My Marie with her fine roguish spirit.'

'I like my spirit in a tankard,' one would jest. 'I like my spirits parsoned,' laughed another, and so they bantered and banged their pewters on the tables or the bar. 'Get along with you all,' retorted Everard, 'My Marie can keep you in your places. Better than a woman twice her age and four times as ugly. Woe betide the pot-valiant who takes it into his head to pinch her as she leans over to wipe off the tables or collects pots and pewters.'

'He's likely to get his lug pulled and a wet cloth over his face,' cried out one, his sea weathered face creased with mirth.

'He can depend on that at least,' cried out another.

The men laughed heartily, and looked round the company hoping that some fresh lad might rise to the bait but no one was foolhardy enough – Marie's reputation was widespread in the town and not many dared risk her quick tongue or her displeasure.

Mother Booth broke in on Everard Deane's morose reverie by knocking loudly on the wooden bar. 'A sup of porter for us both. Come, rouse yourself. Go and see your newborn son. And Marie. You've been in your cups long enough. Sober yourself before the doctor comes. He'll be after his fee!'

'Don't you wheedle at me Mother Booth. Help yourself!' He stumbled out of the room, up the wooden stairs, and to a little back room that would later be his son's room. He did not look into the room where his wife and child lay. He felt ashamed and thoroughly miserable. He should have been as blithe as a bird, but he felt as if he had a lump of date pudding in his throat! He lay on the bed, alone, defeated. He felt as if he had been on a long journey but it was not his usual homecoming. That son of his! To come so soon, before he was ready!'

Outside the back bedroom window a gull rested on the sill and mewed quietly. The noise of the lap of water against the piers nearby drifted in through a chink in the window sash, but Everard Deane was already asleep, snoring gently, fully dressed, on the top of the little white painted bed.

For many months the work of the tavern went smoothly. Marie, when recovered from Alexander's birth, was as loving and forgiving as always. Everard basked in her outspoken affections and took up the threads of domestic life once more. With her husband at home it gave her more time with her son whom she loved in the same passionate, suffocating way she loved his father. She had refused to let her son sleep in the back bedroom in the little white painted bed her husband had bought with the words, 'You, you will have him a man before he's a boy!' But she went to the shops and bought him all the little treasures dear to a little boy, even before he had cut his first tooth. She bought a sailing boat, and a battalion of soldiers on one occasion and excused herself with, 'He'll grow into them, so he will. 'Tis no nonsense to give a lad a boat with water so close to him, or a soldier with so many cockerels parading the town.'

Then, one day, Everard Deane got up early, almost before dawn and started packing a few things together. Marie looked on sleepily, and there he was, not speaking, but folding his clothes into a pack, a grim and resolute line to the angle of his chin.

'You off then?' Marie queried, her lips drawn tight to stop them from trembling. Her eyes were as moist as a spaniel's and had a look in them that would have turned to jelly the bones of other men, but the look was not strong enough to deter that driving force within Everard Deane. That fierce and longing ache for the open road, the fecundity of field and moor, stretching in unending line to the world's rim. An adventure lay for him over the next hill, and he was away from wife and child almost without a goodbye.

Marie then continued with the work of the tavern as before, often pouring out the ale with Alex asleep in the crook of one arm, his head on her shoulder.

In the years that followed the pattern of Everard Deane's comings and goings were unchanged. His son, healthy and strong, grew vigorously in the noise and squalor of warehouse and tavern, and before he was three years old he was collecting the empty mugs and pewters at the Cat and Garter. The men would coax him into singing sea shanties with them in a high-pitched infant voice. This brought him a copper or two from the foreign sailors who saw in this infant the image of their children so far away.

At six years old Alex began to station himself on the quayside. He carried baggage and ran messages. He held the heads of horses whilst the groom or box man wet his whistle as they waited at the Cat and Garter, and so gained money both ways. He carried drinking bowls out to numerous Dalmation dogs which ran alongside some of the carriages of the wealthy. He spoke prettily and minded his manners to anyone who wore a uniform, touched his forelock when he had no cap to doff, which was often. He had a tousled crop of red-gold curls above his winsome face which earned him many a coin from the ladies who fancied him a changeling with his pretty-boy face and plump limbs. They yearned in their hearts to take him to their own homes and away from the foul middens in which he roamed. The ladies whispered amongst themselves, surely he was a child stolen from some high born place, or washed ashore from some ship wrecked on that inhospitable coast? If these ladies had stepped inside the Cat and Garter they would have seen he could have been no other's child but Marie's, for they were stamped clear by the same brand. But they persisted in their fancies, if only to veil their own desires to make him their own. A winsome page or sturdy groom was the extent of their hopes for him, so when Marie heard of their highflown wishes her laugh rang up to the rafters, the sailors carried the tale out to sea, the drovers took the tale over the moorlands and into the villages, and Alex learned to give the milk-faced ladies a wide berth.

In the winter of 1814-15 Everard Deane returned home from Dorset where he had been since harvesting. He stayed at home until May Day when, despite all the protests from his wife and son, he joined the army and sailed for France almost at once.

On the day of departure they watched him go along the quayside, his step jaunty, a whistle on his lips. As he reached the corner he turned, gave a flourish of a salute, then still whistling he rounded the corner and was gone from their sight. Minutes later they could still hear the notes of an old Irish song drifting along the quay as he piped himself out of their lives.

On June 1815, after hours of murderous mayhem, he lay on the battlefield of Waterloo, his clothing tattered and stained, his pockets empty as always, his heart and restless spirit forever stilled.

CHAPTER THREE

In all truth, if asked, Alex could not have said he missed his father. His death seemed to him only a lengthened stay from home, and even when it did eventually dawn upon him that he was fatherless, it did not seem worthwhile making a fuss about it for there were many children he knew lacking of one parent or another. He was already self-reliant and a glance around the crowded alleys and byways instructed him that there were many in a worse plight than he and his mother were. Apart from the money he earned from his own labours, there was many a piece came his way out of the pockets of a homing sailor, who, with more money than intuition, thought he saw in Marie Deane the answer to his celibate prayers. True Marie provided a soft bed at the Cat and Garter, but they slept in it alone. Marie kept faith with a husband who had never kept faith with her but of whom she always spoke with a soft tongue and a faraway look in her eyes.

It seemed natural when Alex had reached the age of fourteen years that he should seriously turn his attention to the sea and all that it held. At high tide the waters of the harbour almost washed the walls of the tavern and most of the men he could call friends were seamen or had been seamen, and most of the women he knew were sisters, mothers, wives or lovers of seamen.

As he looked out over the harbour one morning, a little after sunrise, watching men already unloading a portion of a cargo of a ship that lay at anchor, he was filled with a hunger to travel that was almost physical. The gulls were wheeling and mewing over the decks of several small vessels, where fishermen were unloading their catches of the night before. But as he gazed his vision was on the larger ships. They held his attention with their reefed sails and trim decks. One, named *The Bold Adventurer*, laid claim to his imagination. Of late he had grown tired of helping his mother in the tavern and serving in the Chandlers Shop at the busier times for a few extra shillings. Down was just beginning to peach his cheeks and his muscles were starting to flex. The sea had called to him, day and night, for weeks past, and the only thing that held him back were the trips he took out into the country with Doctor Dawes. He had enjoyed that, holding the head of the pony and looking after the gig whilst the doctor made his calls. It had been like a holiday to get into the gig and bowl away along the country lanes, seeing the hedges laced with flowers, hearing the field birds calling. But these trips were not to be compared to sailing to other lands. Some of the sailors who came to the tavern had told him that of ten men drinking in a bar, eight might be of different nationalities, with a variety of tongues and customs. What might he not learn from their comradeship?

Later, he wandered down to the wharves and fell into conversation with an old sailor whose voice boomed on like rollers on a distant cliff, and a smile that showed stained and uneven teeth, gripping an old and well-chewed pipe. He sucked in a gasping mouthful of air before he spoke which gave his words a certain rhythm as they sat on the bollards peering down into the blackness of the water around the piles of the jetty. Out of the shadows the sunlight made glittering chains of light upon the water, and the warmth of it made lively the smell of pitch and salt to their nostrils.

'Can be a good life at sea. If you be a strong lad,' boomed the old man and a merry light came into his eyes as an old tale came into his mind. 'I remember once, we had a very anxious journey, to South America. Bad weather all the way we had, running up and down the ratlines, reefing in the sails as we ran into a storm every other day. Then we had a strange happening. It was a moonless night, heavy cloud, sea as calm as a millpond, black as the grave, when suddenly the sea was alight . . . Little phosphorous lights, bobbing and dipping. One seaman, Scotch Willie, put a ladder over the side, climbed down and dipped a foot into the waves. He was very quiet when he climbed back. Then he said, "That sea is boiling hot." Well, he weren't scalded we could see that, but he were moody for a day or two, like something or other were bothering him. Then we had a terrible storm. What a day that was! Never seen such a bubbling and frothing and sucking, like a giant whirlpool threatening to draw us under, down into Davy Jones's Locker. That storm shook the ship like a terrier shakes a rat and then it was gone, sudden as it had begun. We were all exhausted when we all lined up for a roll call, but of Scotch Willie there was no sign.' He heaved a deep and throaty sigh.

'Had he been washed overboard?' asked Alex who had been listening intently.

'That was the general opinion,' replied the man, 'but . . .' and here he touched the side of his nose with a grimy finger. 'There was nothing we could find of Scotch Willie on that ship. Not a shirt or a knife or a basket or a hat. Nothing! 'Twas as if he had never been on board at all.'

Rule Of Thumb

'But would not his name have been on the roll call list?' offered Alex instantly.

'Aye, like as not it was! But I never heard of that! It was a queer day with the smell of sulphur on the air, and a throbbing in the wind like a woman sobbing.'

As they had been talking, another old seaman had come abreast of them and heard the last sentence of the conversation.

'Take no heed of the drivelling old saltie, Alex. You gang to sea if you've a mind to it. It'll make a man of you – if it doesn't kill you!' He laughed heartily and strode on, his peg-leg stumping along the cobblestones, his shoulder twisting with the effort as he hurried along.

'How did Peggy lose his leg? Did a shark get it?'

'No!' The old man took out his pipe and knocked the dead ashes out on to the side of the bollard. 'He got drunk once too often. He ended up under the wheels of a fine lady's carriage. 'Twasn't her fault nor that of her driver. She fainted when she saw him laid there grimacing with his leg crushed, just like a piece of firewood. She come round quick like and gave him a lift to his lodgings. She gave him five guineas to pay a doctor. She gave him twenty not to tell whose carriage had done the deed.'

'I'd like to sail on the *Bold Adventurer*,' broke in Alex. 'I'm sure I'm fit enough to be a sailor.'

'Well, if you don't mind me saying, lad, you're a bit too pretty, if anything! First off, have them curls shorn off. Don't smile so much. Them teeth are too even, too sound!'

Alex burst out laughing. The old seaman gave him a nudge.

'You think me an old fool. You'll learn. Lust and envy make poor fellow travellers. Best always to take the middle road if you want to keep your front teeth in place!'

'All you say will not keep me at home!' exploded Alex.

'Make sure then that you don't come back home with them hung from a fine chain around your neck!'

Still laughing Alex walked away from the old man. He looked back once or twice but he was filling his pipe. He had told Alex the worst things that could happen, it was up to him to find out the best himself.

When Alex arrived back at the Cat and Garter there was a lot of work for him to do, it was evening and men were drifting in for food and drink before he could again give his thoughts over to his future. One sailor in particular held his attention. Although his body gave the impression of immense strength he was a dispirited fellow. He told Alex, as he was hunched over his

Rule Of Thumb

pewter mug, that he had been crimped in 1803 and been carried aboard a vessel bound for the Spice Islands. He had been unconscious for two days and sick for most of that first journey. But after that he had been held by the seas of the world, now he had come home again after nineteen years, but he did not think he would settle. He sat there, the aromatic scent of warm rum in his nostrils and the fog of tobacco smoke whirling before his eyes. Harsh-faced drabs and blowsies, stretching their lips in mirthless smiles hovered near him and glanced slyly at each other when he spoke of treasures beyond compare and the pearls of the Orient. One nudged him in the ribs with a jokey finger and asked if he was looking for a wife to settle down with in the town. He wiped his mouth on the sleeve of his coat and took a measured look at the woman and her avid companions.

'I'd take ye all!' he replied with a sepulchral voice, 'if I thought you wouldn't be tired o' jumping into bed with the same man every night within the length of a fortnight!'

Some time after, when the drink had flowed freely, and a mellow tone of conversation had begun to permeate the room, a man entered. Alex was first aware of his presence by the buzz of excitement on his arrival. The man was a Captain Franklin and he was looking for a new crew for his next voyage which was to be to Port Jackson in Australia. Mutters amongst the men became more lively and there was a concerted rush to the door.

'I wish you had been choosing a better time, Captain,' said Marie Deane, giving him a bold look over one shoulder.

'Hold your tongue, woman,' he said, as he sat himself at the fireside where there was a small table. As Marie went to his side, he went on, 'I'll bet you have had every loose penny out of the pockets that left, already! Come now, who's for a sail to the New Land? Best to go under your own stowing than to wait for the Justices to send you.'

There was a murmur amongst those left in the tavern and a sailor put a glass of rum before him. 'Thank you kindly,' said the Captain taking a good mouthful of the fiery liquid. 'Are you game to take supplies to Australia? I have need of a strong man and a man of experience? I have need of two men who are young and lively on their feet. They must be able to take orders.'

'Mother,' whispered Alex. She shook her head, a warning light in her eyes.

'Please,' he begged. Marie stood under the lamp, blinking in the blazing light, her hands tight clasped in the handles of two empty pewter mugs. She watched her son's face, shivering and wavering before her eyes, as a corpse beneath the water. He was slipping away from her into the future that held his life, away from her arms and her love.

'You're a man almost. You do as you think best for yourself,' a voice crooned in his ear, as Alex moved towards the Captain. The voice belonged to the first mate, his forehead wrinkled with deep furrows, his blue eyes narrowed by his years looking out over the oceans. A woman approached the mate with signs of overt wantonness, but the Captain gave her a fierce glare, and she backed away, pulling a thin gauzy shawl over her semi-bare breasts. The Captain then turned his gaze leisurely on Alex who stood at his elbow.

'You want a job as a cabin boy? You look strong and healthy.'

Alex, his heart beating with a quicker throb, the room so still and expectant that he could hear himself breathe, edged forward.

'What would I have to do, sir?' he asked hesitantly.

'Do? why, young sir, you will do as you are bidden!'

'I meant, Captain, sir, what would my duties be?' replied Alex, unruffled as the men about him let out a guffaw.

'You will help in the galley. You will have to be more careful than the last. He burned himself badly with slush-fat,' broke in the first mate, 'be scarred for life, he will.'

The Captain gave an impatient movement of his arm. 'Ten shillings a month and your keep and a share of the profits at the end of the voyage. How old are you?'

'Fourteen, sir, I'm a good worker.'

'Are you, indeed! Are you obedient?'

Alex hung his head. 'Well, that is of no great matter, you will soon be brought to heel on the *Bold Adventurer*, and if you shape up well, maybe on our return voyage you will be a seaman proper! What do you say then, laddie? Will you sign on the dotted line?'

Alex looked across at his mother whose only movement was a slight inclination of her head.

'Yes, Captain, sir!' cried Alex enthusiastically. He snatched up the quill and dipped it in the ink encrusted pot with haste before the Captain or his mother changed their minds. He signed his name with a flourish. The Captain scratched a few lines alongside and then said, 'Here is a list of the things you will need to bring with you. Give my regards to your mother!'

'You may be giving those to her yourself, Captain,' said Marie coming alongside. 'We haven't seen you here before, Captain,' she went on as he turned to face her squarely, and regarded her with new interest.

'You, the mother of this boy here?' he asked with forced heartiness.

'I'm his mother alright and I'll be obliged to you to keep him safe under your rigging. He's a brave lad, my Alex, but he is still young and headstrong at times. He means no harm with his wild looks and flashes of temper.'

'Comes of him not having a father?' asked the Captain.

'No,' returned Marie tensely. 'Comes of having me as his mother!' She moved away suddenly, going about her work with concentrated energy.

'It looks to me, Alexander Deane, that you now a member of my crew. I'll bid you farewell until we sail. Be prompt!' and with that short order Alex was dismissed in his own home.

Alexander Deane spent the next four days bidding friends, neighbours and customers, goodbye. Doctor Dawes was very sorry to hear of his coming adventure. He had hoped to make more use of him in the near future but what was done was done. The lad was set on going to sea. It was no use him wheedling and what could he offer to compete with the Spice Islands and Australia and all the mysterious places in between! Best to wish him good luck and have done with it. Best to look for a more home loving apprentice.

Marie Deane thought differently as she said goodbye to him on the quayside where only a few years before they had both said their last farewell to his father. Alexander was so filled with hope and excitement that he could not squeeze one tear from his eyes as he kissed his mother's tear-wet cheeks or find one word to soften the stone of anguish in her heart. Mother Booth, who had helped to bring him into the world, stood beside Marie and tried to comfort her but Marie wept bitterly and felt a cold hand had squeezed her heart to a small ball of lead that would be the death of her.

In the close confines of her bedroom overlooking the harbour, white as death, shaken by a storm of nerves, Marie sat on a straight backed chair in front of the window and gazed out on the seascape that would soon be bearing her son away from her. She sat with one hand to her face that was marked by lines of care at mouth and forehead until the *Bold Adventurer* hung like a mote of dust on the horizon's verge. Then it was gone. She got up from her weary, cramped position and crossing the room flung herself down upon the bed. She lay there for some minutes, weeping shuddering sobs, then she half rose, drew the curtains around her to cut out the chill of the fireless room, and gave herself over to a sorrow induced sleep.

When Marie awoke and drew back the bed-curtains the tavern was presenting its window panes to the sun which was waning fast. As she watched the rays of the sun turned the glass from violet to copper and then to gold before it tipped downwards into the distant waves, a deep flame of orange with a magenta rim.

She felt better for having slept and her natural fighting spirit had reasserted itself. What had she to complain of? Her son had now a profession in a minor way but the years would take care of that. Her son was not dead! There was nothing final in his going to sea. The streets below were filled with homing seamen. One day her son would return too. He would come bearing gifts from far off lands and tales of the world's wonders. She tidied herself and tried to shed the dry look of despair from her eyes, then went downstairs where she knew her work was waiting for her.

CHAPTER FOUR

It was well for Marie Deane that she was not to know that the Captain of the *Bold Adventurer* was an evil tempered man and as Alex was the youngest and greenest lad aboard he would come in for more than his share of goading until he had proved himself in the eyes of both Captain and crew. Some of the men were ill-tempered with loud voices which grated on Alex's ears. Their lewd talk, some of which was obscure to him, and what wasn't made him go hot in the dark, as he lay on his bunk. Even so, part of him was fascinated by their rough manners, bearded faces, strong hard bodies and their fiery talk.

When he went aboard the *Bold Adventurer* he was much surprised by the cramped quarters of the crew. When he was shown where he was to sleep he stumbled in the dim confines of the area and would have fallen to the floor if he had not been steadied by another sailor. As it was he caught his leg against the guard board at the side of the bottom bunk. He sucked in his breath and rubbed the spot ruefully.

'You'll get a few more bruises afore long to join that one,' laughed the sailor. 'Now here's your bunk, Alex, we got no hammocks here! No, my hearty. Bunks is what we got. Ever slept in a hammock?'

'No, or a bunk come to that.'

'You'll no doubt find it hard on your bones at first. After that you'll be too tired to care where you lie just so long as it's flat!'

Alex looked up at the low ceiling of his bunk which was the base of the one above, and thought that a clean open swinging hammock would be infinitely more desirable. The sailor broke in on his thoughts.

'Now put your belongings there under the head of your bunk. The man in the top bunk will use the other end!'

It was evening before Alex found out who the other man was to be. He was a young man some eight years older than himself. As his eyes became accustomed to the dimmed light he noticed the man smiling at him a few feet away. He was broad shouldered with a mass of curly black hair and

Rule Of Thumb

dark doe-like eyes. His even, white teeth were set in a mouth pleasantly smiling and seemed used to doing so. Alex smiled back at him.

'Ambrose Cunliffe,' the mouth said and a firm hand shot out towards him. Alex took hold of the proffered hand and gave it a swift shake.

'I'm Alex Deane. The new cabin boy-cum-general-kick-about!'

'I can believe that,' said Ambrose with a broad smile. 'This is my first voyage too. I expect we shall both be put upon until we show our mettle.'

'I've never been anywhere as bad as this!' replied Alex, nodding his head around him. 'It's so clean and tidy above and the Captain was so polite when he signed me on, giving his regards to my mother and such. He's a sham, that's what he is!'

Ambrose burst out laughing when he came close and saw Alex with a woebegone face. 'Don't take on so, Alex. It's early days yet. We shall both have to spend as much time up on deck as we can, away from the staleness down here. Come,' he urged, putting a firm hand on the boy's shoulder, 'we don't want a kicking for being shirkers, do we?'

'Aye, I expect we shall have to show ourselves or maybe they will think we have jumped overboard. I know I will have to help in the galley. What have they set you to do?'

'Heaven only knows. What will they set for a sailor as green as new cut grass?'

'Is it a riddle?' asked Alex with a scathing edge to his voice.

As soon as they were up on deck it was a riddle no longer. The work set them was the clearing away of food, washing dishes, and peeling of potatoes for the day after as the cook was not feeling well. As they were in the galley the first mate came in.

'What you two doing?' he asked with a stern voice. 'Where's the cook?'

'He is not feeling himself,' answered Ambrose, putting the table between himself and the first mate so as to be out of reach.

'Not himself! That will be an improvement! Carry on until told otherwise!' He turned on his heel and left the galley leaving them to resume the chores set them.

It was while they were working together that they told their life stories and Alex learned that Ambrose was the son of a farmer who was prosperous now but had spent his younger years at sea. He had been very fond of travel and the freedom of the sea but his father had died and left the thriving Manor Farm of Hinchley to his only son, so he had to leave the roving life behind. He then settled down, wedded and sired one son, Ambrose, who had also thought the sea was in his blood. His father, wise or not, had agreed that the only course was to satisfy his curiosity by going to sea and trying for himself.

So, there they were, scraping dirty platters and pans and preparing vegetables.

'If there was an island in sight, I'd jump ship already,' growled Alex, as he hung over the scrap-bucket.

'Don't despair. Better times will come. We are both homesick yet. Bound to be. I bet you have never been away from home before.'

'No . . .' Alex shook his head dolefully, and he felt a tear well up in his eye. Ambrose turned away quickly, and said, 'There seems a lot of potatoes here, do you think there will be enough?'

Just then a voice cried out dramatically from outside the galley door. 'For pity's sake, is that food I smell? Let us at it afore mi drooling drowns mi teeth!' and into the galley popped a strange looking fellow with a narrow, orange-skinned face and a tarred pigtail sticking out of his leather hat.

'I'm sorry,' said Ambrose, apologetically, 'there's no cooked food in here.'

'Ah, then,' cried out the man, rubbing his grimy fingers together and doing a curious little jig. 'Give us a cracker then, or a bit o' somat as will stop mi stomach fighting its way up mi throat.'

Alex and Ambrose smiled at each other. Here at least was an amusing turn of events and the two were glad of the interruption as they looked for and found the cracker-barrel. They gave the man two crackers and he seized on them and began to nibble at them like a squirrel on a nut, dry and unappetising as they were. As he nibbled he tapped now and again upon the table with them.

'Why do you keep tapping with those crackers?' Alex asked, much bemused by his action.

'Cracker weevil, cracker weevil. None in these. Force of habit.'

'You mean there are sometimes weevils in the crackers, live?'

'Often, lad, often! Sometimes the only fresh meat we matelots get!'

They rewarded his information by a tasty bit of pork crackling which he devoured with the same relish and by the time they had served their intruder to his satisfaction and he had departed they were reasonably cheerful. Alex only just stopped himself in time from beginning to whistle a merry tune. However, when he climbed into his bunk an hour later, it was to be enveloped in the warm stench of oil and sweat and stale air, and it sent a surge of sourness up into his throat. The distraught misery which then filled him was like nothing he had ever before experienced.

The following day Ambrose had his first encounter with the Captain. He was working in the bilges. It was dank and dark and a stench rose into his nostrils that made him gag. A sailor working with him began to taunt him until he could stand it no longer and he sent the man over into four inches of turgid water. The sailor retaliated by reporting the matter to the Captain. When they were both stood before Captain Franklin he asked the sailor, 'What happened?'

'I was just going about my lawful business,' he began ingratiatingly, 'when that land-lubber fell aboard of me for no cause.'

'I can well believe that,' agreed Captain Franklin, as he stood with his thumbs hooked under his armpits and his elbows angled. 'I can indeed.'

'I'm sorry I hit him,' said Ambrose. 'I have no excuse.'

'No excuse! I ask for information not excuses!' the Captain said sarcastically. 'What did he say to you?' he asked the sailor.

'He called me miserable scum.'

'Well, so you are,' replied the Captain, nodding. 'A reasonable enough observation.'

'He told me that hell would freeze over before I made a sailor, Captain, sir,' offered Ambrose.

'And so it might,' agreed the Captain.

'He said I worked as unwillingly as if I had been press-ganged!'

'Press-ganged! Press-ganged!' roared the Captain. 'All my crew are signed on and above board! The devil take you!' He turned on the tormenting sailor with a curling lip. 'He should have drowned you!'

The man cringed, ready for a blow, but the Captain turned on his heel and walked briskly up the deck. Ambrose looked after him and wondered if this would be the last encounter with the strange Captain Franklin. He wondered also if he had not been somewhat strange in the head himself, to take on such a journey. He was to ponder the question again and again, as was Alex, for the first few weeks of the journey were enough to wash every fancy and desire for the high seas from their souls.

Ambrose suffered more than Alex. The work set him was harder, the hours longer, and being older than Alex he saw many injustices that took the heart out of him.

In his unhappiness Ambrose turned to Alex for companionship, and they vowed lasting friendship, until death came to part them, which they expected every day to do so in one shape or another as they went about their daily tasks. The other men, well-seasoned and long-tried in the ways of the sea, laughed at their greenness and their mistakes at first. They thought it amusing, in their coarse way, to see Captain Franklin come up behind Alex and toe him in the buttock as he holystoned the deck, or kicked over his bucket of salt-water with a scathing, 'Put your back into it, lad.'

Alex would alter his position slightly, square his shoulders and scrub the harder, or rise with a smile and went to get more water. No one could call him a sniveller! The Captain could kick him as much as he wanted. He wouldn't whine like a puppy as the men had said he would! Captain Franklin soon moved on shouting orders to others of the crew who caught his bullying attention.

One day, in the later afternoon, a little puff of whitish cloud appeared and proceed to blow itself out, in bursts and flurries, until it covered the whole of the sky as far as the eye could see. The ship was enveloped in a harsh and piercing cold air, as the white, boiling clouds, gave way to an ominously glowering overcast, cleft by vibrating tongues of lightning, quickly followed by reverberating rolls of thunder, echoing across the waves. Then the fury of the wind was upon them, and the whole ship broke forth into sound. Every spar and bolt rattled, freak ice hung on the shrouds, the wind thrummed in the rigging. Most of the crew spent the night tightening one rope here and loosening another there. Alex, because he was young, was sent down below. 'Make yourself scarce, lad, your turn will come tomorrow. There'll be plenty to clean up then!'

Alex had gone reluctantly. Supposing the ship went down with him asleep? Ambrose quelled his fears.

'Get below, Alex, I'll come for you should ought go amiss with us!'

As Alex lay in his bunk, he rolled with the ship, hitting his head against the bulwarks time and again, as the ship tossed in the waves. He punched his thin pillow into some form of neck support and tried not to think of the storm or the need of a bowl of hot meal with perhaps a tasty bit of fat-pork across its surface. Even a piece of crisp crackling pork-rind to chew on there in the dark was better than the biting of his lip near to bringing blood! But, at last, he slept, worn out by anxiety and hunger.

He was not to know until early the next day that one of the sailors up aloft, his grip weakened by long and continued labour in the riggings, had slipped, recovered, glanced fearfully over his shoulder and again lost his foothold and plunged deckwards.

Ambrose shook Alex awake and told him to get dressed and go to the Captain's cabin where the man lay with his spine shattered. It was obvious to Alex as he knocked on the door of the cabin and then entered that the Captain liked all the comforts of a home around him. There was fine, polished furniture and bookcases and ornate brass lamps, and carpets from Turkey and curtains of heavy brocade. There was also a curiously enamelled dresser, with cupboards and glass fronts. The cupboards were filled with delicately carved pieces of ivory and soapstone. It was certainly very different from the grime and darkness of below decks where the sour sweat smell of some of his companions repelled him and their red-rimmed lashless lids filled him with horror.

'Come in, lad,' the Captain invited not unkindly. 'You know something of medicine, I remember you saying. What can you do for our comrade here?' He put his arm round Alex's shoulder and drew him to the bed.

Alex drew away. 'I can do nothing,' he answered biting his lips. 'All anyone can do for him is to make him comfortable for his last hours.'

'Then do just that, Alex,' urged the Captain. Alex sponged the man's face, dribbled brandy between his lips, and bathed the blood from his body, while the Captain watched him. As he watched Alex with his weak, girl's hands fluttering over the shattered body he saw how effectively he worked. He did not give out orders to Alex as he might have done to others but stood patiently by with scissors, binders, and bowls of water. When Alex finally drew away from the bed the Captain voiced his admiration to the first mate saying, 'We have a rum cove here and no mistake. I took him for a ninny but he's done as fair a job as a barber-surgeon.'

'A barber-surgeon would not go amiss aboard this hulk,' answered the first mate.

'We are not sailing a hulk, Mr Giddins. First mate you may be but remember I am the Captain. I do not run a hulk.' He turned then to Alex. 'You have some skill there, as you told me. You will be called upon again. Be ready. In the meantime stay here with this wretched fellow and do what you can for him whilst he lives. It will not be long! Mr Giddins, hand me that Bible, I must acquaint myself with some wording. It would not seem proper for a Captain, even of a hulk, if he were to stumble over the wording of a committal to the deep.'

The sailor lay for two awesome days before death came to him. He cried out as he saw the end approaching, welcoming it, his eyes moist with tears. Alex's knees quaked with fatigue as he stood against the Captain's bunk head where they had laid the man, watching death claim him, smoothing out the pain-twisted lips, drooping the forced back eyelids, stalling the laboured breath in his chest which had sunk low and showed the cage where his heart had beaten frantically for the last time. Alex had not witnessed death before and he began to cry, not from pity but fear. As he had watched he had felt a sudden pang for his mother left on the quayside. He thought how carelessly he had said goodbye to her, never to know, until then, the bond that bound them even though seas separated them. But then he wiped away his tears, loathe to show them before men as rough as gritstone, and busied himself with helping to sew up the body ready for committal to the sea.

Some time later the men were all gathered upon the deck and the wrapped body of the unfortunate sailor was laid on the plank with a coloured covering over whole. They stood around the Captain as abashed as sheep, their eyes downcast, their rough hands clasped before them, over their varied headcoverings which they had respectfully removed. The high-toned words of the Captain drifted out onto the still air, and Alex had to admit that when he was not abusing his vocal chords by violent shouts and guttural growling, he had a very beautiful and controlled pitch to his voice. It seemed to Alex that the words came to him in melodious waves, ebbing and flowing.

'We brought nothing into this world and it is certain we can carry nothing out . . . I will keep my mouth as it were with a bridle . . . Lord let me know the end and be seen no more . . .' The words sang on in Alex's ears but in his head he tried desperately to think of something else. He was greatly fatigued by his watch over the stricken sailor and the scene began to take on an unreal quality as he stood there motionless. Then, the words ended, the plank was expertly tipped, there was a gurgling splash as the shrouded body hit the water, and a life had ended.

Captain Franklin closed the book with a snap and firmed his lips together. 'About your duties, men,' he ordered. The groups broke ranks and went their separate ways.

CHAPTER FIVE

'What did you think of the committal yesterday?' asked Ambrose of Alex as they ate their midday stew on the top of the hatchings.

'I tried not to think of it at all,' replied Alex. 'When the body was tipped into the water, I could see in my mind's eye a blind man running his stick along the railings that bound the churchyard at home. Old blind Stewart. Why should I think of him?'

'Perhaps it was a symbol,' said Ambrose. 'A sign that we all start off straight but life can divert our aims.'

Alex thought for a moment and then threw down his plate impatiently. 'We should both have stayed on land,' he declared, stretching his aching limbs. 'I feel we will get nothing from this trip but trouble.'

'Feel what you may, Alex. Here we are and here we must stay. Do your tasks well as you are able, show nothing of your discontent to the other men. They will despise us for our weakness and are hard enough to add to our miseries. Be willing to learn all the men ask of you. We may come out of this venture unscathed yet!'

'I'll try, Ambrose, but I can't help thinking how my mother would pull Franklin's lug for him if she knew how he has treated me! She'd braid his whiskers for him if she knew!'

'You must not rely on your mother to fend off your assailants. Besides, you are too old to hide your face in the folds of a woman's skirts. You have other weapons you can use. Your time with the doctor can be put to good use on board here. I'm sure Captain Franklin is wise enough to know you have skill there. And you sang well at the shanty singing the other day. Even the other sailors remarked upon it.'

'My voice is changing, Ambrose, I can no longer sing the highest notes.'

'That is a good sign then. Now you'll get a man's power to your fist.'

They burst out laughing and Alex felt more cheerful than he had for many days. Alex continued to do his work well, but fear dogged him by day and he was sick to his bare feet of Franklin who looked at him out of steel grey eyes that brought a chill to his bones. It was no use complaining to the other sailors, they were grown men who had suffered scurvy, been keelhauled, shipwrecked and flogged, if one was to believe them. Franklin held no terrors for them! But there were times on that journey when Ambrose and Alex saw fear flicker in their salt-rimmed eyes as Captain Franklin moved amongst them, his whip at the ready, darting, thin and snake-like over their bare backs.

Just when Alex was beginning to wonder if he would ever see dry land again, the word went round that shortly they would make port for new supplies of fresh water, vegetables and fruit. Alex and Ambrose were delighted until they heard that only five men would be allowed to go ashore and they would certainly not be amongst them. They were already short of one of the crew and it did not seem likely that the Captain would replace him or risk losing other members of the crew.

The First Mate thought that Alex should learn to climb the rigging and make himself useful with the sails when the weather was calm. The Captain agreed, and Alex also, for he thought that anything was better than working in the galley, or holystoning the decks. After climbing about in the rigging at the lower levels for a few days and then gradually climbing higher, Alex felt that he was, at last, a seaman. Ambrose taught him all he had learned himself, but the lithe and quick movements of Alex were all his own.

In spite of the First Mate allowing Alex to learn when the waters were calm, he later insisted that he should take a trial when the seas were less than friendly.

'This is just the sort of day when we may be forced to reef in,' said the First Mate dourly. 'Get to it, no missy poutings here.'

Alex looked at the sea and then at the sky. There was a swell on the sea and a raising wind with the promise of rain at its back.

'Stir yourself, look lively. We all get a frog in the throat the first time up to the crow's nest.'

Alex stirred himself and began to climb, clutching at the ropes nervously. The pit of his stomach felt tight and chill and his knuckles and bare toes were white with tension.

'See if you can see the ghost of our late lamented,' cried one of the sailors in a bantering tone. Alex did not reply, he knew he must show his mettle, even as the rain came sluicing against his body, drenching him instantly to the skin. He hung for a moment and then began to climb upwards towards the crow's nest amid cheers from below. Once he was up there he looked about him, seeing the heaving white-caps, feeling a pulsating exhilaration.

Rule Of Thumb

The wind now had a low, dull moan to it and he fancied he heard his name uttered in a soft tone within its cry. From down below he heard real voices from the seamen ascending towards him in a sort of agitated whisper. He began to descend with an unconcerned air. It was easier for him on the downward journey, he did not have to look up or down but kept his eyes straight forward while his nimble feet and fingers took him quickly towards the deck. As he dropped to the deck, intoxicated by his success, he noticed Captain Franklin there. He was dressed in breeches of white sarsenet and a shirt trimmed with deep ruffles and in his hand he carried a coat of dark blue watered silk braided with gold-thread lace.

Alex, emboldened by his own efforts, offered to hold the coat whilst the Captain put his arms into the garment. He seemed pleased by this, but his pleasure did not last long for he had just ordered a seaman who had been in irons for two days to be brought before him to receive two dozen lashes. Now Alex saw two seamen drag the resisting captive along the deck. His arms were then placed around the mast and shackled there in order for him to receive his punishment. He had been given an order which he had neglected, and when the Captain had asked him about it, had thrown himself into a weak-hearted attitude of defiance on the half-deck, muttering furiously. The Captain, who would not brook the smallest provocation by his crew, sent a stentorian shout below for two of the crew and in a few breathless moments, they had the man pinioned between them and later clamped in irons.

Now Alex watched, as the Captain, his eyes narrowed, paused and considered how best to deal with the dissenter. The man himself felt the threat towards him from the steel grey eyes that seemed always to bore into the object of his scrutiny. But, suddenly, the Captain's stern features softened, and he rasped with a mirthless laugh before he spat out, 'Release the cringing dog! Get about your duties, man.'

Released, the man stood speechless by what had happened until the two men waved him away, when he stumbled along the deck in a state of painful agitation.

The Captain resumed a leisurely perusal of the ship with an air of surety born of long experience of the tempers of men. Alex, watching him, became aware of an undercurrent amongst the seamen, a slight relaxing of tension, an agreeable light-hearted atmosphere creeping into the daily grind. It was a change he welcomed more than he could say. They were but two days from a port of call, and Alex wished, with all his heart, that the port could be that which he had set sail from. To see his mother, standing upon the quay once more, in her black, stiff gown, with the demure frill of muslin around the neck, the black and grey cotton shawl about her shoulders and the pert little multicoloured scarf over her dark coils of hair, was a sight he longed for with almost unabated hunger.

Two days later they were in port. Fresh fruit and vegetables, water, and other stores and great parcels of cloth, and merchandise were carried aboard. Then the Captain and two burly seamen went ashore again. There was much speculation on board as to what the purpose of the second visit could be, but it was after midnight before the Captain and the men returned. By that time Alex was asleep in his bunk and given over to merciful oblivion.

Morning came. There was no turning over and going to sleep again, the duties of the day called for attention. The ship heaved and the creak of the boards and riggings could be heard plainly where he lay. He knew it was a task of his that day to clean the silverware in the Captain's cabin. Polishing was a job he hated! It reminded Alex of the tavern, with pewter mugs, brass lamps and spittoons. Those he had cleaned with a good heart and often enough but the Captain's silverware was all twists and turns, fiddling gadgets and spouts, chased flounces and engravings. No amount of paste and polishing could stop them from tarnishing, and he had suffered boxed ears on more than one occasion when chided for his lack of skill.

Nevertheless, he dressed and went dutifully to the Captain's cabin. He was, he fully realised, a novice in all things, but he had already decided that he was not going to run the absurd risk of enquiring as to the Captain's visit ashore the evening before. Little did he know as his pressure on the door handle of the cabin tightened, that all the Captain had done the night before was soon to be dramatically revealed to him. As he stepped into the cabin Alex was confronted by a man other than the Captain. He was amazed at the bulk of the man before him. He was as black as a sweep, and his hair grew close to his head, his eyes were large and luminous and protruded in an alarming manner. Alex felt at once the danger locked up inside him and flinched away, but he was to be surprised even further when a few seconds later the Captain entered the cabin. The man, low on his knees, as if afraid of the Captain, crept to his side as the Captain sat at his desk. At first Alex felt quite amused as the man abased himself before the Captain.

'Don't you smile, boy, unless you want a tickle from the cat,' said the Captain to Alex, his tone low and dangerous.

The huge man turned to look at Alex and uttered a throaty growl, and then as he saw Alex start back, gave a menacing grimace showing a yawning gap where six of his top front teeth should have been.

Rule Of Thumb

'How do you like my new watch-dog, Alexander, he is not so toothless as he seems,' the Captain gave Alex a lancing look. 'Is he not a fine fellow? Does he not have arms and legs like oaks in a forest?'

'Yes, yes, indeed.' Alex nodded vigorously, taking good care to keep the table between himself and the man who was staring violently as if his very gaze might break the barrier between them. Sunlight filtered into the cabin, casting pale aqueous shadows upon the walls. It lit up the body of the man still further and the Captain gave a pleased laugh.

'Would you like to wrestle with my slave, Alex?' The awful truth rang in Alex's ears like a knell. A slave! He shook his head, afraid to speak less his voice faltered, and walked on trembling legs to the silverware in the cabinet. There was a narrow room off the main cabin which could be used for stores and into this room the Captain proceeded to usher his slave. He went there meekly as a lamb, submitted to fettering, allowed a studded collar to be placed around his neck, and the end to be chained to the wooden wall. The door was then closed and the slave was left sitting on a bench without any light, except that which was let in through the air-holes at the top of the door. If he sombrely surveyed his prison Alex had no way of knowing. He felt pierced by embarrassment and shame that any man should be so treated.

Later when he had finished his work in the cabin he said nothing to any of the men of what he had seen or heard. The men were to draw their own conclusions, when the Captain made rounds of the ship each day, and trotting silently and faithfully as a hound, came Ebony, for such the Captain had named him. The Captain had also calculated that having paid a good price for him, Ebony must earn his keep in entertainment, such as sham, but realistic, fighting! The seamen avoided the Captain's eyes when they heard and would not honour him by showing the slightest interest in his purchase. They glanced cautiously at one another when the pair passed along the deck, gave jerky movements with their heads, and spat over the side of the ship, providing the wind was blowing in the right direction.

Alex had noted that for some days as he went about his duties in the Captain's cabin the atmosphere had become tense and chill. Captain Franklin began to give every little incident amongst the crew a sinister interpretation. Every word of complaint was credited with heavy significance that boded ill for his own safety. Alex knew that he was being used as a go-between and tried his best to assure the Captain that all was well with the crew, and that his fears were unfounded.

Captain Franklin's face always took on a look of constraint at his words until finally all Alex's efforts to penetrate further into his confidence proved

Rule Of Thumb

fruitless. Although Alex continued to work in the cabin he tried to limit his time there, and did not tarry when asked to go up on deck or help in the galley.

One morning, Alex, who was learning to service a rope, was sat up on deck, when the Captain sent for him.

'What does he want me for?' he asked the seaman who brought the message.

'Did I ask him?' queried the man. 'He said for me to get you, so you go!'

Alex went, wondering what new caprice or complaint he was to be harried with. He tapped gently at the cabin door hoping that he would not be heard and so have the excuse for going away, but a voice, low in tone, said, 'Enter, Alexander.' He turned the handle and stepped inside the cabin. The Captain was sitting on the side of his bunk and looked quite pale, but he stood up when Alex came in and said, 'Good lad. I hear you are as good with needle and thread as any woman?'

'I learned that skill from my mother and my good friend Dr Dawes,' Alex replied mellowly, although he felt much perturbed by the fact that the Captain was, with difficulty, peeling off his ruffled shirt. Alex wondered what was to be requested of him. He had heard the men say that the Captain was fond of pretty-boys and hoped he did not fall into that category!

The Captain broke in on his thoughts with, 'I would be obliged if you could dress these wounds.' It was humbly said and relief swept over Alex like a warm wave, and he stepped forward eagerly to show his worth as a wound dresser. The Captain looked less overbearing now that his shirt was off and the thin linen web covering the wounds was exposed. He was at a loss to account for the wounds at first, until he saw on the desk beside a carafe of madeira, a leather collar studded with spikes. Someone had evidently swung it with strength over the chest of the Captain. It had inflicted several penetrating wounds in the right breast and the upper arm on the left side.

'Why do you not ask how I came by these wounds?' asked the Captain.

'It is none of my business, Captain, sir. I was called here to minister to you, not ask questions!'

'My God! Your Doctor Dawes taught you more than how to dress a wound. He taught you ethics!'

'I don't know as he ever used that word to me,' replied Alex innocently, as he bathed the wound in salt and cold water he had found in a basin on the toilette table. At first the Captain repelled the gently but questing fingers but soon realised that Alex knew what he was about, and lay still and let him bathe the torn flesh without further resistance. Alex then opened the medicine chest which was on the table. There was an array of bottles in the

Rule Of Thumb

chest similar to the ones Doctor Dawes had carried with him. There was a drawer with bandages, waddings, plasters for drawing and Belladonna Poultices. Alex took out wadding and bandages and a small tub of healing salve.

'They will not need to be stitched?' asked the Captain.

'No, puncture wounds must heal from the bottom of the injury, if I stitched the wounds up they would heal false and fester.' Alex began to put on the salve over the deeper wounds and skimmed over the surface of the weals and grazes before putting on the wadding and proceeding with the bandaging.

'I'll tell you how I came to be in this state,' said the Captain, lying back on his bunk now and relaxing comfortably. 'My slave did this! The gutter-dog! To bite the hand that feeds! That is base ingratitude! Don't you think so?'

'I do not understand such matters as slaves,' answered Alex, guardedly.

'We are all slaves of one sort and another. I don't believe you are as innocent as you would have me believe. You know more about life than you let on. I'll tame that slave of mine. I have a seaman aboard this ship who will make a sound opponent in the ring.'

There was a noise from inside the cupboard and the Captain got up from his bunk and crossing to the door struck his fists upon the wood. 'I'll settle your account. You Ebony! You dreg of the wharves and markets.' There was a thump from inside the door, and the wood shivered. Alex was glad that he would not be the man to bring Ebony to heel. He discreetly made his escape to the deck above taking with him the sullied water and the blood-stained bandages.

A few days later the cook sent Alex down to the lazaret for a measure of sugar and whilst he was there he heard the Captain's voice, speaking in fairly low tones to one of the seamen in the hold. The seaman appeared very distraught, saying that he would rather submit to the lash than to do what the Captain asked of him. As Alex kept unobtrusive watch it became obvious to him that the Captain was asking the seaman to partake in something that went very much against the grain.

'I will not stay here and argue the point with you!' growled the Captain. 'The men are restless, a little entertainment is what they need. An excitement will help to relieve the tensions. Come, now, do it for their sakes if not mine!'

The man still seemed surly and uncompliant though his answers never quite reached the point of rudeness, his voice was thick and indistinct, his general demeanour expressing clearly a deep-rooted mistrust in the

Rule Of Thumb

Captain's request.

Alex crept closer and could now observe the Captain who stood, fists hard upon his hips, legs straddled apart, and the seaman, the one let off previously from punishment, whose forehead was puckered into furrows of concentrated thought.

'If I were to set up a purse, you would, no doubt, lose your misgivings! One guinea a round – win or lose,' offered the Captain in an exasperated tone.

The man began to waver. 'I ask you to do this because you were once a gentleman, but I can quite as easily put you in irons again!'

'I know that only too well, Captain, but have a care, I still have a few friends aboard this ship, as well as ashore and you could do well to tread lightly in a certain direction!' The Captain seemed shocked by this spirited reply, but lost no time in demanding, 'Who has been braying about me?'

This question seemed to send the man's courage to the winds, for he hackled only for an instant, and then said, 'Very well, I will do as you ask but if murder be done, as it might, it will lie at your cabin door!'

'Do you think me for a fool? I can stop a fight if it gets out of hand! A cocked pistol is a quick diverter!' replied the Captain as he stamped up on deck with a self-assured swagger. The seaman went to take quick solace from a bottle of rum he had secreted away at the bottom of the nail box. After a few moment Alex took up the sugar to the galley where the cook was glumly stirring a cauldron of steaming pottage that smelled more like boiling washing than anything that might be eaten.

'Where you been, lad!' he bawled at Alex as he entered the galley. 'Why, what's happening?' asked Alex, putting the sugar into the bin on the shelving.

'What's happened? How should I know? Nobody tells me anything!'

'Nor me,' Alex replied cryptically. The cook stirred the pot vigorously.

Two days later Alex came out of the galley with a bucket of slops to throw over the side and also to get away from the cook, who had a boil on the rim of his ear which was proving difficult to draw to a head. As he drew in the bucket Alex noticed that some of the men had spread a sailcloth over the grating of the main hatch to make an elevated stage and were engaged in threading a hempen rope through the eye stanchions to square off the area. On turning he saw also that the cook had come out on deck and was wiping his hands on a pea-bag apron.

'Exciting, isn't it, lad? There'll be no entertaining on board this ship unless the Captain has a mind to it!'

One of the men had taken up a fiddle and was playing faintly a mournful tune. A few seamen gathered near him, their talk a low, half-hushed murmuring. Then the Captain and the two contenders arrived on the scene. To one man he bore no special enmity but he regarded his slave, Ebony, with implacable hostility. The seaman was dressed in tight, white trousers which ended just below the knee. Ebony wore a calico waistcloth and stood, fists hard upon his hips as he faced his opponent. Swallowing hard the seaman moved restlessly on the balls of his feet.

The other men, squatting or lounging on each side of the ring, demanded impatiently that the combat begin.

Both the combatants drew in a deep breath. They knew their ambitions locked them in rivalry for the purse, which meant freedom from debts for one, and personal freedom for the other.

Ebony stood still. He was not a fighter. He could retaliate, hurt for hurt, but he had not learned how to strike a cold-blooded blow. The seaman seemed for an instant impressed by his sincerity, then finding his situation irksome, rushed up, seized Ebony and threw him on the deck, pinning him to the canvas. The suddenness of the move gave him the advantage and he showered repeated blows onto the head of Ebony, causing blood to flow out of the unfortunate slave's mouth and nose. Ebony stretched out his hands to ward off his opponent who tweaked his bloodied nose as an additional insult. With a burst of indignation, Ebony leapt to his feet and pushed his assailant aside. The man staggered on his feet and Ebony swept forward and enveloped him in a vigorous hug. He squeezed and squeezed in a redness that veiled his vision. The seaman struggled and clasped both hands over his bulging tight-lidded eyes and his mouth opened and closed in wet lipped sobbing gasps. By then, the Captain had seen enough, and he whispered a word to one of the sailors. The word went round, and Alex heard a few disgruntled voices from the men, 'Captain is going to stop the fight!'

Something hard and painful made its presence felt on the head of Ebony and he pitched forward into total oblivion. As he fell the seaman slipped from his grasp, sprang up, and laid his hand on a stanchion to support himself, only to be attacked by another man who had been watching.

The bearded seaman thrust at him fiercely with a belaying-pin. His blow brought an ooze of blood from his forehead. He covered his face with his left arm and driven to desperate measures, drew the man with his right hand into the ring. It was obvious to all who watched that the second man had been planted by the Captain to sustain the fight and he knew that he must win to show his worth. For all Ebony had done to him he was still stronger than his present opponent, and after half strangling the fellow and nearly gouging out an eye with a long-nailed thumb, the bearded man flung himself to the deck in despair. He was wholly exhausted, wishing he was one hundred miles away, and trying to think if it had been worth the three guineas the Captain had bribed him with. The next thing he knew, Alex was holding a mug of rum and water to his lips. He drank, greedily, but he felt thoroughly put out by the whole affair.

'What did you think of the fight, Ambrose?' Alex asked at the earliest opportunity.

'A fight is a fight,' Ambrose answered, 'what did you think of it?'

'I think it was what my mother would have called "not seemly". There was the fellow who had been bribed to take over, half-choked and the gentleman seaman crowing over his winnings in a most ungentlemanly manner. Then there was Ebony, his head split open unmercifully with a cowardly blow!'

'I agree with everything you say, Alex, but what can we do to change matters?'

'I would like you to come with me once we are quit of this ship. I have no wish to sign on again once we are in Australia. Have you?'

'That I have not! I would be glad to go with you till we find our feet in Australia. You are still very young and no doubt you would sleep better at nights if you thought there would be a day when you are quit of this ship?'

'Yes, that I would. Will we promise then to stay with each other and sustain each other in this New Land?' asked Alex. Ambrose, touched by the sincerity of the boy, promised that they would be friends forever, and ventured to say that as they approached the New Land perhaps their days would become less irksome. But there were further events in store that neither of them would have guessed at in their wildest dreams.

Two days later, in the early morning, Alex saw the Captain standing at the head of the stairs which led to the quarter-deck. He was in a thundering bad temper. He had, for some reason best known to himself, given orders to back-sail. The seamen were hesitant, reluctant to move the ship backwards without explanation, and the mate had the men lower the anchor, cautiously, until the whole episode passed over.

'You see,' the Captain declared to Alex, 'they are all of them against me.' He paced about up and down, in an agitated manner. 'I'll see you in hell, every one of you!' he called out to no one in particular and brushed Alex aside roughly. He wondered if he was included in the Captain's tirade, and that night, as he lay in his bunk, he was beset with new fears, as he became convinced that the Captain was touched with madness.

Rule Of Thumb

He had taken the Captain's supper to his cabin and was amazed to see a woman at the window, looking out over sea, where a rising breeze was driving the spray off the combers. In his surprise Alex almost dropped the tray, but placing it on the table, he hurriedly left the cabin. A few minutes later, whilst he was dumping slops over the side, a woman emerged onto the deck, holding her fluttering skirts about her, and going through a series of feminine movements. Patting her eyes with a lace handkerchief, waving to someone in the distance, coy movements of the head and shoulders, and lounging movements of walk. Alex was curious and crept nearer with his line and empty bucket, to where the woman was posing against the rail.

'Madame...' began Alex.

'Madame!' the head of the woman turned, the mouth open, the word spitting like vitriol into the boy's face. 'Madame! You tinker's brat!' Alex reeled backwards, his heart lurching sickeningly. The face was that of the Captain. It was too much for Alex. He fled along the deck, the line held tightly in his hand, the bucket whisking and thudding after him, as he ran into the galley.

'My stars!' said the cook, seeing Alex's drawn face. 'What happened out there?'

'The Captain... out on the deck... dressed like a woman!'

'Is he indeed? You'll be telling me next you've seen a mermaid,' the cook retorted dryly.

'He is, he is! Will he bring bad luck on us all?'

'No more than he has already,' answered the cook, looking at Alex in a doubtful manner.

'Go down to his cabin and collect the supper-tray,' urged Alex.

'That's your job,' the cook replied giving him a half-hearted cuff over the ears.

'I know that. But if you go down to the cabin you will see for yourself. The Captain in a fashionable gown. Truly he is.'

'Here, let me smell your breath, young man. You been at the rum?'

'No, no. Be quick, see for yourself!'

'You're barmy lad!' said the cook, beginning to laugh. 'What would the Captain be wanting with the frock of a woman? I'll be watching you close for grog-blossom on that pretty face of yours.'

'I believe it is our Captain that is going manic,' said Alex with conviction. 'I have seen people who were mad when I used to go on the rounds with the doctor. They did all manner of things that were not usual to themselves.'

The cook looked serious at last. The grin left his lips and he edged closer to Alex. 'It's not been a good journey, I'll say that. There's been a queer feeling hanging over the ship, that I only felt the like of once afore, and I don't like to speak on that.'

'Please go down to the cabin,' begged Alex.

'Oh, very well. I'll tell the Captain you're wanted above, should he ask where you be at.'

When the cook had gone, Alex looked around the galley. It had been a meatless day, Ban Yan Day, and Alex felt that a large bowl of Burgoo (four parts barley and one part oatmeal mixed with meat juices and spices) would not come amiss, but he knew he would have to forgo any food without the cook's permission. As Alex waited for his return, he remembered a day which seemed long ago, but which was less than a year ago. Doctor Dawes had taken him to the home of a lawyer who, by mischance, had contracted a disease which required regular and painful treatment. While Alex had stayed in the trap outside, the lawyer's daughter had brought out to him a dainty, two-handled cup, filled with a hot, sweet, chocolate drink. The very thought of it sent a thrill down his spine and made his mouth dry with longing. He ran his tongue along his top lip just as the cook dashed into the galley, with the Captain's tray all of a rattle with his agitation.

'You been at the sugar again?' he asked breathlessly.

'I have not!' Alex replied indignantly.

'I seen you, licking your lips, boy.'

The cook was clearing the tray with nervous hands, clattering the dishes and cutlery, and avoiding Alex's gaze.

'Well, did you see the Captain? All dressed up like a lady?'

'When I went into the cabin, he was washing of himself. But, I did see a wicker basket with the straps undone. Peeking out was a floral, gauzy bit of cloth. It might have belonged to a woman's gown.'

'What did the Captain say to you?'

'First off, I says to him that I have come to collect the tray, the boy has been called aft. He replies, civil like, "I think we shall have a favourable wind before long." I said that I hoped we would. Then he hands to me a soaped sponge and says, "Be so obliging, Cookie, as to wash my back." I was so surprised that I did. Aye, and rough-towelled it too, and helped him on with a clean shirt.'

'I do that often,' Alex said with disdain. 'There is naught strange in that!'

'It makes a change from stirring the galley-pot anyway,' said the cook, tidying up the cutlery drawer. 'But, I was fair shaken that he allowed me to do that for him. It was not right!'

'No,' agreed Alex, 'it was not right for him to ask a cook to do such a thing for him.'

'This has been as strange a passage as I remember, it has indeed,' went on the cook, dipping a small spoon into black molasses. He gave it a twirl or two and then handed it to Alex. 'Don't you say a word about this to no one.' Alex took the spoon gratefully.

'No one mind! Not even that Ambrose!'

'I'll not tell a soul,' Alex assured him, as the cook began cutting up vegetables at a rapid pace and throwing them into the stewpot. Alex laid down the empty spoon and ventured, 'You think he's mad then?'

'Mad! Of course he's mad! What Captain would ask his cook to wash his back!'

'But the frock. He had on a frock!'

'Yes, so you said! But a Captain to ask a cook to wash his back!'

Alex gave up the struggle for sense and went up on deck. It seemed obvious to him that they would need more than a fair wind in their favour, if they were to reach Sydney Cove with any degree of safety and he fervently hoped the *Bold Adventurer* would not be written up in some dusty ledger in a shipping board office, as a ship that had floundered. He walked lightly on the very clean deck-boards, over which he had spent many hours, contributing to their whiteness, and slid down the companionway thinking of nothing else then, but a few hours sleep before the next watch.

In the next few days it became obvious to all the men on board that there was something amiss with the Captain. One man found him shaving on the forecastle, another found him in his cabin surrounded by little pieces of paper, which later proved to be leaves torn from the ship's log book and then shredded. He was either lying in his bunk, silent and retiring or up on deck cursing and lashing out wildly with his whip. His actions began to sow dissatisfaction amongst the men. They were down to rations of salt-beef with a few vegetables, weevily hard tack, and thin gruelly porridge which ashore Ambrose would have been loathe to feed the pigs. The water in the water butts had taken on a brackish flavour and many of the men stood in the rain with their mouths open, gulping down the purer drops of moisture as they stood watch or filled bowls and barrels for future use.

Day after day the rain swept over the ship in moist shawls, and buffeting and wet clothing extinguished any flame of adventure Ambrose and Alex had, as they spoke together of home and the people left behind. But always the Captain broke in on their misery, goading them, setting up their hackles until a kind of strength oozed into their sore and tired bodies. Then, suddenly,

Rule Of Thumb

the ship was in calm waters. The men were able to supplement their diet with fresh fish and their spirits rose accordingly in spite of the antics of the Captain whose moods swung from total lethargy to frenzied activity.

CHAPTER SIX

A few days from their goal the weather changed again. Alex was pacing aft and looking over the taffrail when he saw, to his concern, that the seas behind the ship were again leaden in colour and a glance at the sky and the flying clouds warned him that the breeze was freshening. He had not lived all his life by the sea without learning the moods of the tides, and seasons, and the overall capriciousness of the friend and enemy of man. By noon the clouds were being torn to flitters by the wind and the main topgallant had been hoisted so that the ship might run easy before the coming storm.

It was mid afternoon before the gale was upon them, heaving up the ship's stern and sinking her bows into the dark green furrows. Running before the gale the rest of the day, and the fearsome, noisy, night, the next morning found the ship in a very battered condition.

The Captain had retired early to his quarters and proceeded to get very drunk, and the crew had taken advantage of the laxity, for the First Mate was also laid up with a severely injured leg. They had not furled the canvas, in spite of the fierceness of the weather, and in consequence of this the sails not furled were split to rags. A succession of waves, breaking over the tilting ship had carried parts of the deck railing and the binnacle away with them. The Captain came up on deck as soon as he was awake. He was pale and dishevelled as he stood in the doorway. He yawned and rubbed his eyes. He opened his mouth to yawn again, and instead let out a roar as he saw the devastation of the night.

He raved, stamping up and down the deck, his whip, his constant companion, lashing out, frequent and fierce, on the bent backs of the terrified crew. Although the wind had abated, the ship heeled and lurched in the strong swell and Alex found it hard at times to keep his feet, for in spite of his experiences he was still without sea-legs and not like the other sailors who seemed to be able to walk up the side of a ship, like flies on a ceiling, without faltering.

Rule Of Thumb

Suddenly, there was a cry of 'Man overboard!' After a moment of panic and indecision, one of the crew, wide-eyed with alarm, ran to the ship's side, where the rail had been torn away and cried out, 'A rope, quickly, 'tis the Captain!'

Alex felt the blood rush to his knees and he almost fell, but another of the crew stood nearby, his arms folded, legs apace, and the sight of him steadied Alex. Then he saw that across the sailor's neck and shoulders blood ran thinly from the blistered wheal of a whiplash. Fear gripping in his throat, once more, Alex ran to the side of the ship together with others of the crew and as they scanned the choppy water with experienced eyes they pointed out, excitedly, the position of Captain Franklin. He had fallen into the water from where the rails had been torn away the night before, and as Alex looked down into the water, two arms, with extended fingers, began to beat the water, and the gaping mouth and fear-filled eyes of the drowning Captain appeared. A rope was tossed to him and for a brief moment it lay within reach of his groping fingers, but the waves foamed and eddied around him, and then swept him under and away. Sick and afraid, Alex walked from the side of the ship and sat down on a large coil of rope where Ambrose found him. He took Alex by the arm and helped him to his feet and as he did so they heard a voice come clear upon the air, 'Nature is not niggardly or unjust.' There was a ring to the sound and they both turned to seek out the owner, but the crew were already at their work and one man in a defiant tone had begun to sing a ribald song of the sea.

On the death of the Captain the First Mate assumed command of the ship. True he was still in pain and his leg was heavily bandaged for Alex dressed it for him repeatedly. It was a curious injury and although the First Mate had said that it was the result of burns from an overturned lamp, Alex thought as he dressed it that he detected teeth marks, and he thought that the First Mate had tried to cauterise the spot, and not been very skilful in doing the deed.

The day after the Captain drowned Alex said to the First mate, 'Where is Ebony?' He shrugged his shoulders and replied, 'How should I know?'

'Have you not been into the Captain's quarters?' Alex asked, amazed that he had not taken over his quarters.

'I will presently,' said the First Mate calling to two other seamen. 'Go down to the Captain's cabin and see where his slave is, for he is still a slave, in spite of the Captain's assurances.'

One of the men was the man who had fought him first and he went down to the cabin with the other seaman and Alex tagging on behind.

Rule Of Thumb

The cabin appeared empty. 'There's no one here! The bugger's thrown him overboard.'

'Serve him right then,' crowed Alex, 'for the sea to claim him. He was a wicked, evil man!'

Alex who knew that cabin better than the other man went to the cupboard-like room that he knew the Captain shut Ebony in, but it was quite empty and only a sour smell of faeces and urine filled the cabin. 'That will have to be cleaned down to the boards!'

Alex roamed about the cabin and then said, 'I wonder if the Captain killed Ebony and put his body in the window seat?' The other two men milled about, looking at one another, loathe to express what was on their minds. Just then Ambrose entered the cabin and as Alex was lifting the window seat where the Captain had kept some of his supplies, Ambrose took one end of the lid and they forced it upwards together.

A piteous sight met their eyes. Manacled and gagged, the unfortunate Ebony lay almost suffocated. His body was in a fearsome state, covered with sores, and clad only in a torn, striped nightshirt, which was liberally stained with sweat, urine, faeces, blood and pus. His dark and luminous eyes moved from one face to the other, apprehensive, as the men stood over him, too stunned for the moment by what they saw to say one word or offer any assistance, until Ambrose said, 'For pity's sake! Give the man air!' and taking the binder from around Ebony's mouth, he helped him carefully into a sitting position.

'Bring me a glass of madeira, Alex,' he ordered, and then held the glass as the slave sipped the fortified wine gratefully. The other two men felt guiltily that their place was elsewhere, seeing to the ship, and leaving the man in the capable and caring hands of Alex and Ambrose they went back on deck to tell of the terrible fate of Ebony. Alex and Ambrose took off Ebony's bonds and helped him from his erstwhile prison, then sat him on top of the closed seat. His eyes were fixed unwaveringly on Alex, who had begun to tremble out of pity and excitement. Then, to their amazement, Ebony spoke.

'Alex, do not tremble, the Captain will not like it.'

'He is not in a position to like or dislike, Ebony,' replied Ambrose, while Alex stood, his jaw dropped with astonishment.

'What happened to the Captain? Has he disembarked?' asked Ebony.

'He has indeed,' answered Ambrose. 'He lies drowned in the sea, miles from here in body, but his soul, no doubt, outside the gates of Hell!'

Just then the cook came in to the cabin and Alex ran to him saying, 'Ebony can speak!'

Rule Of Thumb

'I told you that this ox was not so dumb, didn't I. Well, get our friend up on deck and give him a good wash and a clean set of clothes. I will go and put on the fish kettle for a nice steam-up of something or other we got from over the side in the early hours of this morning.'

'Not the Captain?' queried Ebony, his raw and blistered hands held to his chest. All three there laughed.

'We wouldn't have the Captain for ransom. Too tough, too detested, and too much to say!'

Alex and Ambrose helped Ebony up to the deck where they doused him with sea-water until he begged them to stop. The salt water made his wounds smart and he longed only to lie upon the deck in the clean air. Alex brought him a clean nightshirt of the Captain's. With its loose sleeves and loose neck band it fitted Ebony reasonably well as he sat upon the deck taking in great gulps of fresh air. His eyes were large with excitement and a certain amount of triumph as Ambrose told him that he was now free.

'He was a bad fellow, hurt Jo-Jo all the time. Jo-Jo good servant. Bad people make bad spirits come calling!'

Ambrose nodded, 'Like calls to like. That is true in all things.'

The man who had fought Ebony last then came close and said, 'So your name is Jo-Jo. Well, you will have a better life from now on. I will take care of you, and you may share all that I have at present, which is little enough, but I have something in the offing once we come ashore.'

'If it is a ship in the offing I hope it is a better bark than this,' said Ambrose, who was hanging out a line of washing from Ebony. Even Jo-Jo laughed at that. Ambrose and Alex helped him to his feet and took him back to the captain's cabin. The nightshirt they had put him in on deck was already spotted with pus and blood from his wounds so while Ambrose helped him out the nightshirt Alex opened up the medicine chest and took out wadding and several strips of linen, and a pottery jar containing a yellowy-green salve. When Alex had bandaged the worst of the sores, Ambrose took up another of the Captain's nightshirts and slipped it over his head.

'You look like an Emir,' said Ambrose.

'Why did you not speak before?' asked Alex, all his tension now removed.

'Captain forbid! He say to my last master that he wants a mute servant. My master has no mute servant but he has Jo-Jo who is a good servant and knows when to hold his tongue! So Captain Franklin purchase me. We come on board and he says that if I speak he will cut out my tongue! He had bad feelings. I think he likes to keep his men afraid but now the bad spirits have heard and taken him as their own.'

Just then the cook entered the cabin bearing a steaming pot of fish broth, fish flakes, potatoes, spices and meal.

'Wrap yourself around this, you'll feel a new man in no time,' he said, as he put the pot down on the table and handed Jo-Jo a large spoon. Ambrose brought up the Captain's carver chair to the table and sat Jo-Jo in it. He ate and rewarded the cook with a broad and toothless smile.

'You two had better get some vitals inside of you if you are to clean up the cabin,' the cook said to Ambrose and Alex. 'Jo-Jo can sleep in the Captain's bunk after his meal while you do it!'

When they returned to the deck they found all manner of repairs were underway. Carpentry and sail mending, tarring and rope splicing, happy and contented the seamen worked alongside each other without a cross word. Alex and Ambrose sat amongst them with their broth, the other men having eaten before.

'Have I stepped on to another ship?' Alex asked.

'No, we have stepped out of the clutches of a sadistic Captain. We must thank God for our deliverance.'

Some of the men watching heard Alex and Ambrose, and began to say the Lord's prayer, others joined in and soon there was a reverent murmur lifting into the balmy air.

Although the recent storm had washed away the binnacle, the seamen knew that they were nearing land. Seabirds had made their appearance, resting on the crests of the waves, like a smother of foam, and were greeted by the crew with shouts and whistles and much throwing about of caps. As Alex looked out, over the glaring expanse of water, he thought in the distance he could discern a faint, grey-purple line on the horizon, and hoped it might be the land for which they were bound. He called to one of the men to come and see.

'There, can you see? Is it land?'

The man spurted a mahogany stream of tobacco juice from between his wide spaced teeth, and squinted his eyelids into slits, but shook his head.

'Nay, nay, laddie, that's not land! It's nothing but the roll of the ocean. That and impatience!' He put his hand on Alex's shoulder and patted it. 'You bide awhile. It's out there somewhere close. The last hours are always longest after a long, bad trip. Thank God the cargo has kept whole and not shifted since we set sail, and is as dry and cosy as a mouse's nest.'

No sooner had he spoken than the First Mate hobbled up and called the men together.

'When we get to where we are going, no man must leave the ship until I have talked with the authorities ashore.' There were deep groans from some of the men. 'We must all stay together. The cargo must stay in the holds until the authorities give clearance. We have lost our Captain overboard. That is a serious business enough . . . the cargo must remain intact lest we be branded thieves also. I forbid tales likely to spread unease on shore. We do not wish to be thought mutineers or murderers.' He glared down upon the men around him. 'Any one of you that sets foot on shore without my leave will forfeit his pay and cargo bonus.'

The men were sensible enough to agree, that if the crew were to come out of the affair without taint, they must comply, although a few, when dismissed, had gloomy and dejected looks to their faces.

For himself, Alex felt exhilarated. To be free of the interminable fluctuations of maritime weather and the ship itself, seemed to him to be the ultimate in comfort.

Alex had found that there was no virtue in necessity, and longed for the comparative luxury of land life, fresh water, fresh food and dry, clean clothing. His growing excitement threatened to infiltrate his defences, and he felt close to tears as he stared out over the last miles between the *Bold Adventurer* and landfall. His eyes grew bloodshot with the strain, and he turned away, knuckling his eyes, and turning his attention to the sounds of the ship. What a noisy crew they were to be sure! What a hive of industry! Hatch bolts rattled, sail was hoisted with shouts and cries and the occasional oath was uttered, like some caterwauling contest while the First Mate hobbled painfully amongst them barking orders to all and sundry.

Alex and Ambrose returned to the Captain's cabin and proceeded to obliterate all signs of Jo-Jo's captivity. Soon the room behind the cabin, the cabin and the window seat that had almost become Jo-Jo's coffin was wholesome again. All the while Jo-Jo slumbered in the Captain's bunk, they washed and polished and dried and tidied. When they had finished they went on deck and Alex was set to trim the wicks of all the lamps on board and Ambrose was set to oil every bit of machinery that had so much as a whisper of a creak. The carpenter and several less skilled men were repairing shattered rails and woodwork, to the best of their ability, with the materials they had to hand. The crew took it in turns to climb the mast head, each one eager to be the first to sight land.

The First Mate drew Alex to one side as he was filling up the oil container, prior to refilling the trimmed lamps.

'A word, Alex,' he said drawing him close to him. He was pulling at his bottom lip which Alex took to be a sign that he was troubled, so he listened attentively as the First Mate, in little more than a whisper, spoke directly into his ear. 'You be careful, lad, when we gets ashore. You done well aboard your first ship for a young 'un! Questions will be asked, and some of us may fare bad because of the answers we shall be forced to give. We be heading for a rum spot, convicts and the like. Boys be sent to the hulks, younger than you, and . . . and transported for seven years after!'

'Well, they can't transport me to Australia, I'll be there,' retorted Alex with a cheeky grin.

'So you shall, lad, so you shall. But it is a bad business and we shall all be reckoned to have had a hand in it. Say no more than you have to, the slave's back and those of others must be used in testimony of the Captain's state of mind. But men ashore may not believe what they hear and we may be forced to take the consequences of that!' He moved away, shaking his head and biting his lips.

As the mate hobbled away, Jo-Jo appeared on deck, and going to the ship's side, stretched his arms wide and took in deep breaths of fresh air.

'Land not far away,' he said.

'I hope so,' replied Alex.

'I know so!' uttered Jo-Jo with conviction.

'You have slept well whilst we cleaned the cabin,' said Alex.

'I have slept most well. You have been very kind to me. You have a good friend in Ambrose, I think. When you go to land you stay together?' he asked.

Before Alex could answer, there was a cry of, 'Land ahoy!' from the crow's nest, and all took up the cry, 'Land ahoy!' and crowded to see the welcome line of the landfall fringed with white and gold. The telescope was handed round and calculations were made upon just where along the coastline the ship might be landed. It had been judged that the storm had come whilst they were in the Bass Straits but now it was feared that they might well have been driven off course. There was much speculation amongst the crew as charts were consulted and past memories drawn upon by seamen who had sailed the waters on previous voyages.

'Might even be an island out there. Bass Straits is cluttered with islands and reefs,' said one.

'Might be Tasmania,' said another.

'Might be a mirage,' said yet another, edgily.

'I don't care what it is as long as I can get both my feet on it!' said Ambrose.

'Aye,' said the First Mate. 'Neither do I. Let's make our best for it before nightfall. Crowd on more sail and get this racy breeze behind us. We may be

Rule Of Thumb

harboured before the moon is up.'

As the ship was manoeuvred, the thin blue line became nearer and at last gave way to a hazy blue then a dark verdant green. About the ship there suddenly appeared water-shoals, and reefs became discernable. Alex went to the side of one of the men who dropped a plumbline into the water to ascertain the depths. Alex watched the trail of foaming waves from the stern as the ship sailed through the larger rocks and a faint uneasiness filled the pit of his stomach. The other men were beginning to have doubts and in a few moments were aware that the harbour they hoped for was the mouth of a river.

The ship was old, built in 1770, of English oak, and built for cargo, not speed. Her bottom was not sheathed in copper as ships were a decade later, and the four inches of timber would be so much firewood to the rocks of some cruel reef. True they carried boats, should the worst occur, but even then they would take short shrift against the tiger-sharp teeth that now barred the waterway. The men began hurling invectives at one another as the ship heeled over at an angle. The cargo below had taken enough and had begun to shift.

'Go down below, Alex, you are only a slim lad and can creep about like a monkey. Take a lantern with you, and see what it is that is amiss, whilst we drop anchor and furl sail.'

Whilst Alex was lighting the lantern the ship juddered heavily, flinging everyone about and the order was 'Back sail.' Whilst this was done Alex hoped that the ship was not holed or held. It was then that they saw in the distance a simple boat with a lateen sail and as it came swiftly towards them on the flow of the current, they could see in the boat three men. The small boat bobbed skilfully between the rocks and soon they were in hailing distance. 'Where are you bound?' they shouted as one.

'Sydney,' came the reply in unison.

'You're off course. Back water,' came the reply. 'You are in Shoalhaven river. You need the Parramatta. You are not far away.' They waved their farewells and as the ship was backed off the reef, Alex and Ambrose slipped down into the hold to see to the cargo. Several packing cases had come adrift from their tight corners due to the constant wearing of the ropes which bound them, and several boardings had been shifted with the weight of the packing cases. This had allowed bales, trunks and sacks of food and small barrels of wine to list about in a very dangerous and disconcerting manner. It was obvious that these must be made safe once more before the ship could be sailed again.

Alex went on deck, told what he had discovered and several men went back with him to where Ambrose was beginning to make the goods secure. Soon all was ship-shape again and the men went up on deck to tell the First Mate.

'That is well done, my lads, we may now back sail to deeper water and make for the Parramatta river and so on to Sydney Harbour. As for the cargo, we may yet be forgiven for losing our Captain overboard, but to lose our cargo as well would have been a totally different matter.'

The men smiled, but their hearts were heavy, and they were too weary to think about port, but went about their tasks with a dreary air, automatically tightening a rope here, slackening one there, pushing a spar or hammering in a nail where it was wanted. It seemed to Ambrose, who had read the classics, that even Jason of the Golden Fleece would have baulked at the journey they had made. There was one thing he knew, that if the ship did hold together until they reached Sydney Heads, and the safety of the harbour, the *Bold Adventurer* was past mastering for another long voyage. As long as there was plenty of draft under her she would carry, but she was a sullen craft in the shallows and with her holds clewed down. She would take on the job of a coastline goods carrier, or maybe a storage hulk down on the wharves, but that was all she would ever be fit for again.

With a brittle, raking sound, the ship was in free water again. Now in deeper channels the slap of the waves came up to the men as they crowded on sail again before the breeze. They sailed on as night fell, and then, at about four o'clock in the morning, in the distant gloom there was a faint glow. It was like a star in their darkness. They drew nearer, and the glow deepened and widened, and they knew in their hearts that what lay before them was Sydney Heads and the Harbour.

CHAPTER SEVEN

It was well for the crew of the *Bold Adventurer* that the Supreme Court was in the throes of a readjustment of policies. Sydney had been a wild town, once, full of convicts in open styled prisons. Now those convicts had served their sentences and settled there and had been joined by emigrants looking for a new way of life. A wind of change was blowing but it had a softer tone, a more beneficent image. It was the beginning of an age when the law could listen as well as pontificate, but they still asked a lot of questions, and even Alex was put in the dock.

'Let the boy speak,' said the magistrate. 'He is too young as yet to dissemble. Was the Captain always kind to you?'

'No, sometimes he was very cruel. He hurt me by hurting others!'

'And how did he do that?'

'He would punish Ambrose because he knew he was my friend. He brought a slave on board and used him to terrorise the rest of us by his cruelty to him. He threatened Jo-Jo that he would cut out his tongue if he so much as confided in us. That was the Captain, sir. A very bad man, but I am told he was a good Captain once. I believe, sir, that Captain Franklin had gone mad.' A murmur rang through the court.

'And who is Jo-Jo?'

'I am here, sir!' he cried, pushing his way to the side of the dock.

'You are Jo-Jo, the slave? Much punished by your late master?'

Jo-Jo pulled up his jacket to reveal the strips, cuts and weals of his beatings. A gasp hung in the air, as the onlookers saw the evidence of the Captain's cruelty.

'Captain Franklin, he very bad man to rule others. He has demon in his head.'

'He had a demon in his head,' the magistrate corrected.

'Yes, you know that too! Demons make him do bad things. He also carry demon in bottle. It jumps down his throat and makes him laugh and cry, then other demons come and he lashes them with his whip and he lashes Jo-

Jo too. Jo-Jo does not see other demons, and they do not leave blood on the floor. Jo-Jo bleed, his blood is on the floor and everywhere.'

When the day came for the summing up of the case, the magistrate said to the assembled courtroom, 'Are we to think then that Captain Franklin had grown mad by the vagaries of his vices? Or was his madness a recent affliction brought on by physical and mental adversities? An eventful voyage, plus the responsibility of an over-cargoed, under-manned, over-old ship?'

The authorities laboured on over the loss of the Captain of the *Bold Adventurer*, and while they were still debating, a man who had not been on the ship pushed the matter to the crew's favour. He stood up in the hot courthouse and blurted out, 'I knew Captain Franklin in England! He took a bull-whip to me for telling him his younger brother had been committed to the hulks!' A harsh whisper crept round the spectators, and a voice rang out, 'Put that man on oath!' The man found himself gripped by the arms and ushered up to the dock. There he took the oath, and squaring his shoulders looked up at the magistrate.

'And when did Captain Franklin take a bull-whip to you?'

'In the month of March, 1815, your honour.'

'You have a good memory. It is now 1823. Most people can find difficulty in recalling events of a few weeks ago, let alone eight years ago!'

'I got good cause never to forget it!' the man replied and a titter of mirth rippled round the room at his audacity.

'No doubt,' replied the magistrate, 'but, we here have only your word for it!'

'Words said on oath!' retorted the fellow, warming to his audience as they to him. 'And, your honour, if I might take off my shirt, I will show you the stripes that can say all without ado.'

'Stripes you may show us but they do not confirm time, place or by whom. But, if you insist you may divest yourself.'

His half-opened shirt was slipped from his tanned shoulders to reveal the thickened, healed stripes, from bull-neck to waist. The courtroom audience sucked in their breaths with sympathy, although striped backs were nothing new to them.

'Went skeptic on me,' said the man squaring his shoulders, for he knew his physique was something quite unusual. The magistrate smiled at the word 'skeptic' but he knew what the man meant. He made several notes on the paper before him before he said, 'You may return your shirt now, and give us your true opinion of Captain Franklin, if possible without bias!'

'My opinion of him, your honour, was that he was no gentleman. He was a fiend in velvet!'

'Thank you. You may step down.'

The man did so. He had a beaming smile on his face as he went to his place in the centre of the courtroom. He had done his duty, he had taken his revenge!

Alex watching the proceedings felt like he was watching a play, except that he did not enjoy his role, and a giant rat seemed to be gnawing away at his vitals the whole of the time. Sometimes he felt as guilty as if he had drowned the Captain in his own bath-tub. Sometimes he wondered why he hadn't. It had been one of his duties on board to fill the wooden structure, after lining it with a sheet, with numerous buckets of hot sea water heated up in the galley. Alex had never known such a man for hot soaks. He himself could not remember when he had last had a hot bath, and he doubted if the members of the crew could.

The voices droned on into the hot afternoon but at last all was resolved. Alex was glad to be away from the restrictions of the courthouse and the First Mate praised him for the evidence he had given.

'Now everything is down in writing and it has been seen that the crew did not give the Captain a sly push or that they mutinied.'

Alex smiled and smiled with the relief of it all, until his cheekbones ached with the strain, as he helped unload the cargo and ran errands for the crew and made himself as agreeable as he could to the men of the crew whom he knew it was likely that after a few days he would never see again. All except Ambrose, their pact still stood firm.

When the work on board was finished and they were paid their dues, Alex and Ambrose hurried towards the town, their bundle of personal belongings over their shoulders.

Sydney was a beautiful, natural harbour, and the blue sparkle of the water, the healthy greenery all around, and the new stone of the many buildings, made their hearts leap with hope.

But the outskirts were very different. There dwelt the no-hopers, the penniless, the homeless, the drifters, and the adventurers. Inevitably, Alex and Ambrose were drawn to them, like sticks to a vortex. They walked down the streets bearing the names of London thoroughfares, and listened to men with the sound of Bow bells in their voices. These men told of beatings, prison, and death, and also pardons and resettlement. Some were taking a chance on exploration. Some believed there was an inland sea, others that precious metals and jewels could be dug out of the dry and desolate wastes of the interior that lay behind the Blue Mountains. In some regions, they said, the ground was strewn with pot-hole after pot-hole of abandoned hopes. Alex and Ambrose sat down under the shade of a blue gum tree and debated their future. It was not possible to go back to England on the *Bold Adventurer*. She was to be auctioned for use as a cargo coaster, if it was found she could be trusted, for she had taken many hard knocks lately and the worm had got in her timbers.

'I suppose we might try our hand at sheep-herding,' said Alex. 'You know something about sheep, and about farming and shearing. Let's go down to the holdings by the shoreline and see if we can meet up with someone like ourselves.'

Ambrose silently assured him of his participation by standing up and gathering their few belongings together. They shouldered them and made their way to a half-stone, half-timbered dwelling, where several men had thrown in their lots and by pooling their slim resources, kept body and souls together. By speaking with these men, Alex and Ambrose were no wiser as to what course they should take, for whilst one confirmed enthusiastically the virtues of the new country, another condemned, and it became obvious that if they were to rely on any experience, it would have to be their own. They did, however, agree to stay at the dwelling for it was near to the shoreline and surrounded by plenty of grass and soft bush and a few blue gums. As they settled round the cooking fire, eating heartily of roasted meat and partaking of the nourishing broth, boiled up in an ancient iron pot, they both felt a contentment they had not felt for many months. They listened intently to the tales the men had to tell of the thirsty wilderness of the interior. A few of them were men already broken in health and spirit by the terrible privations, scratching a living as best they could, sleeping sometimes in the open, cooking over a pile of gum tree bark and sticks. To those who were young it could be a blissfully romantic time, watching the soft plumes of smoke scenting the air as it rose wraith-like from the crackling red sparks and flickering flames as they ate their suppers. They could hardly visualise the perils that awaited the explorers into the unknown hinterland, while they were told by leather-faced, lean limbed men that in the best seasons one could ride girth high through the native grasses and find no lack of water in natural wells, clay pans or creeks. But, then again, at the worst times, dazzling sunrays beat down from cloudless skies, over the rough ironstone ridges that cropped up from the tableland, bringing an enveloping stupefying heat not known outside Dante's Inferno.

Alex's gaze was drawn to one man who sat with head bowed and arms dangling before the glowing fire and when he did, at last, raise his head, his

Rule Of Thumb

face had a starved look and his eyes stared out doleful and dark, like two holes burned in a grey rag.

Alex vaguely wondered at his story, but guessed that it was transportation in lieu of the rope. Whatever it was, he did not mean to tell it to anyone, and rose slowly to his feet and went into the slant-roofed building where they were all to sleep.

There was still the slight odour of roasting meat upon the air although all the last remnants had been either devoured or fed to the flames to heat the weak beer that was now passing from hand to lip in a cracked washstand jug. Alex savoured the moment wrapped in delicious calm. It felt good to be still. Most of the men began to amble into the building, stretching and yawning, ready for a night of sleep. Ambrose and Alex, being newcomers, followed more slowly, waiting for the others to bed themselves before entering the long room. It was almost dark inside and it took a few moments for their eyes to become accustomed to the dimness around them, but they eventually came to a patch of floor not covered by a man. There they prepared to settle down on the hard packed earthen floor, their possessions under their heads for both safety and comfort. Surprisingly enough, they both slept, and most of the men were outside when they awoke to the savoury smell of cooking on the fire outside. They eased themselves up and wandered out into the open with their packs slung over their shoulders. There were a few nods exchanged and a few words of greeting and a place was made for them. There was a certain amount of sobriety amongst the men as they warmed themselves, warding off the chill of early morning, though it was January and summertime. The flames licked the bottom of the soot-encrusted kettle as it sat amongst the branches and twigs and the skillet was handled carefully over the charcoal embers.

Ambrose and Alex took little of the food cooked over the fire, being painfully aware that they had done little to earn it, or add to the now meagre stores. The question of work was now to the forefront, but what to do they had no notion since the men they appeared to have cast their lot with did not seem to have work either.

'We have been thinking about getting work inland,' said Ambrose to one of the more friendly disposed men.

'Work?' asked the man, pulling on his upper lip and looking as if it was a word he had not heard before. 'Inland?' he looked about him with a questioning air. The other men seemed amused and one or two writhed upon the ground in their repressed mirth. Ambrose and Alex looked askance of each other, wondering what they had said to trigger off the sudden outburst.

'You don't work here unless you have to, you ninnies!' said a hatchet-faced man. 'There's things here just for the gathering. Wood for fires, fish in the sea, shellfish, crabs, birds and young roo. Then there are edible berries or roots, and fruits of all kinds. What do you want to work for?'

'Money!' said Alex, glad that the money they had got for their dues was safely stashed in the middle of their packs.

'Well, pardon me!' replied the man with an air of assumed elegance, 'if you're going to bring money into it, that bloody well ruins everything!' Ambrose laughed in spite of himself.

'We thought we might get taken on as herders and I can shear,' offered Ambrose.

'If I were you, I'd shear off, the both of you!' He laughed at his pun and the other men joined in. 'Stay with us and you'll turn crazy as loons in no time. If you want to work and because you have a clean record you'll probably get work. But you'll have to search.'

'Well, I think we will push off after we have stocked up some wood for you all and done a bit to help the dinner-pot,' said Ambrose, but the men waved this aside, saying that it would give them something to do, and foraging was no hardship.

'Scout round in the town for a bit,' advised the leather-faced man. 'You might get a good, clean, rooming house to take you in. You got nice ways, and look innocent enough. Some motherly Mrs Hubbard will give you a room on trust, I've no doubt, if you have means to pay the rent later!'

They set off at once, and after a few moments of overwhelming panic at leaving the men who had shared their food and shelter with them, their thoughts finally became calm and controlled.

Other men discovered gold-bearing quartz, why not they? Other men found adequate work and settled. They could do that too! They made their way down towards the harbour, and the first person they saw was Jo-Jo. He stood alongside his new master, tidily dressed in a tawny outfit with bone buttons and sturdy tan leather footwear on his broad feet. His master was dressed in black breeches, white silk stockings, and silver buckled, square-toed shoes. He had on a short jacket of red velvet, adorned with silver lace and heavy turned back velvet cuffs, over a ruffled shirt which he had opened at the neck. When Alex drew close, he could see the riverlet of sweat that ran down his face into the neckline. It was stifling hot, his face was as red as a lobster, while Jo-Jo stood unperturbed, a straw haulm in his mouth, a golden spicle against the purply-black of his skin.

'I wondered where you two had got to,' said Jo-Jo's master. 'Have you got work somewhere?'

Ambrose and Alex shook their heads, and the man said with a laugh, 'You take my advice and head for home, that is what Jo-Jo and myself are doing. Off to England on the next tide.'

'I'm afraid we must see you go,' replied Ambrose, restraining Alex. 'We intend to try our hand at sheep herding or some such work until we come by a little money. Then, who knows, we can try our fortune in the interior.'

'And so you might, my brave boys,' said the man laughing again. 'But try not your fortune too hardy! I hear there is a grim heart to the land behind that range yonder. A place that throbs with heat so strong that only an Aborigine can survive its arid nature. Yet I hear he is a timid creature, easily frightened, carrying only for his defence a shield and a boomerang.'

'If he is easily frightened, then we have nothing to fear from him,' answered Ambrose, 'and he nothing from us, for we have no defence, except our bare hands, and at close quarters our teeth!'

At the word teeth, Jo-Jo became quite animated. 'See,' he said proudly, 'see what I have!' He pointed to the place in his mouth where once a black gap, filled with a pink tongue tip, was exposed with each smile. Several carved, ivory teeth, secured by gold wire around adjoining teeth, now graced the gap. True, they were not of the gleaming, dense whiteness of his natural teeth, but Jo-Jo now ate and smiled with unusual distinction.

'My master's gift!' he said, spreading his hands wide and then bowing low to that worthy. Ambrose and Alex admired the teeth and the action of Jo-Jo's new master before they hurried away to go on board the ship. They felt a depression settle over them, torn by their desire to follow and the desire to try their fortunes in this new and challenging environment.

CHAPTER EIGHT

The day was hot and sunny, and Alex was loathe to walk very far through the thoroughfares of the town, so he persuaded Ambrose to keep down on the docks and wharves where there was a chance of a breeze from the waters of the harbour. But later in the day Ambrose had to insist that if they were to find shelter and food that night they would have to stir themselves and go into the area of settlements.

They had walked a fair distance, rejecting first one and then another of the 'to let' signs, and their packs were heavy on their shoulders, when they came across a sort of tavern. Alex was immediately drawn there because of the smell of food wafting from the building. The building itself was rudely erected from rejected timbers and straw and canvas but it appeared to be a place where they might get wholesome refreshment.

When they entered the building they saw a large deal topped table, surrounded on four sides with rustic benches. On them sat four men, two of whom seemed to be in their early twenties, a man in his forties, and another of whom it was impossible to tell his age. His face was covered by a beard, matted and greying, and his hair hung down his back in uncombed hanks. On his head he wore a felted hat fringed with antimacassar bobbles and a red neckerchief was knotted rakishly around his scrawny neck. His shirt was collarless and patched, his trousers a thick fustian, his stockingless feet encased in hard leather boots, turned up at the toes. He was holding audience with the three younger men, and Alex and Ambrose ordered savoury hash from the woman who came and stood aggressively over them with hands on hips and growled, 'Savoury hash, or fat fried veg! Take your pick, or have both if you have the money.'

The woman's name, they learned later, was Grace, and she had been transported there for the manslaughter of her husband. Having served her term she now worked at the tavern, serving drink but mainly food. The hash she brought to Alex and Ambrose was, indeed, savoury and filling, and being very hungry they both enjoyed it very much. Grace expanded a little as they paid her and complimented her on her cooking.

'You look like you could do with a bit o' bagging,' she said as she took hold of Alex's thin arm. 'Will you look at that! It's some time since you knew good vittals. It's no thicker than a young roo's tail! Where you been, lads?'

'Down on the docks, and round and about,' Alex said. 'We came over on the *Bold Adventurer*.'

'Oh!' said Grace, wiping over the table with an even sweep of her buxom arm. 'Heard about that journey! Lost your Captain! Well, don't you grieve none over that. I knew that scally-onion too!'

The old man turned then to Alex and Ambrose. 'Jack Tars, eh! I was once the same. Landlubber now, and glad to be so, though I stuck it for twenty years before I came ashore for the last time.' He lit an ancient pipe and puffed contentedly for a few minutes, while Ambrose and Alex sat digesting their ample meal. Then the old man said teasingly, 'I once had a journey that was so bad I was fair pickled in brine by the end of it. True as I'm here, the moment I steps ashore, a yellow-maned dog come up behind me, and gives me such a hearty nip in the calf of me leg, I nearly faints from the pain of it. Well, I hollers to one of me mates and he comes and sees the sneaky tyke off, and there I am, hopping like a pelican with me bill open and no sound coming from it. My mate he bursts out laughing, and sings out, "Sure he thought it was a shank o' bacon, it's that full o' salt." It was too! That's what saved that leg o' mine! Hard as teak, and not a bit o' poison from off them mangy fangs, survived the night, and next day, apart from a bit of a limp and a headache, I was as good as new!'

Grace let out a guffaw, and slapped the old man across the shoulder. 'You were never new, Tommy Connelley,' she scoffed good-naturedly, 'and that aching head you found in a bottle!' They all laughed at that, and Grace once more turned her gaze on the boys. 'You two got a job?' They shook their heads. 'Like to work for me?' 'Doing what?' Ambrose asked warily.

Grace hunched her shoulders, 'Chopping and fetching wood, cleaning vegetables, humping provisions from the docks, what ever there is to do.'

'What do you think, Alex, you're good at cleaning vegetables?'

'I can't pay you anything,' went on Grace, 'but I'll feed you until you can find something more to your liking, and there's a shack out the back where you can bed down at night. Agreed?' she asked looking intently into their faces as they hesitated.

Alex and Ambrose looked at one another and deciding they had nothing to lose, agreed.

Rule Of Thumb

'Right,' said Grace, 'jump to it then! First job's to earn your supper, wood box filled, meat trimmed and vegetables cleaned. Collect the eggs from the pen. You'll find the eggs in nests under the bushes in the pen. Don't let them chickies scare you none. Be firm, and pop whatever you can find that looks like an egg into this basket here!'

'Grace Bluette!' said the old man. 'That is a lot of jobs for a scrawny bite of supper!'

She laughed a full, round laugh that rose up to the rafters, and crinkled up her face, pushing fat folds upwards, closing the black, twinkling eyes.

Fortified by the wholesome meal they had just eaten, and the jolly company they seemed to have fallen into, Ambrose and Alex set to with a willing heart. At last, things were brighter and assured. To have a bed and board and a job all in one day was a good and welcome benefit. The two lads worked quickly, and Grace was eager with her praises as she fanned her red and perspiring face, put up her fat legs upon a stool, and laid back on a bench with her ample buttocks against the wallboards.

'I'm right glad you fell in here, lads. You both be willing and what's more handsome. Now don't you go blushing! That's something rare around here! Don't you think so, Tom Connelly?'

'That it is. That it is!' echoed Tom, giving Grace a wink. 'And I'm thinking two such might draw in a few ladies to your parlour for their supper, as well as the hungry men around here.'

'The thought had crossed my mind,' agreed Grace. 'Many a match is struck over a bit o' bagging, and if I can help in the marriage stakes around here, who is to complain? I don't mind losing a few of the good men who come here to other ladies and their cooking!'

'Grace, Grace, you are a sneaky sort of cupid, and that's a fact,' said Tom with a whinnying laugh. 'But, many will have cause to bless you, hash and all!'

'Tom, that is the nicest thing you ever said to me,' Grace replied roguishly, as Tom Connelly slipped out of the door and into the street.

'He'll be back,' said Grace to Alex, who was stirring the new-cut onions and potatoes into boiling water at the stove.

Night came, the men crowded into the tavern, and were fed well and given their ration of beer. It was eleven o'clock before Alex and Ambrose sought their beds in the shack behind the tavern.

There were several rough beds but the place smelled clean and the walls had been given a coat of whitewash recently. They settled down in adjoining beds with contented sighs and slept well until morning. On awakening they were surprised to find that five more beds were occupied. The men had come silently into the shack during the night, returning from the outback with tales of semi-precious metals, pebbles, tales of opals, gold, inland seas, aborigines, new songs, and the agonies of their daily meanderings. Best of all, from Grace's point of view, they had brought with them several additions to the astonishing cook-pot. Ambrose and Alex stood amazed at the selection of meat and fish Grace placed on the table outside for them to chop up or carve. Wombat, kangaroo, snake, rabbit, small shark, and several fish, large and small. There were several species of wild bird, all of which were used in Grace's savoury stews.

The five men stayed for two weeks, before setting out once more, on their various trails. Well fed and rested, eager to try for fortunes, to battle with the elements, they made their way singly, and at their own pace, towards the magnificent mountain ranges many miles away.

Two days later Tom Connelly humped his pack onto his bowed back and set off into the hazy blue distance, to fossick about the mountain ranges, also entirely alone. Grace had helped him to gather together all he might need without question. She felt he ought not to go even though she had, from time to time, felt he was under her feet. She had even said so, though not unkindly.

Alex and Ambrose watched him go. Ambrose marvelling at his determination in spite of his years, Alex knowing that the urge Tom felt was not unlike that his father had known, and recently himself, as he craved to go to sea.

A few weeks later a straggling party of hunters came into the tavern, one of them bearing a battered pack. As soon as Grace saw it she threw up her hands and 'came over all peculiar', and had to be revived by deep sips of strong gin. The hunters then told her that they had buried an old cove they had found, stretched out dead beside a dried up water hole. His water can was empty, and his provisions gone. It was an old story. Men perished in the arid zones of this land. They had buried him above a deep gulley that contained only a thin trickle of rusty-coloured water, wedging him under a narrow neck of dry rock, under the slope of a spur, so that the dingo dogs would not get at him.

Grace threw up her hands in horror, then clutched the pack to her. It contained nothing of value, but the hunters agreed that she should keep it, and in return tell the authorities that Tom Connelly had gone to meet his maker.

Ambrose and Alex on hearing of the fate of Tom, were less inclined to

Rule Of Thumb

try their hand in the interior, or even step beyond the boundary of the town. They continued to work for Grace, filling out in limbs and faces and enjoying life at an easy, carefree pace. They were well pleased with their lot, listening to the tales of hunters and adventurers but never wishing to join them. They had plenty to keep them occupied. Grace seemed to get larger by the week, until she could hardly raise herself from her chair to go to the stove, and she was loathe to let two lads get into 'habits of idleness that led to wickedness of all sorts'. Since Grace had once taken a chopper to her idle and wicked husband, Alex and Ambrose gave her no cause to complain of their willingness to take on any task asked of them. Grace was not hard to please, she was a good woman at heart, driven to her former actions by desperation, bred of poverty and fear.

Out in the bush dogs howled in the night, but by day they swarmed about the shack, 'romping, sniffing and fornicating', as Grace said, as she took a broom to them. The dogs had no passionate return of feeling for that object and eventually one of them, larger and bolder than the rest, wrested it out of her hold and ran triumphantly on to the steaming dunghill with the broom in its jaws, followed by a yelping, whining pack, eager to share his prize. Some time later, when the dunghill had been scattered over a wide area, the broom bitten into firekindling, and the shaft splintered beyond repair, a large pack of filthy creatures ambled amiably along the alleyways and streets. They were of all sizes, but all of them smelled equally nauseating.

Ambrose and Alex patiently restored the dunghill to its former site and size, but this time they fenced it in with boards. The Indian Summer sun grew hotter. The suffocating heat pervaded the surrounds of the shack and the fenced in dunghill drew innumerable flies, swiftly followed by chirping birds, taking advantage of the airborne feast.

Grace puffed and panted in the sultry heat. As well as her colossal size, hot spicy food, alcohol and the torrid climate had affected her blood pressure, and her liver and kidneys to such a degree, that it became plain to all that Grace was much afflicted. When she slept, her nasal yowling, from congested lungs, seemed to shake the whole of the structure.

Ambrose and Alex ran the place as best they could, cooking the savoury stews and keeping the tavern reasonably clean. It was not the sort of work they wanted, but they had grown fond of Grace and felt that to abandon her now would be ungrateful and insulting.

Now Grace was enormous and unlovely, lying on her bed, puffing and blowing, like an enraged grampus, her face wet with perspiration and so red and swollen that her eyes were just dark slits.

Rule Of Thumb

Her voice came in little gulpy breaths as she urged Ambrose to bring a clerk from the town to see her will. Ambrose was loathe to do this, but she insisted, saying that she wanted to make matters right, should she die soon, and she feared she might.

It was Alex who went into town and brought a solicitor's clerk to the tavern, Grace being shrewd enough to pay 'money up front', to be sure of immediate attention.

They climbed the rickety stairs to the room where Grace lay, her head thrown back, her mouth slackly open. There was a stench in the room that made them all gag. Flies buzzed frenziedly around the stinking form on the bed, and then zoomed erratically away, as the mound that was Grace, heaved and grunted. Ambrose took up a fly whisky and hastily smashed all the flies he could hit to a pulp. Alex pinned a lace curtain to the open window shutting out some of the terrible invaders, while the clerk quickly authorized the will, and promised to send a doctor to see Grace. 'Best for you to send an undertaker,' said Grace, heaving her fleshy form about the soiled bed. But, the clerk was as good as his word and the doctor duly arrived. He sat in the now cleaned bedroom, and the flies were no longer able to invade the bed as before. He looked at Grace and shook his head.

'How long have you been in this condition?'

Grace looked at him out of her pig-slit eyes and said huskily, 'Too long.'

'It is too late for me to help you to get better, but I will make your last days more comfortable.'

Ambrose and Alex were aghast at his callous approach. Hope had been abandoned, but they clung to his offer of help and Alex said he would go back to town to receive the prescription the doctor recommended.

Ambrose and Alex were stunned by the fact that they were now owners of the Tavern, but they were not allowed to forget there were dinners and suppers to prepare and this they did with the help of conscripts from the diners themselves. They also brought in a 'nurse' from the town. A strong, mannish type of a woman who could manage Grace's bulk without difficulty, and kept her clean and well dosed with the doctor's elixir. It did not save her, as the doctor had predicted, and within three days she was dead.

As Ambrose and Alex looked at her in her coffin in the tavern dining room ... the face paled, the tortured body still, the rough tongue quiet, they considered their good fortune due to the kindness of Grace Bluette. At 22 years and 15 years it seemed incredible, but this indeed, was an extraordinary place, where fortunes were made or lost in the twinkling of an eye.

'I know what I'm going to do now,' said Alex, taking up a spade and heading outside for the dunghill. 'Bring that old bucket, Ambrose, and then help me take down these boards.'

'Whatever have you got on your mind, now?' asked Ambrose, picking up the old bucket and following Alex outside.

'I think we should move this dump over the way, to that clough over there.' He pointed to a depression in the ground, a little way from the shack. 'It will take a fair time to shift it, but we could make it a rule that if anyone wants second helping, they have to take one bucket to the dump, and if they want a meal and they can't pay, they'll have to take five buckets!'

Ambrose stood pondering for a moment. 'It will be a good idea, if it will work! I wonder why Grace would never have it shifted, even when the fly plague started?'

'Well, Grace said it was handy for her, and it was, she just opened the door and flung out what she didn't want onto the top. The chuckies had a good scratching place there but they can just as easily go over to the clough.'

The little scheme of free dinners and suppers worked very well, and even in two or three days there was a sizable chunk out of the pile and the flies had removed themselves away from the dunghill to the disturbed, stinking mess of recently thrown out garbage which was arriving daily at the clough.

'It's a pity that Grace, so recently and decently laid to rest, with due ceremony and respect, could not have seen the benefit afforded to all by this removal,' said Ambrose as he looked upon the lessening pile.

They both felt very proud of their enterprise until a man, of grizzled beard and sundried skin, lean of frame, without a penny in his pocket, came to do his stint to earn a free meal. He had taken four buckets of the rich smelling contents of the dunghill to the clough, and had wearily stuck in his spade to fill up the last bucket, for he was in dire need of a dinner, when a horrific sight met his gaze. A human skull, with some hair remaining and remnants of flesh still adhering to the bone, rolled down out of the mulch and came to rest at his feet. He let out a yell, that ripped into the silence of the day, and brought both Alex and Ambrose quickly to his side. That the head had been severed from the body was evident by the few spinal bones still attached by tendons to the skull itself. Further probing brought to light several other bones, some of animals and some unmistakably human.

'What a bloody awful thing!' said the man bursting into tears, due to shock and the weariness of his state.

'It is indeed,' replied Ambrose, much perplexed, as he led the man inside the Tavern for a wash and a tasty meal, after a small dram of brandy.

Ambrose and Alex knew that they would have to tell the authorities at once, and this they did, with great misgivings, for it was obvious that the human remains had been in the heap for some time. The question was, how long, and had Grace started the heap there? They knew she objected to it being removed. Did she know of its grisly contents? Had she put it there herself?

The authorities arrived, serious of face, but with an undertone of excitement in their voices. People began to gather outside, standing in little knots along the dusty road, whispering, pointing, shaking their heads. It was known that Grace, good natured though she had been to Ambrose and Alex, was capable of killing! She had once been judged guilty of manslaughter, but this had been reduced to the leniency of transportation, due to her husband's prior behaviour. Had she killed yet again? The previous owner of the tavern was said to have gone into the interior to seek his fortune. Everyone he dealt with knew of his intention. Grace had worked for him for two years without pay, just board and lodging and the occasional guinea if things were good. It was also known that he would leave Grace the Tavern when he left. But, when the questions were asked, who had seen him go? When anyone had asked the whereabouts of Waterloo Jack, Grace had replied with a terse, 'He's off on his trip at last!'

Waterloo Jack had two outstanding features, his left lower leg was bowed slightly forward, and he had a ridge in his skull, caused by an old sabre wound. Certainly there was a bony ridge on the skull from the dunghill, but several other bones could not be found, one hand appeared to be missing, as were the lower bones of the left leg. Ambrose told the authorities of the day the dogs had got into the dunghill, but forbore to tell them of the distress of Grace, who had moved quicker with the broom than they had seen her move since they arrived at the Tavern. He had not actually seen the dogs run off with any bones, but they might well have. They had done a lot of sniffing and scuffling about the mound. It was after that they had put boards around the whole of the mound. Grace would not let the mound be moved, it was too convenient and she was, as all knew, too large and slow to go any distance.

All the evidence was mulled over and for every 'if' there was a 'but'. The mound was convenient to the kitchen waste but it was also convenient for Grace to keep an eye on the ever-growing pile, knowing that in its heart lay the evidence of her secret crime. It was a mystery not to be solved. The two main characters were colourfully dead. The streets were full of the buzz of gossip and surmise, but that was all that came of the affair, except that the tavern became well-known. More and more people flocked to the door and

Rule Of Thumb

the verbal name of Grace's Place was taken over by a boarded sign with Waterloo Jack's painted across it.

It was to Waterloo Jack's that a certain man came a month or two later, offering Ambrose and Alex the sum of one hundred guineas for the place. At first they were suspicious, then interested, and finally, when the money was placed before them, quite overwhelmed by their good fortune.

Putting their money into safe keeping and adding to it what they had left from their sea voyage, and their work at the tavern, they had a goodly sum of £170 between them. They felt like they were millionaires as they stepped from the bank into the street, and made their way through the hubbub of the town to the outskirts where they hoped to get work in sheepherding.

Alex and Ambrose sat in a waterfilled gully. The heat was intense. Basking lizards hid down under the sheltering stones and under the cool roots of water loving trees. A flawless silence hung in the air like a shimmering curtain. Ambrose flicked his fingers against his cheek to brush away a troublesome insect. Alex amused himself by standing on the boards placed over the sun simmering swamp, watching the watery mud ooze out between the worn wooden planks. The mud dried almost at once, eventually sealing up all of the gaps, until the structure was strengthened by the adobe filling.

Soon, they were both maddened by a cloud of mosquitoes who made an onslaught on them, making them leave the gully and make for the dusty road. As soon as they were on the road a restless baaing of sheep and lambs caught upon their ears, and they became aware of a young man, wearing a stitched smock and leggings and stout shoes, a battered straw hat upon his head, and driving a small herd of sheep before him, and towards the town. They waited for him to come abreast. He looked at them apprehensively. He had heard tales of hungry and desperate men, laying in wait for just such an opportunity. Ambrose saw the look and stepped forward with a cheery, 'Good day.' The young man nodded and kept his charges in a tight knot with his dog, silent at his heels.

'Me and Alex are after work on a sheep farm. Are you in the way of employing? I can shear sheep and Alex will be a good runner!'

The man brightened visibly. 'We need good men for shearing! I expect the Boss would hire you! I'm off to market to take in this lot and buy a horse. I'm a horseman myself. I know a good mount when I sees one and the Boss knows it.'

Ambrose forbore to say that he was a horseman himself, in fact had ridden a horse from being seven years old and ponies before that. Instead he asked politely, 'How would we be getting to see your Boss?'

'It's a tidy way. Go up along this road, through the blue gums on the bluff, then down into the valley beyond and you'll see the ranch. I'll probably overtake you on the way! I'll be riding, see!'

The two hopefuls shouted their thanks as they parted and went their separate ways, turning once or twice as they started on the road to give a cheery wave.

The young man did not overtake them and they had reached the ranch and been taken on as new hands before he made his appearance. For several days Ambrose was confronted by the glassy eyed stares of obstinate sheep, and the seemingly endless shearing of fleeces with handshears, whilst Alex helped with the dipping and earclipping.

The days were still hot and at night when Alex lay on the cot in the shack provided for sleeping quarters, he went over the day's events in his mind. They had been there over a week. It was Tuesday, and August. The unfathomable dome of midnight, pricked with a faint scatter of stars, hung directly above him as he gazed upwards through the narrow planes of glass. Why there was a window in the roof he could not guess, but he was glad of it, making the room seem less oppressive with its dull shaft of lesser darkness penetrating the hot, reeking room.

The odour of sheep pervaded the room, but Ambrose, in the cot beside him, had fallen asleep immediately, worn out by handshearing and the sitting of countless sheep on their tails, whilst he did the work. Alex had been taught how to take up the shearings, fold them neatly into a packet – topside inside, then a swift twist and a pull of wool to bind the whole together. He moved restlessly in his cot, tired and thirsty. And he itched! He thought, blissfully, of his money in safe keeping. His escape hatch to England and freedom. Eventually, he too slept, and when he next opened his eyes, the dawn was coming up, the colour of dulled brass.

The room had become clammy and cloying and he began to toss, and turned about in the rickety cot from side to side so often be became afraid of upsetting it altogether. He threw back the thin covering and began to dress, whilst others slept on, albeit fretfully, snoring and grunting. He sallied out into the dusty warmth of the yard and longed for the silken feel of water on his skin.

The day before the yard had been filled to the enclosing wall with sheep and men, and the place had seethed with the noise of them. Now all was quiet except for one or two sleepy murmurs from birds, and the plink, plink of water dripping into a tin. Alex looked around to see where the noise was coming from. At first he could not believe his eyes, and stood transfixed,

Rule Of Thumb

staring rudely at the dusty, naked limbs of an aborigine male. He was stood beside the water-pipe, holding a pannikin under the drips. He was very thin, almost to the point of emaciation, with a tightly curled head of hair that was as dusty as his body. He seemed nervous, and rolled his eyes in his puckered face until his gaze was full on Alex. Alex then walked over to him and held out his hand but the man seemed to think that Alex wanted the water and held the pannikin to himself, protectively. A guttural speaking noise came from his thick lips, and since Alex did not understand the words, he quickly turned on the tap. The water spurted out and over the aborigine's feet and he shot one or two feet into the air, as if a snake had bitten him. Alex smiled at him encouragingly, and holding his own hand under the tap, cupped water to his mouth and indicated for the man to do the same. He did so, and beamed a broad smile. Alex turned the tap on again, water flowed, the man's smile returned, and he indicated that he had got the idea. To turn the tap brought water or stopped its flow, but the water did not disappear! He wanted to try the tap for himself. He turned slowly, watching the tiny drops gathering speed as he turned it into a ribbon of liquid crystal. He passed his hand through the flow sprinkling water drops onto his face, over his body, and on to his red-dusted head with little pleasurable grunts of glee.

'What the bloody hell you doing out here, Daffy? We can't have beggars and mumpers around here!'

'He just wants a drink of water,' interceded Alex.

'Be on your way!' the man growled out at the aborigine. 'I got your line, matey . . . either working the shallow (begging half naked) or doing the scaldrum dodge (begging with feigned or self inflicted wounds). You know what's best for you! Make a space between here and there.' He pointed well out of the yard.

The man appeared to know the sign and picking up his pannikin shambled out of the way. Looking at the man who had sent him away, Alex was also able to read a few signs. He had obviously not come to Australia of his own accord but had been asked to 'get the boat'. He was a loud-mouthed man who called a knife a 'chiv', a policeman 'a crusher' and empty premises 'dead lurks', all of which coloured the picture of his not so distant past to Alex.

'Don't you go mixing with the likes o' that,' said the man coming closer, and jerking his thumb in the direction of the fast receding figure.

'He only wanted a drink of water,' said Alex.

'Drink of water? What a flam (lie). A fellow like that would have your gallies (boots) off you while you were still fastening your laces. You mess

Rule Of Thumb

with that sort and you'll have the ruffles (handcuffs) on and a terrier crop before you knows it.'

'I don't give a fadge (farthing) for what you think,' Alex replied, his temper rising. 'I say he came for a drink of water, and I'd give a dog that!'

'You little muckswipe,' (one totally down and out) the man growled. 'I'm in charge here and you'll do as I say or leave.'

'Then I'll leave the moment I get my pay,' declared Alex. 'And that goes for Ambrose too!'

'Don't you speak for others, monkey,' said the man, 'I'll give you that thrashing you deserve.'

'Sod off, lushington,' (drunkard), spat out Alex. 'I've sailed on a ship where a whip had the most to say.'

Ambrose came into the yard. 'What's the matter here?'

'I'm leaving. You coming?' answered Alex tensely.

'We'll draw your pay and mine first. After that we'll leave!'

The Boss stood by listening as Ambrose said, 'I don't think I ever liked sheep before. I think I hate them now.'

'There's a few here I feel the same way about,' spat out Alex as the Boss started to walk across the yard. 'He wouldn't give one of those native men a drink of water, but I filled his panny for him. I called the Boss a lushington and told him to "sod off".'

'I hope he doesn't dock our pay, it would be like him,' said Ambrose apprehensively.

'He called me a muckswipe!' said Alex.

'I hope you didn't tell him different. It wouldn't do for him to think we were independent!'

'Leave off, Ambrose. I'll not tell anyone about money matters, except those that need to know!'

As they were talking the under-manager came across the yard. He had in his hand two packets. 'These are for you, earnings less keep. Be off the premises within the hour. The Boss will not stand for "retaliatory eruptions".'

Ambrose took the packets and gave one to Alex. They walked silently to the sleeping shack and gathered up their baggage. Some of the men wished them well but most just looked on. Work was work.

CHAPTER NINE

As they left the Ranch, Alex and Ambrose made their way once again for the coastline. The day was warm, and there was a touch of spring in the air, making walking more pleasant. The areas they passed through were quite lush, with small springy turfed plateaquxs, and in the hollows, the gurgling flow of water, and the shade of over-hanging trees. They kept plunging into pebbly brooklets to bathe their hot feet, and as they bathed they talked. They talked of panning for gold, and sharing their lives, and meals crouched over meagre fires and scantily filled cook-pots. They talked of setting up in business again, but not in the tavern line. A respectable house for respectable clerks, newly arrived. Or perhaps they would set up as clothiers, or chandlers, or guides. Their capacity for dreaming was boundless. It forged a strong bond of friendship between them, even though their backgrounds had been totally different.

It was getting on in the day when, whilst they were walking, and not talking they became conscious that the sea was very near. A tantalising cool breeze wafted over them from the sea, they stood still, testing the air like young colts, and then they were away, running through the slim trees, and plunging down onto the beach below. The sand was crunchy, strewn with shells and bits of flotsam and jetsam. The air smelled salty sweet, the varied greens of the trees, the flowers and grasses, and the soft murmurings of the sea, made a harmonious whole.

Alex lay on his stomach looking out over the shallows. It was a far cry from the narrow entry and uncompromising headland they had encountered on their arrival. They made their minds up at once to shelve any thoughts of 'business' and live off the land and river as best they might. 'It's beautiful here!' cried Ambrose. 'We need travel no further. We are already in Eden.'

Their ears were, as yet, for the sounds of the country, but their eyes saw, and marvelled at the clouds of large butterflies drinking from dew ponds, and the many species of birds also new to them. The chattering budgerigar and the rouged-cheeked cockatiel, and the sulphur-crested cockatoo were the sauciest of birds to entertain them. Animals of infinite variety, the wombat and wallaby and kangaroo, the cuddly looking but long-clawed koala, and many others they could not name or had but the merest glance of as they travelled daily along narrow tracks.

A bushman would have heard all that stirred, and known at once the source of origin. They knew from experience that the quiet pools under shady gum trees, lushly bordered with plants and having every appearance of being permanent, could disappear in ten days of heat, to a sticky mudspot overlooked by withered leaved guardians. They also knew, that by scratching up the surface of the pool base and inserting a hollow dried reed, they could draw drops of water up to their parched tongues. They knew where the succulent fat, white grubs lay, under dried out roots, and where to get their fingers on honey-ants, and edible fungi. They were at one with the country. They did not perish in her as others did. She nurtured them, sparingly but adequately, as was in the beginning. Diamonds, opals, and gold, were of no value to the aborigine, or even interest. Mirages, that floated on the horizon, did not tempt them astray, as they did the new, weary, explorers, drawing them further and further into the deserts to die of thirst under a quivering haze of heat. They did not get bogged-down in quicksand, or bitten by water-snakes, or wander round and round in decreasing circles, until they reached the eye of death upon their knees.

The aborigine's compass was built-in, by sense and smell and sound. It was accurate, having served its purpose well since man first stood upright on that continent. To see them squatting upon their haunches amongst the scanty porcupine grasses, or lying curled around a camp fire in embryonic slumber, one might envy them their completely relaxed state. To see them straining after food was a lesson in eloquent patience. It was while Alex and Ambrose were watching them, so successful and at one with their environment that they decided that what they needed most in life was a ship that could pile on sail, and skim over the waves, like a great bird, to ENGLAND.

They were, however, reluctant to lose sight of their carefree days in the bush, and whilst they were sometimes to be found at the harbour-side for many weeks more they lived off the country. Then it was winter.

The far mountains took on a mantle of snow and drifting grey mists shawled the landscape. The elaborately thatched shack they had cobbled together themselves in the lee of sheltering rocks, began to soak up the rain, and gained a decided list. As they walked amongst the trees there was no longer a flurry of wings as birds were disturbed from their perches. They conserved their charcoal as zealously as any native, in order to have at least one hot meal a day, and each night toasted each other in large gulps of tawny liquid considered by the local people to be the foe to all chills and all ills.

The rain flooded over the ground that had been baked by the sun into the hardness of adobe tiles. At sea, the waters slapped and chattered against the shore-line, and inland there was the continuous thundery rumble of boulders being tumbled and ground by raging torrents along the river beds. The way to the harbour was filled with pot-holes and mud-soaks. The ditches were brimming, and the air was always chill from plaguey north-west winds, the waters of the bay choppy and white with foaming crests.

Ambrose and Alex stayed close to the shack, swallowing the occasional hot jam dumpling with howls of protest, and gulping down unsavoury broth without enthusiasm. The continuous dampness, coupled with their inertia and inadequate food supplies began to show itself in several ways – sudden bouts of temper, clumsiness, sleeplessness, toothache, earache, split skin on toes and fingers, constipation, and morbidity of intellect.

The latter was recognised by Ambrose, being the elder, and at that point the most sensitive of their situation, and he resolved to end some of their hardships by a daily hunt for fish and game. When they had devised a system for their hunts their condition improved. Better food relieved many of the niggling irritations, and the exercise was beneficial in raising their spirits.

Their only madness came late one afternoon. It was on the edge of a clearing and they saw a ewe, nibbling delicately at the thinned grasses. She had obviously escaped from some pen or pasture. They could not believe their eyes but stood transfixed, thinking of hot mutton! Ambrose fingered the hunting knife at his belt ensconced in its leather sheath. They both walked over to the ewe. She stood, her green-eyes glowing in the fading light. Ambrose took hold of her and sat her on her tail as if he were about to shear her. He turned her over, her neck resting on one leg, her rump against the other, and plunged his knife into her. She jumped once, twice, the blood spurting out in pulses as he cut into the animal's throat. They took the carcase down to the shore and gutted and skinned it, then cast the fleece out onto the water.

That night, as they rested, warm and satiated, for the first time in several weeks Ambrose allowed himself to feel a little ashamed that they had stolen the ewe. Sleek and fat as she was, delicious and tender as she was . . . He sighed and throwing his blankets over his head, fell into a sleep as dreamless, and innocent as a new born babe.

But, morning came, and with it guilt. The fleece was there upon the shore, the bones were there upon the floor, and more of the carcase was stashed away in the back of the shack. 'Do you think,' asked Alex in a tremulous whisper, 'that we might be transported to England if we were to be found out?'

Ambrose smiled. 'I think it would be unlikely, though many have been sent here for just such a crime as we have committed. And, now I come to think on it, what a fool am I to think on such things here, when, on my own farm in England, I can eat all the mutton I wish for!' Alex burst out laughing and began to bury the fleece deep into the fine sand above the water line. Ambrose felt better when the fleece was no longer in evidence and as they walked back to their shack observed, 'I am bound to say that as an adventurer, Alex, I am a poor and timid kind, only driven to bravery by fear. What do you say if we make our way back to the settlements? We could draw out a little of our monies and make our bid for a respectable rooming house, while waiting for a suitable berth home.'

Alex pondered for some moments, and then slowly nodded his head. 'We could take the mutton to the men who were good to us when we first came here. They would be glad of a good mutton stew.' Ambrose agreed that would be a good idea and would serve two purposes. They would help to feed someone, and they would clear their consciences.

They took away the props of the thatched roof and let it tumble damply over the whole. They dismantled the fire where they had roasted the few bits of mutton they had saved for themselves, after packing the rest for the men at the coastline. In a few weeks, no one, except perhaps the aborigines, would know anyone had lived there.

They walked into the town as quickly as they could and made their way to the men on the coastline. They were happy to see them and over-joyed at the mutton and other provisions Ambrose and Alex had brought. They shared their meal and settled down for the night with them knowing that they would have a better chance at getting lodgings when they had called at the bank and tidied themselves up.

The following day they walked into the town before ten o'clock. The clerk greeted them like long lost friends as they asked for ten guineas each from their account. 'Where are you bound for now?' he queried.

'We are going to get lodgings and await a ship to take us home,' answered Alex.

The clerk threw up his hands. 'Why not stay? There is a new building project on hand, and new roads to be built, as you will know that the present ones are woefully inadequate.'

'We well know that!' said Ambrose with a laugh. 'But the roads in town are a joy compared to some of the ways we have travelled. Mud-holes and potholes, pebbles and boulders, we have traversed them all, in fact we have taken to open country sometimes, rather than travel by the known way.'

They left the Clerk, still shaking his head. 'He is in a wax because he does not want to lose our accounts,' said Alex with a laugh as they made for the main street.

It was fine weather, but though the sun shone only weakly, they both felt good. Hope nestled around them like a contented cloud. They tried singing a couple of shanties, they talked about the vagaries of the ship's Cook. They discussed about where they might take lodgings. Certainly, they did not want rooms that were expensive, nor yet too inexpensive. They felt they owed themselves the luxury of full board, and clean linen.

By three o'clock in the afternoon they had found a place that was neat, though sparsely furnished, and with a savory smell coming from the kitchen that promised to fulfil all expectations.

Sally Mullins, the landlady of the house, a homely woman of forty years, was recently widowed. She had one married son who had two children and they lived near her. She helped them and they, when they could, helped her. Besides taking in lodgers in her home, she made bonnets and dresses, and sometimes yards and yards of hairpin lace, all of which brought in a small but regular income. She and her husband had come with their son as settlers some seven years before. They had hoped to start a fruit farm but the land they were allotted had been covered by scrub and old trees, and they had given up in despair that anything useful could be done. Her husband had worked for a time helping to fell timber, but had died of a fever, suddenly and without warning, a few months before. 'It's a hard country lads!' she said. 'But I'm stuck with it now! My Jeffrey married a local girl when he was eighteen and now they have two little girls. If I leave here, I'm alone in the world. So, I'll take my chance with the rest. Maybe, I'll find a second husband one day. Maybe, one of those reformed convicts! I've seen some good marriages made from them. Seen a bit of life and know a thing or two! Hard men, it's true, many of them, but many a man has been sent here who was less of a criminal than his master!'

Sally looked askance of the two before her, so they hastened to tell her that they had come there of their own free will, and that their unkempt appearance was temporary and not from choice.

'No matter!' she replied cheerily as she cut them another slice of pie.

Rule Of Thumb

In their past journeys down to the harbour, Ambrose and Alex had managed to scrape acquaintance with one of the men in charge at the wharves. He had a forehead that sloped backwards, and two glittering, cobra-like eyes, and an astonishingly broad chest. When he spoke, his breath hissed from the barrel of his chest, and one or two of his fingers were always bandaged due to a condition known as 'grocer's itch' an eczema cause by the sugar mite, which he came in contact with in the sugar store. With his sore hand and unusual appearance, it was difficult to be unaware of his presence, and Ambrose and Alex approached him one morning with a view to employment or a berth on one of the ships.

'I do not know of a Captain who is in need of a crew at present,' he hissed, and he went on, 'I hardly know if you are suitable. Such an ill-starred pair as you two may be considered bad luck!'

'How are we ill-starred?' asked Alex, at once on the defensive.

'Well, don't blame me if disappointment comes,' hissed the man. 'Losing one's Captain is bad enough, but the tale had it that you lost a landlady as well!' He leaned over the bulwark and spat a gob of green phlegm into the water below.

'We had nothing to do with either of those things!' exploded Ambrose. 'One was an accident, and the other was a natural death.'

'That's not what I've been hearing, and others around here!'

'What are they saying?' growled Alex, his temper rising.

'Leave it, leave it, Alex,' placated Ambrose, drawing him away from the side of the man, and turning his attention to the water where a supply boat was drawing away from the wharf. It was heading towards a ship which lay at anchor some way off. They watched enviously as the boat receded, the slap of the oars growing fainter with each stroke. It reminded them of the times when on the *Bold Adventurer,* waves had caught them unawares, the white heads slopping aboard, the spray wetting untidy hair or woollen caps with salty drops. They remembered also the exhilaration of starting up the rigging, springing agilely among the spars, shrouds, and ropes like monkeys. The aching weariness, terrors and anxieties were forgotten in their desire to be at sea, sailing for home.

It was two more days before they found a berth, in a fine ship of 700 tons and carrying its own Chaplain. 'Surely, God will be with us on this journey,' said Ambrose fervently. Alex was well taken with the Captain, a quiet, but firm spoken man, broad of shoulder and of smile. They drew out what money they had in safe-keeping, bought a few odds and ends of clothing and other necessities for the voyage, then went to sleep their last night under the roof of Sally Mullins.

What a fuss! What a shedding of tears, and slurping sobs, as Sally threw her apron over her head. 'There now,' chided Ambrose, don't take on so! We're only going home.'

'Home, home!' wailed Sally with increased vigour. 'Home, and we stuck here in this place, warped with damp in the winter and dried out to the bone in summer, and everything out of season!'

They sympathised with her but they had never really noted the times of the year. Both their birthdays had come and gone before they noticed.

'I'll never get used to Christmas Day with the sun pining the rind off me, or Midsummer's day, muffled up to the eyebrows against the cold,' wept Sally. But, presently she dried her eyes and was calm. 'You'll be wanting to get home, to see your families and your friends. I've got no one in England to give a monkey's waistcoat whether I go back at all! Petticoat Lane has seen the last of me!'

They ate their last evening meal together in tense silence, broken only by the chink of glassware and the scrape of metal against the thick white plates.

After their supper Alex and Ambrose wandered down to the waterside. It was noisy with a different tone now on the dockside. Men were taking their leisure seriously, drinking, playing cards, womanising, fighting and just plain bragging. They could see the ship they were to board on the morrow, her furled sails creamy in the brilliance of the oil lights around the harbour, dock-walks and wharves. Later, they walked into the quiet roads, sniffing the damp air that carried salt odours, smells of cooking and fermented herbage and the dusty way.

On the air came the formidable sound of a Bullroarer. 'I hope they are having an initiation ceremony, and are not petitioning for wind and rain,' said Ambrose wryly.

'We shall have to try the strength of our Chaplain,' said Alex with a laugh, though he felt far from easy.

They turned towards the home of Sally Mullins. The oblong of light from her porch window glowed like a beacon, beckoning them promising warmth and security. A brief spatter of heavy rain, promising winter, skittered across the porchway as they hurried inside.

Outside, not far from the town, under the ancient, protecting rocks, round the communal fire, the old men of the Korrobori spoke of times gone and times yet to come. They spoke darkly, secretly, their words hissing and spitting like the rain, slanting on the flames of their fragrant, gum-tree fire. But they were old these men. The young men were drawn to a new way of life. The white-skinned dominating people drew them away from the laws of the dreamtime, into the reality of New World ideals, putting them in bondage, covering their naked bodies, giving them daily work, and their daily bread. 'They should be glad of it, those savages, moving about from place to place since God knows when,' said Sally Mullins. 'Even then, they can't give a decent day's work in return for what they get. After all, what have they ever given us? Only trouble, that's what. Trouble!'

'Freedom is a priceless commodity,' offered Ambrose as he climbed the stairs to bed.

'Freedom!' scoffed Sally, her voice tight with emotion. 'Freedom! What's that, I'd like to know? You're young yet lad, you wait – Freedom – Fool's Garters!'

Ambrose shook his head and smiled. 'Goodnight, Sally – our last goodnight. Come on Alex, we'll have a deck above us tomorrow night, and the sound of the sea to sing us a lullaby!'

Sally Mullins wiped a tiny tear from her cheek as they leapt up the stairs two at a time.

CHAPTER TEN

The following morning, having taken their farewells, and final instructions from Sally, Alex and Ambrose took the first steps towards their homeland. What a joy to feel the familiar hardness of a deck beneath their feet! With what aplomb did they climb ladders, ropes and ratlines. No more did they cling, shaking and trembling to the riggings as they walked the dizzy heights above the deck, or hung out over the slappy waves below as they checked the sail furlings. A new confidence surged through them both, and as they put water between the ship and the shore, a great sense of relief flooded into their lives. It was a relief that was to stay with them the whole of the voyage, which was pleasant, and as ordered as either of them could have wished.

As the ship reached dock, Ambrose hared for home, urging Alex to keep in touch with him, telling him of what occupation he had decided to follow after he was home again. Alex was glad to oblige, and said so, with many smiles and handshakes. He had found Ambrose Cunliffe a good friend, who had steered him away from vices he might have succumbed to, not from viciousness on his part, but from innocence, for with all his felly ways he was still a boy.

Alex made his way home on a coaster, and on arrival at his home town, slipped ashore eagerly, and made his way to the tavern, The Cat and Garter. He had scarcely walked two yards, when he was espied by an old woman who stopped him, picking at his sleeve pettishly, her gin-soaked breath reaching out into the cool air.

'Now then, young Alex, you come to see "fair-done-by" your ma, at last?'

Puzzled, Alex looked at the old woman and asked, 'What do you mean? Is my mother in trouble, Margery-Daw?'

'You may well ask,' she replied, secretly pleased that Alex had used the nickname he had used as a child. 'Your mother has gone, you'll not find her in this quarter of the town. She lives over by Scrivener's Yard now.' She stood back to see a reaction from her words. Her arms were folded righteously across her breastless chest, her grey, straggling hair escaping in tangled hanks from the frilled crocheted cap on her head.

'Why ever is she there?' cried Alex in alarm. So much had happened to him whilst he had been away, yet he had expected that here, where his mother was, all would be just as he had left it.

'Got the chest... has your mother, she has!' whispered the woman in a conspiratorial tone.

Alex's heart sank. What a dreary homecoming. He left the old woman abruptly, without a word, and hurried off in the direction of Scrivener's Yard. He found his mother living in a garret of one of the houses. The windows were small, and half of the panes were out of the sashes, the openings stuffed with rags and boardings to keep out the draughts. Alex was appalled at the sight of his mother who lay on the iron bedstead, her breath squeezing out of her thin, stretched lips, her facial bones pushing up the pallid skin, which disease had drawn tight over them. Two hectic spots, one on either cheek, made her look like a rouged tart, and Alex longed for them to pale into the creaminess he had known from his childhood.

He pushed the dampened curls from her forehead, but drew back as she warned. 'Don't kiss me, my boy, I have the fever bad!'

He drew back only for an instant before enfolding her into his arms. They sat bound together for some moments, not speaking, and allowing hot, scalding, tears to course down their cheeks. Then Alex's mother pulled away, and Alex took off the overcoat he was wearing and placed it over a chair. 'Is that the rent-man I hear on the stair?' asked his mother. 'If it is, don't let him in,' she begged, her claw-like fingers clutching the thin and ragged coverlet.

'Why mother? Can you not pay him? Does he bother you?'

'Oh, I can pay him,' she sighed. 'It's the sight of him, with his muffler to his face, and him trying to pick up the money with his gloves on. What a sight! Enough to make a donkey laugh! It makes me laugh too, and now it hurts to laugh, and it makes me cough.'

'I'll kick him down the stairs if he so much as shows his face!' Alex answered wildly. 'Collecting rent for such a squalid hole, why my own shack in the outback was a palace compared to this! Things will be different from now on, mother, you'll see!'

'Made a fortune have you?' enquired his mother softly as the tears sprang to her eyes.

'Well, no, mother. I had a lot of expenses. When I wrote to you I told you of my adventures. You got my letters, didn't you?'

Rule Of Thumb

'Yes, I got letters from you, Alex, three, I think. I still have them. They were full of wild talk and strange places but I could tell you were enjoying the life out there, meeting new folk, seeing new places.'

Just to hear her rattling talk made Alex feel exhausted for her. 'Don't talk, I'll deal with everything now I am home. You just rest and get well again.' He went to the window and rubbing one of the grimy panes looked down into the yard below. It was strewn with the cast-off articles of life, bottomless buckets, burned-out pans, rags, old wood, and a one-wheeled cart, listing over on its side. To his right he caught sight of the sea and watched a vessel with red-grey sails leaving the coastline. The drifting movements of the ship along his vision helped to compose him, and he turned to his mother once again.

She was looking up at him, her eyes critical and sharp, dark with fever. 'You've grown into a man since you went away,' she observed, pettishly.

'I've done a man's work, mother.'

'It's too soon!'

'Too soon?' echoed Alex, to his mother as she lay back on the pillow, her breath whistling between her teeth. She was going to speak again, but a cough stopped her. The cloth she put to her lips was already spotted with blood. Alex felt guilty, ashamed and angry, all at the same time. His heart beat in his ears. He felt stifled in the room. 'I think I hear the landlord,' he said. 'Shall I pay him or kick him down the stairs?' As he dragged open the warped, plain oaken door, and stepped out onto the landing, he heard his mother say, 'You always had a kick in you! I remember it well!'

There was no-one on the darkened stairway, and he ran out into the untidy yard. He took a deep breath of salt-ladened air. He had no excuse to linger but he stayed there, looking at the items in the yard, watching the gulls perched on the roof ridges. Finally he returned to the house, climbed the stairs two at a time, to make amends for his tardiness. As he pushed open the door, all was quiet. Not even the tick of a clock disturbed the pulsing silence. He looked to the bed. His mother's head seemed gracefully relaxed as if she slept, her hand still gripping the blood-stained rag. Her heart, already weakened by malnutrition and disease, had proved too frail to sustain the added strain and excitement of Alex's return.

When the rent-collector did arrive a few minutes later, he found Alex holding the hands of his dead mother, too numb to resist the request for the paltry coins for a week's tenancy of the room. He could hardly speak, but nodded and sniffed, and made jerky gestures, with all the awkwardness of grief-stricken youth, as the rent-collector said, 'I'll call a doctor to look in

Rule Of Thumb

on you, lad. Best be getting things together now. Mother Booth is a good friend of hers. You know her, lad?' Alex nodded. 'Get along to her after the Doctor's been. She'll know what to do.'

The rent-collector left the house, and Alex began to search through his mother's belongings. He would hardly get ten shillings for his mother's effects. He raked through the drawers of the dressing table, and came across three of the letters he had sent her, written in his round and school-boy hand. They were almost worn through at the folds with his mother's constant reading and re-reading of them, although she had known the words by heart. Alex put them into his pocket. She seemed close to him then. Her brand was on nothing else in the room.

Although her belongings were so few, Doctor Dawes was entering the room before he had finished. 'Just on my way, Alex,' he began cheerfully, 'met the rent-collector. Blessing you getting here to-day. She wanted to see you. Talked of nothing else for the past weeks. Seemed to know you were on your way.'

He leaned over the still body for only seconds. 'You make your way to Mother Booth's and I'll make all the other arrangements.'

His quick efficiency overwhelmed Alex with relief. He had been ashore five hours. He was now motherless, homeless and almost penniless, or would be after his mother's funeral.

'Mother Booth was a true friend to your mother, but she was not able to climb the stairs when she moved here. Come along, now, Alex,' said the Doctor as he shut his bag with a snap.

It was some little way to Mother Booth's home in a quiet corner of the small coastal town. As Alex picked his way along the alleys he knew that many sailors lodged there, spending their days ashore in the stink of bugs and filth, in the dim corners which served as bedrooms. Not that it was any different to what some of them had been used to at sea. It all seemed to rest with the values of the Captain. A good Captain drew the best crew. Bad Captains would crimp and cheat men aboard. Alex realised that now that he was alone in the world he would have to learn to fend for himself, and not be put about by sly words and flattering manners.

When he reached the door of Mother Booth's home, he rattled the catch, waited a moment, and then entered. The whole house spoke of self-denying economy, and indeed, Mother Booth had often been only a crust away from starvation. Yet, in spite of this, she had never been known to turn anyone away from her door that was in want or in trouble.

'Alex, my dear laddie,' she crowed, as she raised her flushed face from the fire over which she had been stooping to rake the coals together. She held out her arms to him and he fell into them with shuddering sobs. 'Well, well! What's this?' she said as she held him close round the neck to her slack-breasted bosom.

'Is it your mother? Is she gone, at last? Heaven be praised! It's been a weary road for her, and she is at the end of it now. Don't you shed one more tear than you need for her going. Do you hear me? It's not right to grieve over her. Her tasks here were done, her reward is in heaven!'

'I can't see it that way,' said Alex drawing away from her.

'Then feel guilty about leaving her if you must, but it would have made no difference to her. It may have made a difference to you! Instead of the strong lad you are now, the odds are that you would have got the "cough" yourself. Now, where would have been the sense in that? I ask you! Did not the Good Lord bend you to his will, to take to the good clean air of the oceans? It's singing praises you should be this day, for her that is safe in the Almighty's care, and you who is saved and liberated for your life's work. For work you must, laddie. You have the mark of one to do well if you can harden your heart and soften your head.' She slapped him playfully. 'I'm an old woman, given to talking in riddles! I don't know the answers any better than the next!' She got up from the chair and busied herself with buttering bread and placing a few slices of brawn on a plate and cutting thin slices of raw onion. 'Just a bite to push you on for the moment,' she said going to the fire to attend to the kettle.

Alex realised then that he had not eaten anything that day. He felt the need for food and wolfed the whole lot down in a couple of minutes. 'Starved are you?' asked Mother Booth. Alex started to chew more slowly. 'Oh, I'm sorry . . .' It dawned on Alex that he had eaten her share too. His face flushed with shame. 'Let me go and buy you something,' he mumbled as he took coins from his pocket. She placed a staying hand on his arm, 'Give over, laddie, Ned, my grandnephew will be here before long. He generally brings a nice boiling of fish with him. He's a sail maker now. Been staying with me since his accident!'

'Accident? What happened?' asked Alex, pulling his chair nearer to the fire.

'Fell from the rigging six months back. He was that bad we all feared for his life. But, he's a Vickers, that one. Hard as they come. You should have heard him cuss and scream when Doctor Dawes reset his leg! Shaking with fright, he was! The Doctor, of course!' she added with a chuckle.

'Who set his leg in the first place?' Alex asked, beginning to smile in spite

Rule Of Thumb

of himself.

'The ship carpenter. He had the wood you see! Ham fisted he were, and that leg were set four inches too short before it were bound. I'll never forget the look on Doctor Dawe's face when he took off the wrapping, and the smell would have knocked down a pig.'

Alex was now laughing uncontrolled, though close to the edge of tears, when Ned came into the house, with the boiling of fish, and a measure of winkles. 'Welcome home, Alex,' he said heartily, as he put down the fish and took off his jacket. 'You'll be the one to sit at the fireside now telling of your travels!'

'His mother is dead, Ned. It has been a sad day for him, and now he has to go to Doctor Dawes who has arranged everything for Marie's funeral.' Ned nodded his head and clasped his hand over Alex's shoulder as he made to leave the house. No word was spoken, but Alex knew that Ned, a man who had looked on death many times and in many forms, was offering his sympathy and wished him 'God Speed.'

Few people followed Marie Deane's body to her grave. Galloping consumption had driven most of them away, and lack of money and comfort had done the rest.

As they left the churchyard Mother Booth drew close to Alex, and he gave her his arm to steady her. She looked up at him from under her black felt hat, trimmed with one long and arrogant blue green feather. She was not a handsome woman. Her nose was hooked, her teeth long gone. Her face was pitted with the scars of disease and time, but she had a generous heart and now she hugged Alex's lithe, young arm up to her side. 'Now, pretty lad, you just be careful along these flag-stones,' she warned him. 'They all need re-bedding. On a wet Sunday, you've never seen such a belle-and-beau trap, a wiping down of trousers and boots, and a ruffling and shaking of petticoats and showing of ankles. Enough to make the Good Lord frown 'til Tuesday.' Alex allowed a weak, tremulous twist to his lips. 'It's my opinion,' went on Mother Booth brightly, 'that the old well-spring is under those flagstones, and that one practice night the whole of the choir will go, plop, plop, plop, one by one, into a gaping hole.'

The vision of this evoked a shadow of a smile on Alex's face, and Mother Booth noted it with pleasure. Her boy would survive the storm – she was sure of it now.

A few days later Alex paid up all he owed at his lodgings, packed his belongings, and with eight sovereigns in his pocket, plus some small change, made his way to Mother Booth's home.

Rule Of Thumb

When he arrived she was fast asleep by the sea-coal fire, occasionally half-awakened by the sound of her own snores. Alex looked around the room. The lamp that hung from the rafters was black with soot and he took it down, cleaned it and refilled the base with oil. He filled up the coal bucket and went out into her little yard at the back of the house and tidied it up. When he returned to the house Mother Booth was awake. 'You off then?'

'How did you guess?' asked Alex.

'I've read a powerful lot of faces in my time,' she sighed, wrapping her arms about herself and rocking for a few moments.

'I've cleaned the lamp and brought in your coal and tidied the yard, is there anything else I can do for you?'

'You can give me a kiss for old times sake.'

'Well that is easily done,' he said kissing her fondly. She clung to him for an instant, and then shook herself upright.

'You were the best babbie I ever birthed. A bad-tempered nawt that turned into a real man! I'm proud of you, Alex. Real proud! You'll not be afraid to punch the truth a bit!'

Alex kissed her again. 'I'll see you again when I come ashore, often.'

'Nay, lad, you'll not see me again when you leave here.'

'You'll live forever.' Alex teased.

'Perish the thought. Can't think of ought worse than that.'

'Well, if we don't meet on the earth again we're sure to meet in heaven.'

Mother Booth began to wipe her eyes. 'Go now, Alex, you wouldn't want to see a pudden-faced old wretch like me crying in her porter.'

As she stood at the door to see him go, he slipped five sovereigns into her gnarled hand. She looked at him, and made to give them back, but Alex closed her fingers over them, and pushed her hand away. 'God Bless you, lad,' she cried her lips trembling. 'These will be to me as the five loaves, I can shift for the fish myself.'

Alex left her then, running backwards and waving until he turned the corner.

He then made his way to the churchyard, and to his mother's grave. He had left money with the undertaker for a stone to be put up at a later time, when the soil had settled. Now the grave was slightly raised, covered with already decaying flowers. At the head of the mound a simple wooden cross had been erected bearing his mother's name. He felt older than his years as he stood there. He felt lonely and cheated, after returning with such hopes for his future. There beneath the dying tribute to his grief, lay the only bit of England he could call his own. He took one last look, and turned and

Rule Of Thumb

walked quickly away.

His footsteps led him to the quayside. His heart led him to the sea. His head told him that to this spot he must never return again!

CHAPTER ELEVEN

Alex Deane was to sail in many ships, carrying strange and exotic cargoes, or mundane baggage, or passengers, to lands far and near. In the next twenty years he made many ports and saw many people, but was as dissatisfied with them as he was with himself, until 1845, when he was thirty-seven years old, he arrived on the shores of India for the first time.

Nowhere had he been fascinated with life as he was to be here. The day the ship docked, his companion, Salim, a Hindu of some forty years of age, accompanied him from the deck to the harbour wall. Laughing, showing his square white teeth, Salim nodded placidly at Alex as he gazed at the incredible harbour scene before him. The city beyond lay white and dazzling in the hot sunlight and was in direct contrast to the harbour with its myriad colours, squalor, noise, and stench. Up and down the ghats on which the two men stood, walked the inhabitants of the city, Indian, Bengalese, Persian, Chinese, Arabian, Mongolian, African, quadroon, mustee, and mulatto, all walked and talked there presenting colourful facets of harbour life. Down in the sacred river the Hindu people bathed and changed into clean garments.

Salim did this also.

The two companions turned their attention to the city. In the distance they could see a Dravidian temple with a wheel of vultures above it, and all at hand, spires and cupolas, and towers. Mazes of passages led on to large squares where the latticework of the buildings hid the Zenanas, where incarcerated women glimpsed the outside world. In the bazaars were the sellers of Dhurrie, Gurrah, and Seerhand. Traders, seated or propped upon bales of material or dingy cushions, haggled the prices with their customers, who seemed to have time enough to spare. On the road outside, richly clothed men walked along beneath the shade of a slave-held chattah, or sat in brightly decorated howdahs strapped to the accommodating backs of painted and bejewelled elephants.

Alex's eyes were not the well tutored eyes of his companion, Salim, who

Rule Of Thumb

saw in the rapidly changing scene a varied collection with no unifying theme between them. He saw them with good tempered clarity. They were his people, but he did agree that most of them did seem to live their lives with considerable powers of persuasiveness and patience. Life for them was sometimes violent, nearly always disconcerting and at once dramatic and tragic. There was the Pathan with his chick to spend, and the dark spindle-legged little fellow with an anna in the warm palm of his hand, looking for an attractive bargain in the bazaar. Then there was the well dressed Nawab, with no bottom to his purse and no light to his eye. 'Such Maya,' said Salim, as he surveyed the people before them. 'To believe that those three could ever in life be in any way equal, or even in NAKAKA for that matter, if it exists, and I doubt it, as much I doubt your Christian heaven.'

Alex smiled, looking around him with a great feeling of awareness. It was a curious fact that though Salim and he were detached enough to observe these people, they were still to be assailed by the same gusts of emotion, and even at that moment as they walked along the harbour side, a wind of change was blowing in their direction.

Alex had returned his gaze towards the river, and it was then that he saw Nighma. She stood, a burnished living statue at the head of the ghats. On her black, smooth haired head she balanced a flat woven basket, filled with numerous, colourful, and fragrant flowers. She wore a dress of lemony-coloured silk, sprigged with green embroidery, the folds of which hung from neck to ankle. The seams to just above the knee were open, the waist secured by a girdle of plaited, gold and silver cords. Born into bondage, she went unveiled and as she stood there, one slim, shapely arm uplifted to hold the basket secure, she showed to the populace not only her face but an expanse of thigh also.

She was oblivious to Alex as he stood beside a stack of cut bamboo and the cage of a night fisherman. The cormorant inside seemed as dejected as his owner, who sat upon a tiny piece of palm leaf matting putting oil on his hair. As the slave moved Alex's heartbeats quickened. There was a dull ache in the pit of his stomach as he noticed the chains and bracelets at her ankles. There was no shade beyond the city streets, and she looked tired but resigned, her full lips parted, as if to let a sigh escape. He watched her as she moved towards a thin, bent man, and began to speak to him as he stacked sweet sandalwood, and poured ghee into earthen pots, ready for the funeral pyres. He listened to her queries attentively. His eye sockets were sunken and his cheeks wasted, his back bowed by his lifelong tasks. He pointed down towards the water, shaking his head vigorously the whole time, as he spoke to the woman. Then, abruptly, he went on with his work and she moved, hesitantly, away, the brass anklets with the restraining chain between them clinking and skittering against the shallow stone steps. She made her way to the edge of the water.

Alex took the opportunity to follow her within a close distance, and Salim came quickly on his heels. 'What now?' he grumbled, taking Alex by the arm. 'Come away from her – there are a million women here less dangerous than her!'

'Dangerous?' Alex spun round to face Salim with a low laugh. 'Dangerous, that soft skinned beauty?'

'She is a slave,' growled Salim, 'perhaps the daughter of a slave, she will be the mother of slaves!'

'How can she move with such grace under the indignity of irons?' puzzled Alex, ignoring Salim's agitation.

Nighma had made her way to the very edge of the water where a plank rested on the shore from the deck of a small boat. A man, whom Alex wrongly presumed was her master, watched her approach from the deck as she started to negotiate the sloping wood. He moved to the head of the plank and began beating the side of the boat impatiently, with a wound up leather thong.

To Alex, watching, the man assumed enormous proportions of evil intent, and in that moment he conceived such a hatred of him that sour bile came up in his throat and set him coughing. Nevertheless, he started for the bottom of the plank and would have set foot upon it, but Salim caught hold of his arm firmly, and warned him sharply. 'Be still, friend! You are a guest here! Be still.'

Alex stood watching the woman go, the tension mounting in his throat and ears. He knew in his heart, as did she, that something was about to happen, but she never faltered, her small chained feet moving surely over the springy board. Up on the deck she removed the basket of flowers from her head and kneeling, placed it at the man's feet. Churlishly, he kicked the basket away from him and Alex saw the light basket go spinning up into the air in a kaleidoscope of colour, scattering the blooms about as it went. Not content with this, the man also struck at the woman with the long, leather thong, and Alex saw her draw back as the lash curled about her shoulders. He dragged the lash back, and struck out again, but this time she took hold of the thong and held on. He was too strong for her and pulled her slight body close to his corpulent belly and then cuffed her about the head with his free hand. It was a half-hearted affair, but it annoyed Alex, who demanded of Salim, 'Who is that monster?'

'He is a servant of Srinivasan.'

'A servant! Almost a slave himself! We must help her!' Salim shook his head and edged his way back to the ghats.

'There is nothing we can do. See, he has tired of his game, the slave is picking up the flowers again. She will have forgotten the incident by tomorrow!'

But, Alex would not believe that the servant and the slave were anything but snake and bird. Even whilst he pondered, orders were given and the boat pulled out of the harbour and joined the stream of water traffic and within minutes were lost to sight. Alex was furious with his inadequacy to cope with the situation. He already hated Srinivasan and his henchmen, and resolved in his heart to do all that he could to help her, in the blindness of his compassion, he was prepared to champion her whatever the cause.

He caught up with Salim and asked, 'Who is this Srinivasan?'

'He and others like him dominate the coastline with their boats and houses. They are moguls who know no timid prudence, no pigmy calculation of cost. Their notion of government is to squeeze money from the already poor!' Salim spat, a gesture of disgust, but there was a smile on his face too!

'You speak so well, Salim, you are something of an enigma yourself. You know so much, yet you live a hard and back-aching life.'

'One cannot live by the heart, only by the hand. All nourishment cannot be found in one place. One must search for soul food also. Our Gods provide, but they do not bring it to our feet. Come,' he coaxed, as Alex hesitated, 'such scenes are to be witnessed daily. You would be well advised to forget what you have just seen.' With a firm pressure he led Alex up the ghats and into the city.

But Alex could not forget. The battle blood was singing in his veins, and as Salim left Alex to visit an old quarter of the town to visit past friends, Alex took the opportunity to ask about Srinivasan and his slaves.

He asked questions of the dhobie who knelt at the edge of the sepia water with his washing stone. 'Yes, I know English, French, German, but English was my first foreign tongue. I was "saved" by English Missionaries. But the old ways die hard and then Allah put out my eye!' He turned a ball of white to face Alex.

'My uncle tells me it is with reading the hell-fire books of the Missionaries. What should I do? I give up the Englishing and take up the washing!' He flung the wet linen in and out of the water and squeezed it up on the smooth stone, then hung it to dry on the ghat walls. 'We are all slaves,' he grinned.

Rule Of Thumb

'Why should I care for the fate of others?'

Alex walked on to talk to the sellers of ghee, surma, and gingili. He asked impertinent questions of the competition-wallah, who listened to him patiently, his round little head to one side, a puck's smile to his mouth. At last he spoke. 'My friend, this is a time of great misrule. It is not for us to say what is, or is not, right! Go away, get drunk, buy yourself a girl of your own. Be happy – life is not forever!' He brushed flies from all about them with his chowry, and grinned with such appealing boyishness that Alex felt he must laugh, or knock him down. He decided he must laugh and the man laughed too, and walked jauntily away, picking his path along an alley crowded with sacred cows, litter and people.

Alex too walked amongst the people and spoke to vakeel, merchant, and the lowly, but no one wanted to know what he had witnessed or pass an opinion. It was of no consequence – there were worse things in life than being a slave. Yet, no one was incensed at his impudence to think he could change a system which was not only necessary, but was flourishing. A passing beggar whined at him, 'Bakshish' and when it was not forthcoming, gave a harsh, rasping cough. That always stirred the foreigner to part with a coin. A grubby claw, outstretched was one thing, but a rasping cough quite another. It screamed disease and made its hearer want to pay the wretch off, to get him away to haunt the shadow of others who walked there.

Finally, Alex, with his face averted and his head bowed, asked apologetically of the people whose balconied rooms jutted out over the water. As he asked, thinly clothed, half-veiled women, who worked behind narrow shutters, from dawn to dusk or from dusk to dawn, giggled and squealed, and pushed one another to get a look of the foreigner. 'Such hair!' purred one. 'Such limbs,' giggled another. 'Why bother about a country girl?' asked a bolder, older woman pushing her way forward, her bejewelled figure undulating sensually into his vision.

Alex's speech faltered and his voice sunk almost to a whisper. The squeals of laughter rippled out of the lattices and into the heat-ladened air. Suddenly, a girl appeared out of the crowd in which Alex now stood. 'The woman you seek is Nighma. She is a dancing girl for Srinivasan. She dances for his guests. I was a dancer too, but my leg was broken.' She danced a few limping steps, while the others round her stood silent. The girl turned out the palms of her hands in a gesture of despair.

Alex felt a wave of pity wash over him, but now he was more determined to rescue Nighma. If her leg was broken, would she end her days here, in these sordid streets and houses of sin, these so-called pleasure houses? He left the scene abruptly, walking quickly to the harbour and his ship where he found Salim waiting for him.

CHAPTER TWELVE

The following day, after wresting with his conscience half the night, Alex, when he had attended to his ship's duties, went ashore to search out Nazir the scribe. He found him sat in the market place, a gaunt faced, sad eyed man, with one arm withered and useless but the other skilled enough for two in writing. He wrote in many languages and had a host of secrets locked in his heart, and he nodded his head slowly as Alex dictated his demands for a contract to be drawn up for Nighma's freedom.

'You will be well advised to forget the whole matter,' he said at length. 'Srinivasan is great of temper. He is large in frame and in money matters. Who do you propose to send to negotiate this contract?'

Alex told him that he intended to go himself, at which Nazir threw up his hands in terror. 'You will never be seen again, dear sir, never!' he cried, fidgeting about with his writing materials and looking anxiously about him.

But Alex was determined. 'Come, Nazir, I hear on all sides that you are the best scribe in the city.'

'I am also alive,' replied Nazir tetchily, but the gentle flattery had brought the desired effect, and at last, with much twitching, Nazir complied.

Alex stood besides him and watched with admiration as the black characters flowed onto the paper as neat and ordered as the printed word. 'Do not, dear sir, reveal who has penned this letter,' begged Nazir, as he folded and sealed the epistle. 'I am too old for battles with wealthy men.'

Alex gave him the required payment and said confidently, 'Do not fear so, all will be well, and if you could now tell me where I shall find a reliable guide I will again be indebted to you.'

Nazir bent close and put his withered lips to Alex's attentive ear. His guide was to be found in an alley close by in the middle of three arches. It was a squalid alley but the place was easily found. There was a pokey little office behind the arched doorway and a young man there proclaimed to be the best guide in the city.

Alex had sudden misgivings. It was all very well for others to tell someone

Rule Of Thumb

is the best, but to claim that accolade oneself made Alex wonder. It was early in the afternoon, just before resting time, and there was plenty of time before sundown, so Alex agreed to hire the man.

'It will be in order to pay me now,' said the guide, and showed him a large tariff card, and pointed at the required sum.

'It seems unusual to pay beforehand,' said Alex, hesitating.

'Oh, no, very usual. Very usual indeed!' assured the guide. So, Alex opened his pouch and paid and the guide opened the door and stepped out into the street. Alex followed and the young man closed the door of his office and hung up a sign, which Alex could not read, but which he presumed said the office was to be closed for a certain period of time.

The young man set off and Alex followed. To either side of them as they walked, narrow streets disappeared into the gloom of overhanging balconies and fetid heat. Into this gloom walked the snake-charmer with his reed flute and basket of performers, the betel-nut vendors, coolies with trays of charcoal on their heads, the fakir and the sacred cows. Here and there, in the darkness of a house, a yellow speck of light glowed and the rough smell of hemp would catch Alex in the throat. His guide, a garrulous fellow, would every now and again, call a greeting to his barefooted friends, and sometimes disappear altogether into squalid shacks where these men plied their trade. On these occasions, Alex would plunge into the acrid gloom after him, reminding him, in severe tones, and with a boldness he did not feel, that they should hurry on their way. The guide would then pop out of odd corners, laughing all over his face, apologising profusely, and within a few minutes the same thing would happen all over again. There seemed to Alex to be a good number of hounds scavenging, the males tearing each other piecemeal, whenever the possibility of victory was apparent, and this added to his apprehensions. There were many children too, some in the streets, some in their homes, crying, calling to each other or rushing to the doors of their homes as they passed. Some of them were completely naked, all underfed or at best ill-fed, as shown by their pot-bellies and staring age-old eyes. Alex did note a few adults who still retained a lightness of step and a vivacity to the face, but in the main the persons he did see stirring that afternoon were victims of opium and hemp that quelled their hunger, dimmed their sorrows and created false hopes of their days to come.

When the alleyways seemed to crowd so close that even light had difficulty in penetrating, Alex found, to his dismay, that he and his guide had acquired a following of idle folk, children and hounds. In the city, along the sunbaked avenues and squares they would have announced their following with a cry for alms. Here they were insidiously quiet, shuffling silently from point to point along the alleyways. Alex wished fervently that they would leave their trail, as instinct warned him that here the opportunity for murder was too perfect. He could pity them in their ill-ventilated shacks, lit only by lamps of bitter poon oil, but pressing close behind in litter-ladened streets, he feared them in their wretchedness.

When his fear was at its zenith and he was beginning to doubt the veracity of his guide, the rotting buildings began to thin, and one by one the followers dropped back into the shadows. To the delight of Alex the streets began to widen, and the afternoon sun filtered through the buildings in broad ribbons of yellow, and the air had a sweet, fresh smell to it. Suddenly, they emerged on the edge of the city. Brightly coloured flowers sprang up from the red earth, and in a primitively erected shelter with open sides, five white bullocks ate a meal of chaff and hay. It was here before the shelter that his guide left him. 'Be careful, verra careful,' he warned him in conspiratorial tones. 'There are thieves ever-ra-where.' Then with a cheerful smile he pointed to the home of Srinivasan which was less than half a mile away. His guide then darted back into the warren of streets leaving Alex calling his thanks after him.

The house of Srinivasan was large and new enough to still carry the sweat marks of the perspiring slaves who had help build it, thought Alex grimly as he strode purposefully towards the square white structure. As he came closer to it his pace slackened, partly due to the heat of the sun which beat down mercilessly now that he was out of the shade, and partly as a result of sudden fear that chilled his spine and tightened his thigh muscles. He stopped once and shaded his eyes to look at the house which was assuming overbearing proportions as he came nearer, but after a moment's pause he went on. He felt he had come too far to turn back and soon he reached the high wall that surrounded the house, and walking through a small arched entranceway and along a passage found himself in a narrow court. Here the walls were smoothly plastered, and small fountains played in massive, mosaic basins. By a wrought iron gate a man stood stiffly to attention, round his waist was a thick, green sash, and in it a wicked-looking dhar. Alex looked apprehensively at the large curved blade, as he stepped forward and offered the man the letter which Nazir had written. The guard gave Alex a long hard look before he half-turned and called a white-robed servant boy from the cool recesses of the court behind the gate. As the boy came close the guard thrust the letter through the ornate leaf work and nodded his head towards Alex as if to intimate the letter was from him. The servant took the letter, and went away. The guard resumed his attentive posture. Neither spoke.

For some time Alex was kept waiting and during that time he took stock of his situation, which was none too comfortable coming as he had, unarmed into the enemy camp. He reasoned with himself that to come unarmed was to show his mission was genuine and perhaps his lack of defence would, in the end, be his only safe-guard. There was the gently, flip flop, of a sandal against tiled floors, and the boy servant reappeared. He opened the gate from the inside, 'The master will see you. Please to follow,' he said, in a low, pleasant English, which startled Alex for a moment, but as he followed the boy through the gate all his misgivings were washed away by the scene of infinite peace which greeted his gaze. In the inner courtyard, amongst the flowers a little boy played happily. Colourful birds in large wicker cages hung about the walls, sang and chirruped and filled the air with harmonious sound. Another young boy, with a bamboo rod in his hands, pretended to fish in the ornamental pool. A long, green, vine, trailed from the rod and rested idly on the lotus-leaved waters and as Alex passed by, he caught a glimpse of golden fish and on a large flat stone in the centre of the pool a terrapin sunned himself.

The servant went through the Moorish archway and into the house, and Alex followed close behind, every fibre again alerted for combat. There was a fragrance of attar and cinnamon on the air and tatties cooled the spacious open rooms on either side of the corridor down which they walked. Large painted vases stood in every alcove, brightly enamelled tables were placed at intervals along the walls, and ornate lamps hung from the ceilings on brass chains. Under their feet, colourful and fringed, Indian, Persian and Arabian carpets and rugs covered the tassellated floors. The boy-servant ushered Alex through a silk-draped archway and into a large room. He bowed and, without a word, left him.

In the room Srinivasan sat cross-legged on a well padded couch. He smiled expansively as Alex entered the room, which was fresh and cool after the baking heat of the city and the countryside through which he had just walked. Outside the mesh of the window, behind Srinivasan's head, the heart-shaped leaves of a peepul tree cast purple shadows in the veranda and threw patterns onto the pale cream, and orange coloured flooring. For an instant, Alex's thoughts churned in his head and he felt faint but the clipped English-speaking voice of Srinivasan cut into his consciousness. 'If you will be so polite as to fall down before me, we will talk,' he said with a little smile that did not quite reach his eyes. It was an order rather than a request and Alex complied

Rule Of Thumb

readily, not seeking to offend him. After a few seconds he looked up at the well-dressed figure above him and saw that the smile had broadened and widened to show his teeth.

The servant had quietly returned and now showed Alex to an ivory stool, low, and well carved and set well below his master, for no one there was allowed to sit above him. Srinivasan gazed down on him and smiled an interested and beatific smile. He leaned forward towards him and Alex looked up into the dark, luminous eyes.

'So, you wish to buy my Nighma?'

'I wish to buy her freedom,' Alex replied, his spirits soaring and glad to be at the core of the matter at once.

'She is a bad buy at forty rupees,' he rasped down at Alex in threatening tones, the bejewelled collar at his throat flashing in the light.

'That is good, I can pay it,' Alex replied, delighted at the low price.

Srinivasan laughed aloud, throwing back his head, showing small, wide spaced teeth in betel red gums. He leaned forward again and chided Alex with a thick, brown, forefinger. 'Hold hard, my friend. Forty rupees you pay for Nighma. For her freedom four-hundred.'

Alex swallowed hard. He had been caught. But, no matter, he could pay the four hundred also, although it came as a shock to find that a paltry handful of coins could purchase human flesh and blood. From his leather pouch Alex sorted out the various coins and after counting them carefully, put them on the top of a low, inlaid table just to the right of him. Immediately, the servant stepped forward and counted the coins, setting forty rupees aside on another small table. Srinivasan watched, first rubbing his chin with a well-manicured hand, and then sitting back complacently, his plump hands resting on his knees. All the while he smiled, he had a great deal to smile about.

The servant then collected the four hundred rupees, and took them to his master who received them into his cupped palms. As he took them he broke out into a laugh, his belly on the shake, his teeth a ferocious gleam against the betel-red of his gums.

Alex felt like screaming at him and almost at breaking point, stood up to go. Srinivasan stopped laughing and said, 'Will you take coffee?' The question was so mundane that Alex sat down again without answering. 'Coffee! Coffee!' cried Srinivasan clapping his hands to the servant who was already half way to the door, eager to do his bidding.

'When will the woman be freed?' Alex asked warily, stiffening his back and looking Srinivasan straight in the eye.

Srinivasan stretched, lazily, looked about him, and yawned. 'Tomorrow. Tomorrow at sun-up. Today is not convenient.'

Alex longed to take him by the throat and shake him, but bodyguards stood only a call away and Alex had no doubt that their fingers also itched to do mischief. It was easy, he thought to himself, for the rich in these painted palaces to deny the existence of the shacks Alex had passed on his way there. There was a stir by the curtains at the doorway, and a young girl ran into the room, followed by an enormously tall and well built eunuch, who carried a tray on which stood an array of cups and a highly decorated coffee-pot. Also on the tray was a dish of sweetmeats which made Alex drool to look at for he had always had a sweet-tooth.

The girl ran to Srinivasan on his couch and as she approached he threw down the coins Alex had given to him then held out his hands to her and called 'Little bird.' The coins fell amongst the multicoloured cushions, and some of them bounced and fell on the floor. With a small trilling laugh, the young girl scrambled quickly forward to retrieve them, raking into corners under heavy ebony furniture to retrieve them. 'Shantilal, leave them. I have more,' Srinivasan urged her but she would not be satisfied until she had collected all the coins she could find.

Whilst she looked the eunuch poured strong, black coffee into fragile cups, and then as silently as he had come, departed. Mute and mutilated he had a sorrow all his own.

The girl finished her search and came and stood before Alex with some of the coins cupped in her hands. The soft bloom of childhood had scarcely gone from her cheeks, and she wore a jewel on her forehead on a thin golden chain, threaded through her sleek black hair. Her dress was richly embroidered with blue and silver threads and it was obvious that she was there by arrangement rather than servility. She cast a merry eye on those about her, and had not the downcast look of Nighma, though with a few years on her age, they might well have been one and the same. Certainly, Srinivasan's hold over her was not one of iron-fisted tyranny, for in the moments that followed his warmth of conversation to her and to Alex was nothing short of amazing. In spite of this, however, Alex was glad to take his leave and went with some misgivings. He was not readily lulled into tranquillity by Srinivasan's assurance that Nighma would be released from his house the following day, although Alex had thought he detected a gleam of satisfaction in Shantilal's eyes and hoped a certain pressure from that quarter would be brought to bear. To this end Alex gave a further ten rupees to Shantilal to give to Nighma on her release, so that she would not go empty-handed from their walls. She gave a merry laugh as she took the coins from him, and bowed prettily above them. He thought she was what his mother would have called winsome, but she lacked the patient elegance of Nighma. He would not have stirred two yards to secure Shantilal's freedom, but now she took his hand and said, 'I will do as you ask.' Srinivasan rose from his couch now and said blandly as he touched Alex's fingers briefly in a handshake, 'Nighma will be released tomorrow. She will not leave here empty-handed. Never fear.'

But Alex did fear, and the guffaw of laughter that followed him along the corridor as the soft-footed servant boy led him back into the inner courtyard made him think that his fears were not unjustified. When Alex and the servant entered the courtyard, the young boy who had been pretending to fish had gone, the pools of water made by the constant splashings of the vine, in and out of the water, almost dried away by the hot sunlight. The servant let him out through the wrought iron gate into the outer courtyard where another, surly faced guard stood, ready to let Alex out of the archway and into the passage. Not a word passed between the three of them.

Outside the cool archway the sun beat down fiercely on Alex's shoulders, ironing his shirt to his back, and within minutes he felt the sticky sweat run down his spine and into the waistband of his trousers. When he had walked some distance from the house he saw a familiar figure. It was Salim Khoshla coming towards him, across the dry, baked earth. Salim raised his arm in greeting and when Alex did the same, Salim stopped and squatted under the shade of a solitary and ancient tree. When Alex reached him he stood up and asked, 'It is done?' His face was kindly and composed, but his eyes dark and penetrating.

'Nighma is to be released tomorrow,' replied Alex taking hold of Salim's arm. 'It was good of you to come to meet me.'

'Not goodness, Alex, alarm!' replied Salim dourly, shaking his arm free.

'Alarm?' queried Alex. 'Can I not run a simple errand?'

'Life here is not so simple, it is like the truth,' said Salim guiding Alex to another easier path. 'I saw your guide returning. I can guess that he took you through the worst parts of the city. He is accustomed to doing that to foreigners. He hopes they will relent whatever mission they are on, and so he makes half a journey on full pay, which is what he asks before he will stir one step!'

Alex laughed aloud at this. 'I thought my guide had earned his money well, Salim, and I must say this, that for a disappointed man he kept a most cheerful countenance!'

Rule Of Thumb

Salim shrugged his shoulders. 'It is the way of things. Keep close to me and I will guide you back to the city by a pleasanter route for nothing but your company.'

As they were returning through the dusty roads on the outskirts of the city they came abreast of a native leading a heavily ladened bullock cart from out of the surrounding foothills. Salim had known this man in his youth and hailed him and after a puzzled look had crossed his face, he began to shout, 'We thought you had been swallowed by a whale years ago! How fare you?'

'Been swallowed and spewed back again,' shouted Salim, taking the man's outstretched hand. Whilst they pumped each other by the arm, the two white bullocks stopped, drooped their long-lashed eyelids and began to doze. Salim called Alex to him and said, 'This is an old friend, Vishwa Nath. He lives over there.' He pointed towards the west where a blur of green rose above the dry red earth. 'Most of Vishwa's brothers and sisters are migratory in their ways, living on the outskirts of the tract of jungle beyond, tending their herds and cultivating crops according to place and season. Vishwa has been taught a more stable way of life by the missionaries. They took care of him when Vishwa had been up in the foothills with his parents one drought period and he had been plagued by dholes (wild dogs) savaging their goats. The whole pack caught Vishwa unawares one day and mauled him badly. Show him, Vishwa,' urged Salim. Vishwa grinned and obligingly bared his arm to expose the mangled muscles, dimpled and scarred a snowy white. It was not pretty, but it was ten times better than when the missionaries had treated it thirty years before. After his display, Vishwa intimated that he must proceed with his journey to the city, and all three set off together, Vishwa on one side of the road and Salim and Alex on the other, the wooden wheeled cart pulled by the enormous, white, bullocks trundling on between them.

As they went along Salim told Alex a little of Vishwa's life. He had left the charge of the Mission when he had been well enough, but many months had elapsed since he had lived with his own people. He had become used to living in one place and the shifting, precarious existence of his kin no longer appealed to him. He was at an impressionable age and thought for a time of being a Priest, and had, in fact, joined the Mission life for some years. But, old habits, the senior Priest being recalled to England and a new less likeable Priest being installed unsettled Vishwa and he drifted away to live in a small village on the outskirts of the city. There he eventually married a mulatto girl who had borne him sons and daughters with monotonous regularity.

Rule Of Thumb

They were now able to fend for themselves, but the girls were now producing their own babies and they all lived together in a hamlet of their own. In a lush area besides a small tributary they all tilled the land and grew vegetables. By day, Vishwa or one of his sons freighted produce and in the evening sat by the fire relating the happenings of the day or telling stories and legends of the past. Some of the stories were centuries old, some skilfully engineered from the happenings of the day.

Then they were on the fringe of the city. The noise smote the ears like a blow after the quiet of the countryside, for they had become used to the cart rumbling between them, as it jogged along the dusty, rutted roadway. The river traffic was seething as always, people shouting their business at the tops of their voices in order to be heard. Crowded streets were difficult to negotiate with the cart, but at last, the market where Vishwa was to sell his goods was reached and Salim and Alex said their goodbyes as he began to unload his cart. He took off his lightweight jacket now, flinging it across the back of one of the bullocks. He pulled at the binding ropes, the muscles of his back and arms knotting like kinking cords, and the produce spilled out onto the ground in a jumble of colour.

'That is how I want to remember him,' said Alex to Salim as they turned to go. 'Strong and wholesome, going about his work with a will and not yet touched with disease or age!' Salim walked on, kicking his way through a pile of dried and sacred dung.

CHAPTER THIRTEEN

The next day, a few hours before Alex's ship was to set sail, there was a commotion on the quayside. Nighma had appeared there and was asking the whereabouts of the young sailor who had bought her. Everyone was talking at once and Alex's cheeks burned under the criticisms and witty remarks of his companions as he went down the gangplank towards her. As he stood before her, seeing her at close quarters for the first time, he realized that she was more beautiful than he had thought. Her skin was warmly toned, her hair sleek and black, her eyes the soft brown of a woodland creature, and just as trusting, as they looked up into his. 'Oh, God!' he thought frenziedly, 'I've made a pig's ear out of a silk purse!' In vain he tried to explain to her that she was a free woman, but all the response he received was for her to hold out her hands to him palm upwards. In them were the coins he had given her for her support on her release. Alex stared at them bewildered, and called out to Salim, 'Tell Nighma she is now free! Explain!'

Salim came forward, reluctantly. Soon a voluble conversation was taking place. What Salim was saying Alex could only guess at, the tone of his voice seemed firm but kindly, and he hoped Nighma would be satisfied with his explanation. But, as he watched, Alex saw, to his consternation, the girl begin to weep, quietly, two great tears rolling down her rounded cheeks, to the tip of her trembling chin. 'What is it?' asked Alex, a cold area in the pit of his stomach. 'Why is she crying?'

'She has nowhere to go! She has been bought and sold twice already.' There was a sadness on Salim's face as he mouthed silently, 'What was I telling you?'

At first Alex was incensed and then distraught. So this was why her late master had laughed. He knew that to remove her chains was no surety to Nighma's freedom. He had precipitated her from Srinivasan's tolerable bondage to the freedom of the streets and all the uncertainties of destitution. Alex struck his forehead in despair. 'What am I to do? I cannot sell her to another!' he exclaimed as a wave of anger passed through him.

Rule Of Thumb

On board his Captain spoke his piece plainly, 'No woman sails aboard my ship! Free or bond she will not be getting a berth between these boards!' Alex opened his mouth to speak, but the Captain put up a hand, 'What a sentimental fool you are, to be taken in by a slip of a thing like her. But then, you are not the first man to be bowled over by a woman's sigh, or the last, but I think you might have been less impetuous.' Alex tried to explain that Nighma had not seen him until a few moments before. 'Bah! Even worse! Have you no sense? You interfere in the life of another and expect to remain uninvolved. Have you learned nothing as a sailor? You do not sail into the eye of the storm, that is asking for unnecessary trouble! Did you ask her if she wanted her freedom? I have no patience with you man. You had best take your papers.' He reached into a cabinet and took out a piece of paper and signed it. 'Consider yourself discharged, Alex Deane. I shall be sorry to loose you this trip but there are others will be glad of your berth. I hope you will find an answer to the riddle you have set yourself.' He held out his hand and they shook briefly. 'I will not say goodbye, Captain. I may yet see you again, and in any event I wish you a good wind and fair skies. We have travelled the seas together this three years past, and you have always been an admirable Captain.'

As he left the cabin the Captain began to feel very put out that now, just when he had lost him, he had found out what a worthy man Alex Deane was. And he was also a first class seaman. Perhaps, he thought to himself ruefully, Alex was not the only one who had this day been impetuous.

Alex stood at the top of the gangplank and looked down on Salim and Nighma as they stood at the bottom on the quayside. Nighma was looking anxiously around her, her unchained ankles placed close together from habit, her bare feet at right angles, a gesture that had a pathos of its own. Alex ran his hands through his thick, tawny curls, and growled, 'What a mess!' He had been so eager to see justice done and had committed something tantamount to a crime. At the back of his mind he knew where his duty lay but it was a struggle to bring it out into the open, knowing that his misplaced chivalry had blinded his commonsense. He gave some other seamen who were watching a jaunty salute and picking up his belongings went down onto the quay. His steps were followed by curt words of unsolicited advice from his late comrades, only to be quelled by Salim who now left Alex and boarded the ship.

Nighma now stood alone on the quay, a slim, green draped shape, against the white walls of the quay buildings. A rousing cheer went up from the men at the rails as Alex shouldered his baggage and went towards her. Once at her side, Alex looked up at the ship and his heart leapt at what he saw. Salim was coming towards him, his roll on his shoulder, a broad smile on his face. Suddenly a feeling of freedom surged through Alex. He had escaped from the sea! He had never been a willing sailor, he had been competent and obedient, and had enjoyed arriving at foreign ports, but Fate had tied him to the tides as some men are tied to the soil. Now Fate had cast him ashore. He must fare as best he could.

They were a strange trio as they set off, Alex and Salim, walking in front together and Nighma walking a little distance behind them both. The only friend they thought they might have who would be able to help them was Vishwa Nath. Salim knew where his hamlet lay, close to the vicinity of a large village, and they set out without delay.

It was a weary walk, not helped by the thought that they may be laying a further burden upon a burdened family, but at last they arrived. All their fears were unfounded. They were taken into the family as if they had been born kin, given food to eat and a place to sleep, and room besides the communal fire. The village near to Vishwa Nath's hamlet was compact and self-supporting also, although it was true that when the monsoon was late they had been driven to eating fried rats, termites and any edible grubs they could find. Normally, they ate curried vegetables, fried bananas, wild rice, fish, numerous fruits both wild and garden grown, and flaked nuts which they purchased in the city. The huts were reasonably well made of bamboo, and thatch and woven grass lattice-work. The floors were made of beaten earth and cowdung, which had certain antiseptic properties. When the weather was good the necessary duties were carried out into the open air and only sleep was confined to the huts. By general consent, sleeping in the open was to court disaster from both the living and the dead. From the hamlet hilltop a long view of the city spread out to the east. The golden domes, minarets and towers, shimmered in the heat haze that hung low over the hotch-potch of buildings in a smokey-blue blur. Up above, the sky was a dull orange colour, reflecting the red dust of the earth below.

When Vishwa and Salim met, under the shade of a scrubby tree where Vishwa's youngest daughter had tethered two young goats, the two men clasped each other round the shoulders and then stood back and bowed over their joined palms. Alex, when he came near, imitated the same movements, and a pleased expression came to Vishwa's face and the faces of his family who had gathered near. Nighma knelt, and taking hold of one of Vishwa's feet, placed it on her head as she bowed to the ground, the red dust powdering her rounded brow and the tip of her nose. 'Do not kneel to me, jewel of

Srinivasan's necklace of women, I am a simple man. None kneel to me but the camel and the bullock.' He held out his hand to her, and lifted her upright, and a murmur of approval whispered around the gathering. A shadow of astonishment crossed Alex's face as he noted how many men, women, and children came out of the huts, and he wondered how they could manage to take three extra guests. As Vishwa ushered them to his own hut, Alex noted that they grew millet in small but neat plots, and a variety of vegetables. Further down the hillside near a brisk stream they had made a paddy-field and here grew small-grained but very adequate rice.

Vishwa Nath's home was not very big, and none too comfortable, and Alex felt sorry for Nighma as he thought of the tiled and carpeted floors and the clean and silken drapes in the house he had freed her from. She herself did not complain, however, but settled herself gracefully with the other women who moved aside to make room for her.

It had been a tiring day and Vishwa assured them he would soon have food prepared for them. 'I have made a sacrifice today at a nearby temple. Old habits die hard,' he faltered as he saw Salim's searching look. 'The priests and priestesses claimed the head, blood and offal, and washed the carcass for me in holy water. Would it not be a pity to then throw such a carcass to the wild beasts? I do not know, perhaps it is my imagination, but it seems to me the priestesses grow uglier by the year!'

Salim coughed as he tried to stifle a laugh. He had long ago outgrown such fervours. He embraced all religions, yet was a follower of none to the extinction of another. Once Alex had asked him his religion and he had said, 'A pinch of this, and a puff of that!' Alex himself thought that, all things told, his own religious views might be summed up in the same vein.

They were all very pleased with the goat stew, and the chapatties handed round bearing frugal helpings of curried goat's meat tasted delicious and were very welcome to the hungry guests.

Soon it was evening and the air cooled. Night sounds began to issue from some of the animals in the nearby jungle. Small lamps were lit in the middle of each hut and children were gathered up into the protection of their families. Vishwa Nath made a space for his guests in his home, and they settled down to sleep.

As Alex lay in the darkness he thought over the happenings of the day. The quick reversal of fortune and favour, ousted by his own countrymen, accepted by almost total strangers. He would have thought he was dreaming had he not felt the moulded form of Nighma who lay up to the wall, and the solid figure of Salim who lay on his right. After a while he fell into a dreamless sleep.

Alex was awakened almost at dawn by a small boy clambering over him with many chuckles and squeals. He had often been awakened at dawn, but never by such a merry bedfellow, who could hardly stand on his legs. His fat little belly was liberally covered in grease and his kohl-rimmed eyes shone with mischief. He was one of Vishwa's grandchildren, and close by, still sleeping, lay several of his elderly relatives whose welcome to the trio had been irreproachable. They were originally of nomadic stock who were mutually tolerant and inclusive. Each had their place in the Nath household, each had a certain amount of work to do each day, and each took their rewards in life with a joyfulness which made Alex feel ashamed, both of himself and others of his ilk.

The trio were soon to find that there was plenty of work they could do both in the hamlet of Vishwa and the nearby village. Each inhabitant, no matter how feeble and old or how young, had his or her task which enriched the days of the others in the group. Children who were too young or too clumsy to tend crops, gathered dried cow dung for fuel. The quieter and more patiently inclined children, whose eyes shone, darkly luminous in their heart-shaped faces, were set to watch flocks of goats. The older women watched over the fire and cooking pots or the youngest children. Able men fished, women tended crops, and the strongest men, and Vishwa was one of these, freighted wood or vegetables into the city. With the rupees they got for this work they bought brass plates or earthen pots, and materials for the women to make up into clothes and blankets.

In Nath's home, with green lizards walking up the walls and across the rafters, bright birds nesting in the roof fronds, and golden and blue beetles walking leisurely up the mud and cowdung filled cracks of the walls, lived the oldest inhabitant of the hamlet. He savoured life. Every grain of food, every ray of sun on his old, bent back, every sigh of a monsoon wind, every sunset and every moonrise, he gave thanks for a full and good life. The peace and calm in his face reflected in the whole of the Nath household, and never, whilst Alex stayed with them, had he found life so rich and rewarding. Through their eyes he began to see the land as something other than a place to anchor a ship and go ashore. He took pleasure in the growth of plants, and the smell of jungle fruits and spices, and almost at once went daily into the jungle with the fruit and nut gatherers, or fished for the fat and wholesome denizens of stream and river.

At night the men from both village and hamlet sat round a large communal fire, smoking the hookah and talking, but one night, when Alex had been there for about two weeks, he sensed an excitement in the air. The men began passing round arrack in bamboo pipes or earthen jars or even wooden bowls. A party was being held in honour of some God or other, Salim explained, and it would be best for them to honour the God too. Later, women joined the men folk and the night became alive with little stirring noises, and the tap of a drum and the thin, reedy pipe of a flute. Some of the men and women began to dance. At first they moved in staid fashion and then with livelier and jerkier steps. As the night advanced the dancers sat down and only solo dancers took the floor. As one old man stood up and took his place on the ring of bare earth, near to the fire, the rhythm on the drum changed to a pulsating throb. The man began to gyrate on his bare feet, his body thrust about back and forth, making his movements symbolically sexual. His shape leapt up against the red glow of the fire and as he made his way round the ring of people the beat increased in volume and then as he returned to the spot he had begun from, another took his place and as he completed the ring, another. The watchers thought it highly entertaining, and rolled about in spasms of laughter, pushing their fingers into their mouths and wailing with hysterical delight. Alex took refuge behind his own pipe, smiling and trying to look interested, but feeling embarrassed by the whole dance. He was glad that Nighma had been spared an appearance, but Salim clapped his hands to the drum beat and even tried a turn in the ring, much to the amusements of the others, especially when a log rolled out of the fire and touched his foot. His hopping movements added both oddity and verve to the occasion and he was applauded boisterously as he returned to his place. Later, Alex saw couples pairing off and slipping away to quiet corners. It was none of his business, he was still a guest there, albeit a working one, but he thought he knew now why there were so many children in the hamlet and village. The Gods of Fertility, had certainly heard their pleas, and 'May your belly always be full,' had come to have another connotation other than food.

The following day Salim told Alex that Vishwa had heard of a house in the city, which was empty, and which they could move into without delay. 'It is an old house with a large yard. No one wants to live there. It's been empty for years!'

'Why has it been empty for years?' asked Alex, immediately suspicious.

'Well,' faltered Salim, it's old and neglected, and . . .'

'And?' queried Alex.

'It is a long tale! It was a beautiful house but one day there was a sad happening there. A young woman died in mysterious circumstances. Since then the house has been let to go to ruin.'

'And?' queried Alex yet again.

'And it is reputed to be haunted,' Salim went on hurriedly.

'Haunted! You expect me to live in a haunted house!'

'There will be three of us! We have no money to speak of but there will be no rent to pay.'

'And what other delights are there, apart from a large yard and a ruinous aspect? Must we cry 'Ram, Ram' under the house walls to drive away the ghosts, and call tigers, creepers, and snakes insects to guard ourselves against evil?' said Alex with a sour face and much trouble in his heart.

Salim shook his head. 'I have been to see the house. It is not much neglected. None of the house is fallen down, and the walls remain intact because all fear to touch it because of its reputation.'

'Do you think Nighma would live there?'

'I do not know. You must tell her as much as you want her to know. She has followed you thus so far, Alex, perhaps she will brave ghosts too!'

'Well, Salim, if you are willing to live in that house, I think I will be able to live there too. As for Nighma, she is a free woman, she may go or stay as she pleases.'

'Come what may,' answered Salim, 'we can only better our lot and Vishwa says that if we move he will bring his fruit and vegetables to us instead of the market. That will save him time and he will spend that growing more vegetables to sell!'

'It was indeed a good day when we met up with your old friend Vishwa. We are indeed fortunate to have found a dwelling and an offer of work so soon. Many starve upon the streets, under the very windows of the opulent.'

When they saw Vishwa, he was digging in his vegetable plot. He raised his back when he heard them approaching and looked up at them wondering if they were to take up his offer. His face, usually surly looking in repose, burst open with a smile, like the opening of a flower, when Alex said, 'We are grateful of your offer of business. If we give you two-thirds of the value and then sell the vegetables ourselves, that will leave you even more time to grow food, and fish, and gather fruits. We will take all your people can spare. This way we all shall prosper.'

'The house is a good property, made bad by association only.'

'Yes, Salim has told me the story. It is of no consequence to me. What is past, is past,' Alex asserted with a confidence he did not feel.

'I must apologise for the happenings of last night,' Vishwa went on. 'I fear we shocked you with our enthusiasm for life. Forgive us, we are a simple people, living close to nature in her many moods.'

'Who am I to criticize others, I who have followed my heart in such a wayward manner and caused such distress to Nighma?'

'Ah, but my friend,' said Vishwa, drawing nearer and lowering his voice, 'there is a woman who mourns as one who can be comforted. Are you so blind that you do not see how she looks at you?' he asked rakishly closing one eye.

'I have never seen her look at me!' cried Alex on the defensive.

'But she does look,' said Salim. 'And such looks!'

'Do you think she cares for me as a Master?'

'The ways of woman are a mystery to me? You will have to find out for yourself. If she is willing to travel to the house with us that may be your only answer.'

'Then we must ask her at once, for here she is,' cried Alex as he saw Nighma stepping lightly towards them wearing the new sari that Alex had bought her. It had been more expensive than sensible but Alex had felt he owed it to her. She was still conscious of having worn the bracelets and he saw no other way of returning her esteem than by material goods, for he did not wish her to be his mistress and he had not yet come to love her.

She greeted them with a languid motion of a thin manicured hand, and her eyes were less downcast, under the dark satin, of the upper lid where kohl had been applied.

'We have found a house in the city, Nighma,' Alex began. 'It is old and neglected, and has a reputation of fear and sightings. Would you be willing to live there, with Salim and myself?'

Nighma inclined her head gracefully and smiled a shy smile.

'It is not ghosts that are to be feared, Sahib, but people. The evil is in them, not in the reputations and sightings.'

'Well said,' cried Alex. 'We will travel there the first light tomorrow!' He breathed a sigh of relief in spite of his inner qualms as to the wisdom of such an arrangement.

The following day, as the first golden beams of light flooded over the green oasis, they set off with a stock of fresh food to last them for a few days when Vishwa would begin trading with them.

'Now, let us proceed,' cried Alex, 'and let us hope our fortunes fare as well as here, for we have been fortunate to have met with such unstinting kindness as shown by Vishwa Nath and his family.'

They set off, Salim walking to the left of Alex and Nighma, as when they had entered the village, walking several trailing paces behind. But a curious

Rule Of Thumb

change had taken place in her, she smiled and tossed her head and soon the distance between Alex and herself was not so great, not more than a pace or two.

CHAPTER FOURTEEN

The way to the city was hot and tedious, after many stops under shady trees and one when they reached the city, for water from the water-seller, and other refreshments, they arrived at the house in the mid afternoon. They stood, with their entire possessions on their backs, and Alex felt slightly sick as he looked up at the tall almost windowless walls that backed on to the busy street. Down in the street, the air was sticky with heat, and the noise of the people passing to and fro was like the murmur one might hear from a seashell held close to the ear. A sea of sound, rising and falling like a tide.

Alex walked up to the high wooden gates, and pushing them open they walked inside. They looked back into the street as the noise around them became subdued, as people stopped what they were doing in order to stare. The stories which were told of the house had been retold and added to for almost thirty years and nearly everyone present knew of some horror that had been witnessed there. Alex shut the doors behind him with a defiant 'wham', and hoped his lack of fear would be justified.

When Alex had inspected the yard he felt more cheerful.

'There is ample room here for turning two bullock carts, Salim,' he said, and Salim agreed that apart from that, the whole of one side wall could be used for stalls, for the selling of the fruit and vegetables. Alex's heart became quite light as they proceeded into the house and found themselves in a hallway which was large and tiled with lozenges of white and blue and a deep maroon border. There were other rooms which were very much defaced and half-obliterated inscriptions and vestiges of relief sculptures only added to the general appearance of decay. Gone were the days when bronze or gold figurines, dressed in garments of enamel or porcelain had graced the shaded niches. Silent the bells whose heart-shaped clappers had once swung in the breeze and sent tinkling music through the inner courtyard. A creeping vine had strangled the silvery tongues and woven a carpet of green across the roof tiles, and several of the windows that overlooked the inner yard.

The reason for its strangling green clasp was that its roots had clawed deep into the side of the fountain basin, and from here it drew its nourishment. Even when all else was baked brown by drought, this vine flourished.

'That vine will have to go first,' said Alex and Salim agreed that the house would be dark enough and dismal enough without a profusion of leaf curtain over the windows. Inside the three were more alarmed to find evidence of rats, and later the sight of them as they scampered over the floors and built in furniture. They jumped from inside the clothespresses the moment the creaking doors were opened, or sat, washing their long and twitching whiskers, upon the tops of the eating tables. The trio were also alarmed to find the house was already well occupied by a large family of snakes. They took naps in the empty bath tubs and water-pitchers, and slid unceremoniously into the bedrooms just before the mosquito nets were pulled around the beds, and gave them all many nasty frights during their first few weeks in the house. During these weeks their whole attitude towards the deity of snakes was altered. They considered them vermin and treated them accordingly. But, as the rats became less of a problem, the snakes too moved out of the house their main source of food being depleted.

Only two small windows looked out onto the side street, and at a high level. From there Alex watched the inhabitants in the street below. They were a motley of humanity who walked there, and noisy too! All around were cries of business, the rumble of bullock carts and other wheeled vehicles, and the grunts and groans of camels. It was as well that the windows were few and high on that side but the inner sides of the house were sheltered from the smells and noise, and so quiet that the tiny voice of mouse or bird could be heard without strain to the ears. For this boon all three were grateful, although they were aware that their future prosperity and security must come from the noise and squalor outside.

The women who walked the dusty, red street below in their white burquas and muslin or in sari and veil, or even in rag and tatters, were all intent on the same purpose – to shop to feed their families, to live a little, to gossip, to hope tomorrow would be as good as that day or at the very least, no worse.

So the days crept on. They sold those women food for their families, provided them with gossip, gave them hope in their despair, and laughter in their dullest hours.

Some of the men who walked down the street were quite capable of amusing themselves. They shuffled down the street each day and seated themselves on the veranda of the house opposite. They were mostly bearded men, with thin, scarecrow bodies, and gnarled hands and feet. Alex asked

Rule Of Thumb

Salim about them. 'Oh, those men,' he said peering out of the yard gate at them as they sat in two neat rows along the veranda. 'They are old men, usually men who have travelled when young, as we have. They have no families, just each other. They sit there telling tales of their progression through this life. Their bones are brittle, their eyesight fails, their teeth drop out like grain, but they go on croaking out the tales from their childhood and manhood, defying death that waits around the corner, waiting, patiently, and never evaded! They will go on jabbering to the end, the red betel juice running freely from their, wet, slack lips. One day, a space will appear amongst them, in their neat rows, another of their members will have dipped his feet in Mother Ganga for the last time. But, like the dragon's tooth, yet another old man will join their ranks, to amuse or sadden his listeners.'

'How fruitless it all seems,' remarked Alex as he looked once more towards the old men. 'I wonder, will we be as they are now, in our old age?' Salim smiled and shrugged his shoulders up to the level of his ears. 'Why worry about that now? It is life. They have had their span, we may never know old age. They have taken their years, we are not sure of ours!'

'That is true!' answered Alex, 'but let us hope that if we do become old, we shall be venerable, if not rich!' and they both laughed and shook each other by the hand before returning to the more pressing work of the day.

Salim was a great help to Alex. Within a few weeks he had made many contacts in the city, and when they had a little money in hand, Salim made arrangements for a quantity of spices to be sold at the house also, and later on small trinkets of the cheaper variety. In all transactions Salim stood at Alex's side, his bearing dignified and unperturbed. To all his duties, he gave the quiet, scrupulous attention that only the best of manservants give, with one exception, he was a friend, cheering Alex and Nighma with his native wit and charming anecdotes.

Close now to Alex was Nighma, who spoke on all things with remarkable fidelity and was unlike other women he had known whose behaviour, in his eyes, had veered alarmingly between pragmatic and pathetic.

One day Nighma came to Alex in his office and said, 'There is a man at the gates, he wishes to speak to you about precious stones.'

'We have no stones here, tell him to go away,' answered Alex impatiently.

'He wishes you to take some jewels from him to sell, but he will not come inside because he fears the reputation of the house.' Alex looked at Nighma, graceful in pale pink sari, and silver slippers on her feet, and said, 'Does this timid man have a name?'

'His name is Ranjit Rashid. He is very insistent.'

'Very well. I will see him, Nighma, though I know nothing of precious stones myself. He could peddle me coloured glass and I would be none the wiser!'

'He will not do that! Where is the profit in that? He is a business man,' said Nighma as she hurried before Alex to the gate of the yard.

When Alex was shown the man he gave a formal greeting. The man did not look as if he was well-informed about anything. Alex invited the man into the yard, the man shrank back, with a roll of his dark eyes. 'No! No!' he cried out in alarm, 'I cannot step inside. There is danger, that cannot be seen, within the gates!'

'There is nothing here but the shadows on your mind, Rashid.'

'It is fatal to get on bad terms with those departed,' cried the man huskily, his Adam's apple jumping in his throat.

'It is more dangerous to get on bad terms with the living, is it not?' queried Alex with a slightly threatening tone which he did not feel, as he knew the man's alarm was genuine. The man rubbed his chin with a hand that shook with indecision, then peered furtively into the yard.

'Do not we live here and prosper?' Alex asked. 'Does not the choking, strangling vine, curl back from the window spaces? Does it not rot upon our roof-top, then dry and be blown away by every breeze? The rats and snakes have fled, and birds have filled our inner courtyard with their songs, and flowers bloom from every corner! What evil could take residence here?'

'I hear from others that you prosper,' offered the gem-seller, as Alex took him by the arm and into the house and into his office. There Ranjit Rashid threw caution to the winds for 'business' had risen to the surface of his desire to prosper also.

'I have a reliable contact who is willing to deliver uncut gems to me. I have very worthy friends who will cut the gems and polish and set them. It is our wish that you will sell the finished articles in your market.'

'Why cannot you sell them in the bazaars?' asked Alex. 'The people who come here are not in the market for gems. They come for spice and vegetables, and jungle fruits, and gossip, and the refreshing cordials, Nighma, provides.'

'I will be getting the first consignment in two months. Will that suit you? Will you have the money ready?'

'No, I will not have the money ready!' exclaimed Alex. 'We are hand to mouth for vegetables and fruit, let alone gem-stones.'

'You will have no trouble with the selling! The women will flock to the house like butterflies!'

'I have a better idea!' exclaimed Alex. 'You bring me the gem-stones and

I will sell them for you! In return you will give me commission on each piece! I can do no other way! We prosper but slowly, and we have some backsliding. Do you understand me?'

Ranjit Rashid kneaded his neck, 'Oh, verily, verily.'

Alex remembered the verily from his early churchgoing days and wondered where Ranjit had been sitting to hear it also. Those missionaries had a lot to answer for.

'Well, is my offer to your liking?'

'No, it is not to our liking, but, if that is how it must be, then enough. I shall be here in the two months and we will see how the selling goes from then to the next consignment.' He bowed to Alex and Salim who had just entered the office and hurried away.

'What did that "sneaky-up-on-his-toes" want?' asked Salim with a chuckle.

Alex told him. Salim sat silent. They had a few setbacks at first when they came to the house. Money was laid out on goods which sat in the storerooms for want of a buyer. But, as more people came they had eventually reduced the stock-pile, and every day a further 'white elephant' was sold as a desirable gift. Later they had become known to the Europeans also who sent their servants in for spices and fresh fruit, and later on came in themselves to view the trio whose unusual lifestyle made them the vortex of speculation and gossip.

The house and yard began to be a meeting place for camel-boys, and vendors, who began to whisper in Alex's ear of bargains, and in Salim's ear of transactions that might further their popularity and prosperity.

In a matter of months they were able to furnish adequately the rambling old house. Carpets and silks and homely works of art, or the more expensive enamelled brasses and small silver and gold trinkets, were brought to the yard and haggled over. Daily they sold hand embroidered shawls and cushions, and the lawn dresses and blouses much prized by European women. They also dealt in the skins of tigers, crocodile, and elephant foot umbrella stands, as well as the heads of various small animals. These were placed on show in one of the ground floor reception rooms, and daily the more sporting minded of the Europeans, gathered there, drinking cordials and harassing Salim, who did not care for this part of the business. Alex was indifferent to it as he had remarked to Salim on several occasions. 'Where is the harm in it. These men, although delicate of skin and weak of muscle, brought down by fever and repeated attacks of diarrhoea, still retain that aura of sportliness in their outlook. They need a trophy of distinction, to send back home to their relatives, to let them know what a damned fine job they are making of

Rule Of Thumb

their time in India. To let them know what fun they are all having hunting down the wild life, when they aren't running up the flag!'

'But they have never fired a shot for these animals,' argued Salim.

'It does not matter. They have paid good money for the privilege of lying to their own folk. The responsibility lies with them!'

Although Alex sold to the Europeans, he could not bring himself to consider that he was one of them. The blood of India had in some way entered his soul. He objected fiercely and openly to the way some Europeans treated the people born in the land.

The snatches of conversation which he overheard from the window of his indoor office sometimes made him very angry. Some of the women treated their women servants abominably for the sake of caprice or petty spite, and the men treated them even worse. One day Alex heard a man in the yard below the office window boasting of a new servant he had acquired; with an almost black skin. As he dusted a little snuff off the front of his canary-yellow waist-coat, he observed to his companion, 'You can punch him as hard as you like. The bruises won't show!'

'Except in his soul!' shouted Alex grimly, throwing the window open and revealing himself. The man looked up at him assuming an air of injured innocence but his Adam's apple rose in his throat in a gulp of alarm as he realised the speaker was Alex. Alex took advantage of this to assert further, 'What a pot you are putting on the boil for yourselves!' He slammed the window shut and left the office to go into the yard, but the two men, having suspected his intention had already made a hasty exit. They had hired one of the passing carts to take them along the road, and by the time Alex entered the yard they were goading the driver to an urgent pace and were rapidly being covered by a generous pall of red dust. Alex thought of the beautiful yellow of the beater's waistcoat, and what the dust might be doing to it, and allowed himself the smallest of smiles.

True to his word Ranjit Rashid, in two months to the day of his transaction with Alex sent the first consignment of gems. It was brought by a young fellah who wore only a shifty look and a loincloth. 'Something is wrong!' asserted Salim as soon as he saw the made up gems. 'What?' queried Alex angrily.

'I think we are being made fools of,' said Salim more calmly. 'We may be being set up by dacoits, or even market people who think we prosper too quickly and at their expense.'

'How can we find out?' asked Alex, his knees turning to water with anxiety. 'Shall we tell the authorities?'

'No, that is not the answer,' said Salim his mind working overtime. 'We must always play the innocent. We suspect, but we do not condemn outright!'

When the next consignment was due, Ranjit Rashid, appeared in the yard early one morning. He was alone. He hoped that he would collect two-thirds of the value of the pieces and leave the new pieces with Alex. Alex had rehearsed his part well.

'My dear friend,' he began, looking past Ranjit Rashid as if searching for others, 'Come into the house, we will be safe from prying eyes there.'

Ranjit hurried into the house after him, already tense and on edge. 'What has happened? Have you been robbed?'

'We think so, but we are not sure. We are not able to sell the settings. Everyone who sees them shudders and turns away. We can only think that they are stolen pieces. Who is it you have dealings with?'

'I have been sworn to secrecy! I will have my tongue cut out if I divulge the names of my setters!'

'Then, Ranjit Rashid, I pity you, for you have been duped as we all have. They have not used the gems you have given them but substituted stolen like pieces.'

'Oh, I am an unhappy man,' wailed Ranjit Rashid. 'My troubles fall about me like the rain from the monsoon. My hopes die and wither in the dust. My heart is heavy and without power.'

'Come,' said Alex, 'all is not lost. I will return these pieces to you. You have the second consignment too! You are still a man of considerable property, are you not? Return to the setters and make known to them people's suspicions, and hint at authority and incarceration for those that harm you. Trust me, all will be well.'

Ranjit Rashid took the settings and made his exit hurriedly. 'For a man whose heart is heavy and without power he moves exceedingly well,' observed Alex to Salim with a little smile.

There was a sequel to the dealings with Rashid. Men in the foothills heard of Salim and Alex and Nighma and their combined commercial enterprise. They began to bring to Alex their gems, unpolished and sweated and strained for in the most inhospitable of conditions. Why they came, Alex could only guess and be thankful. It was not only the fair price paid that brought them, but the strange partnership that had blossomed into something wonderfully successful. That, together with their dwelling unharmed in a house reputed to be haunted, made a tale worthy to be told by the evening fireside.

Later, carvers of jade brought their work to be sold behind the high yard gates of the house. Chinese by birth, these workers in jade held out their long, slim fingers in friendship, their slanted eyes calm, their hearts remembering their own alienation. Soon they were buying the blocks of blue, green and grey-cream jade from Alex himself, and returning with the finished objects. Their skilled fingers brought to life the dead stone, people and Gods, symbols, and dragons, bursting out of the plain blocks with vigour, and movement denoted in every line. Delicate flowers opened their petals, birds fluttered their wings, and fishes flicked their tails.

It was the gems and the jade pieces that brought Srinivasan into Alex's life again. One day, in the midst of a morning's bustle, there he stood, with three of his servants. Alex's heart skipped a beat, but he went towards him with a smile on his face.

'Welcome! What is your business here? How can we serve you?'

'My servants tell me that you deal in jade and gemstones, as well as vegetables and spices,' Srinivasan said in a teasing tone.

'That is so. We deal in anything we can! It is hard to keep a foothold on the first rungs of the ladder. That is why we also carry a rope!'

Srinivasan laughed. 'I have heard many tales of your exploits in the city. I admire your tenacity and capacity for making friends with the ordinary people of the city. They have a name for you, I hear. Have you heard it, Tiger Dee?'

'No, I have not heard it, but I think I shall like it!' laughed Alex, as he ushered Srinivasan into his office.

He was to visit many times after that first day. Sometimes he bought gems, sometimes jade. Sometimes, when he came early to the house he even purchased fruit from the jungle tract and nuts and spices.

Alex was to find that he had a shrewd eye as well as a full purse and was glad of the opportunity to make use of his acquaintance. And then a curious thing happened – one day he brought into the yard with him a new body-servant. He was tall and black and the moment he saw Alex he fell upon his neck with joyful recognition. The surprised Srinivasan was quickly told of how they came to know one another. Jo-Jo told Alex of how his master had allowed him to go as a body-servant to Srinivasan a few days before when they had completed a business transaction. 'I am a free man, as you know! I receive wages for my attention!'

'He is as my shadow, already! He knows every tick of my thoughts and every beat of my heart!'

'My late Master is very rich now, as is my present Master! I am well pleased with my new position!'

Alex took them both under the shade of the inner court veranda and offered them a cooling drink. Nighma served them politely, quiet and smiling. Srinivasan made no protest that his body servant was treated as his equal by Alex. He had long accepted that here was a man whose worth was beyond rebuke.

Life passed pleasantly enough for Alex, Salim and Nighma. They worked hard but they had the comforts of a home, good food, and company. It seemed to Alex that Nighma had an inner vitality, that radiated from her, and made everyone forget the heartaches and indignities which had once been imposed upon her. She, like Salim and Alex, made friends with people from all walks of life, giving freely of her time and energy to their well being. To Alex, she was a constant source of encouragement and his love for her grew daily.

CHAPTER FIFTEEN

On July 2nd 1846 Nighma and Alex were married. It was a time of great celebration. Their neighbours and friends, all castes, creeds, and colours, gathered in the outer yard or wandered at will throughout the downstairs rooms, and out to the inner courtyard where the wedding was to be held. Nautch dancers came to grace the entertainments along with musicians. There were singers and jugglers, tumblers and snake charmers, and a teller of futures, all draped in a scarlet cloak over a black satin tunic. From the harbour came the children whom Nighma loved best. These children had been born in boats, and would be in and out of the water the whole of their lives. They darted amongst the harbour traffic like fireflies, living on frugal fare and under harsh circumstances. They were afraid of no one and admitted to no superior on land or sea. Nighma had a place in her heart for them all, knew them by name and listened patiently to their ambitions. Already she was a legend among these, the poorest of the poor, the bravest of the brave.

There was a sudden stirring besides the yard gates and Srinivasan appeared in the clearing made for him. He was garbed in an over dress of fine orange wool, and under it a pale cream coloured silk garment with wide sleeves embroidered with orange and brown thread. The collar and waistband were encrusted with seed pearls and orange gemstones. On his head he wore a turban of bright lemon-coloured silk from which sprang a tuft of egret feathers anchored by a clasp of matched pearls in a gold-wire base. Jo-Jo, dressed entirely in matched purple entered behind him, holding over Srinivasan's head a huge umbrella of golden silk embellished with tassels and patterned with flamboyant red, orange, green and brown tracery. Shantilal also crept into the yard, bearing a cushion on which rested two gifts, one an enamelled snuff-box, and the other a fine emerald encased in a filigree cage of gold, and suspended upon a gold chain. Alex greeted them kindly and led them into the house and out into the inner courtyard. He led Srinivasan to a chair and Shantilal sat on a stool at his feet.

'If you will wait here until Nighma is ready we will accept the presents together,' said Alex. 'There are many here who have gifts for us, as you will see. We will not be long.'

Alex went back into the house but within minutes reappeared with Nighma at his side. Alex was dressed in a cream silk tunic, thickly embroidered on sleeves, collar, and breast panels, and wore it over cream Turkish trousers, and camelskin shoes. Nighma was dressed in a red sari, richly embroidered with gemstones and silver and gold threads. Her bare feet were painted with henna. She had arranged the end of her sari veil lightly over the soft contours of her breast and over her head, pinned here and there with fragile ornaments of gold and silver. As Srinivasan watched her walk out of the house and into the inner courtyard he felt a twinge of envy pass through him, as she took Alex's arm and they began to receive the gifts from the people collected there. The table before them was soon filled with tokens of the people's esteem, from a wicker work basket to a bowl of baked rice ready for grinding into rice flour for sweet cakes. There was a precious collection of cowrie shells from the children and a pot of Alta (red lac used to dye the edge of feet by women). Then Srinivasan and Shantilal stepped forward. The gifts they presented were truly magnificent compared to other offerings, but all were accepted with the same graciousness. Nighma raised her head from bending over Srinivasan's emerald pendant.

'Our thanks to you,' she whispered softly. 'Protector of defenceless women, father of many sons, guardian of daughters, light of Shantilal's life.'

'I wish you both joy,' was all he could say in return. As she meekly turned away, he remembered a night when she had shaken loose her hair from under such a veil as she now wore, until it flowed a fathomless, Stygian river, over the pillows of his bed. The thought left him vaguely unhappy, and with a feeling almost akin to shame.

The wedding progressed, the entertainments began, then the music and the dance and later fireworks and sweetmeats.

Evening fell, and Srinivasan, in the confines of his palatial home forgot his disappointment as he watched Shantilal dance across the Persian carpets and tasselated floor of his room. The soft enticing lines of her body, sinuous under the peach-coloured gauze entranced him as he watched. Her abundant hair, shaken loose from the binding wreath of flowers, spun in a dense, dark cloud around her head. But, she was not Nighma – cold, distant, indifferent, Nighma. Light of his past life, still mistress of his soul!

The months passed, pleasantly and profitably and what problems they did have were surmountable. During the first few months, Nighma became pregnant. There was great joy and speculation as to a strong and healthy son for 'Tiger Dee', but, one stormy night, several weeks before his time, a puny man-child arrived. He did not cry or open his eyes and expired within the hour. His parents were left shocked and grief-stricken, their friends consoled them as best they might. Their neighbours, superstitious still, whispered amongst themselves, that the storm was a storm which carries evil and that the house of reputation had taken its sacrifice of a new-born child.

When Nighma became pregnant a second time, she only made a simple announcement, 'Alex I am with child.' They told no one and the fact was never mentioned again until her pains were upon her.

On March 16th 1848 their daughter was delivered, healthy, and without fuss and was named Dorinda Anne. Now there was a new topic to discuss in the yard. The place was overflowing with buyers and well-wishers, and although Alex was grateful for this, as he looked down at his baby daughter, crowing in her cradle, a sudden fear clutched at his heart. Supposing her delicate skin were spoiled by some disease brought in by the customers who lived in crowded conditions and were prey to all manner of complaints.

A new search was made, this time for a home in the countryside where, with the help of an ayah, Nighma could bring up their daughter in health and safety. The old house could then be made over for a place of business entirely.

Srinivasan, having heard of Alex's and Nighma's search came to them one morning with the news that he had heard of a white-walled double-veranda dwelling for sale, not far from his own fortress-like home on the outskirts of the city. When Alex heard of it he went there at once and indeed it proved to be just what was required. It had a large lawned garden, amply shaded by trees and shrubbery. The northern wall overlooked a rocky shrub-free terrace, the western wall a roadway and the river. To the east of the house were forests of mature trees which were in the process of being thinned out. Each day elephants moved ponderously with their loads, goaded by ankus and urged by the conversation of their mahouts, which ranged from sharply satirical to deeply compassionate. In the evening they lay in the river shallows, spraying and bellowing, as the mahouts scrubbed the dust of the day from their thick, grey, hides, and attended to their massive feet, looking for thorns and stone damage.

The gates of the house were on a road without stones. A soft country road which led into the river road, which was fairly well maintained and its potholes filled with chipped stone and in some places flagged areas. This was the eastern side of the house.

Alex, Nighma and the baby moved in without delay. Salim stayed at the old house for some weeks until a suitable couple could be found to be caretakers, then he too moved to the new house.

It was good to get away from the city each evening to the colourful reaches of the river, or to lounge in the high-walled garden, under the shade of the trees, to listen to the subdued sounds from the river, the gentle musical tones of the numerous birds and the shrill sound of the cicadas. When there, it was easy to forget the harassments of the day and the daily grind within the city walls. Alex especially looked forward to Sunday. Most Europeans went to church on a Sunday but Alex spent his day entirely in the company of Nighma and his baby daughter. He delighted in the chubby round-limbed child who carried her heart in her eyes.

The days went by happily. Dorinda left her cradle for a cot. She began to walk, talk, and take an interest in what was going on around her. Her hair was of a soft brown colour as her father's and curled about her face in urchin tendrils, and as she grew older and her uncut hair longer, her ayah did not restrain it in plaits, but let it bob becomingly on Dorinda's shoulders. Alex watched with pleasure as she ran about the garden, hair bouncing, voice trilling with laughter, at yet another new game devised by Salim, who took as much interest in her welfare as Alex himself. Nighma would watch them all, quiet and smiling, as enigmatic as an eastern woman could be, as Dorinda was plied with gew-gaws and sweetmeats brought home from the more savoury of the bazaars.

As Dorinda grew older she put away her toys and began to read. Reading was her joy in life and something she could never have enough of, peopled as books were with the interesting characters of the outside world of which she had seen so little. The servants of the house and her ayah were all her confidants but she longed to go to the city. To this end Salim built her a tree house from which she could see the city, over the wall of the house and in the distance. Dorinda loved the little house, away from everyone but her best doll, and she would take tea there, with cakes and cordial and much shushing of Clarinda, her best doll, whilst she took stock of the city beyond. Her father had built her a rope swing in the old fig tree, but while she adored the dreaming whilst touching her foot to the smooth lawn, it did not fulfil her desire to have the reality of walking through the teeming, city streets. When her father held her in his arms on the upstairs landing and they looked out together at the spires and minarets, Dorinda would wind her arms about his neck and say, 'How pretty it all looks, papa! Let us count how many masts there are in the harbour!' They would try to count the masts like thin, black needles against the sky, and the little native boats, no bigger than leaves upon a swollen river. 'What do all those boats carry, papa?' 'Everything you can think of, firefly!' It was a game to them, her asking and him answering, but each time Dorinda was older and her questions became more insistent and more pertinent.

It was nearing Dorinda's seventh birthday when her father asked, 'What would you like as a present this year, Dorinda?'

'I should very much like to go on a sailing boat. Not a big boat, just a little one like the boats that we see when we go down to the river shallows to see the elephants washing.'

'I do not think that will be possible, Dorinda. Your mother would have thirty fits and your ayah fall down in a dead faint if I so much as mentioned it.'

Her brown, round, eyes came on a level with his and she put her arms about his neck, and laid her forehead hard against his own.

'Tell me about when you were a boy in England and you wanted to go to sea!' she urged, as she slid down to the floor with her head against his knee.

'Well, in the beginning I wasn't nearly seven I was twice as old when I went to sea! I thought there was excitement and charm in the sailors who came ashore to drink at our tavern. I thought they were romantic as they sang their shanties and dinged our pewter about on the tables. When they left us and went aboard and drew anchor, then sailed away proudly, riding the tide with billowing sails, I longed to be with them. I would stand and watch until the ship was a speck on the horizon. Then the ship would be gone. Swallowed up by time and distance. Drawn over the rim of the world for all I knew!'

'Oh, papa,' cried Dorinda, chiding him gently. 'You can't go over the rim of the world. Salim says so! The world is quite round and you can sail on and on for ever, if you have a mind to!'

'What a knowledgeable little girl you are! If only I had known that at your age, I would have been spared a great deal of sorrow!'

'But, papa, if you had never sailed to India, you would never have met mother, and I would not have been gifted to you. I wonder where I would have been sent. Perhaps I would have been sent to a poor family in the city. Where our punkah-boy was gifted with his little withered leg.' Her father looked down on her indulgently. 'And suppose, just suppose, you had been gifted to a Prince. You would have lots of servants and nothing to do all day but laze about and grow fat and beautiful!'

Rule Of Thumb

'Oh, papa,' Dorinda cried, jumping to her feet. 'That would not do at all! I have nothing to do here all day! They are always telling me, "You are too young to do that or this," but, when I cry they tell me to be a big girl and not be a baby!'

'It's a difficult world, Dorinda, one has to compromise all the time.'

'And not only that,' she said, nodding sagely, 'one has to be polite as well!'

CHAPTER SIXTEEN

On February 14th 1855, a one hundred and seventy ton ship named *The Seeker*, anchored down by the harbour. In the evening, many of the sailors went ashore, visiting brothels and taverns, and toasting here and there an absent friend or comrade buried at sea some days before the ship had entered into the sight of land.

Within a day or so another of the sailors fell sick, and then in two and threes and by March 14th smallpox was raging in the city. The streets became empty of Europeans, fetes, markets and clubs and meeting places were taboo to them. The hospital was full of Europeans, later diagnosed as suffering from chickenpox, measles, food poisoning, or in many cases, rashes caused by over-washing with disinfectant. Only a handful were smallpox cases, but these nearly always proved fatal. Everywhere that dreaded name was whispered as one after another of the natives of the city succumbed to the disease.

Business was lax now for Alex, but he concentrated on making the old house more tidy with the help of Salim. They stayed there, cutting themselves off from Dorinda and Nighma, and their staff while the epidemic raged.

Vishwa Nath came every two days with his stock of fruit and vegetables and one day came with the news that a 'gem village' north of the city had been sorely affected by the outbreak and looked to Alex to help them. 'Do they know what they are asking?' cried Alex despairingly. 'They ask no more of you than of themselves. They need supplies urgently, Tiger Dee!' Vishwa used the natives nickname of him hoping to make him realise that the lives of these people were bound with his own. 'I must consult with Nighma,' Alex replied, warily. He need not have done so. Her heart was already set on his going the moment she heard, and she already had a scheme of her own, which she was loathe to discuss in case she was refused.

'You must see that our daughter is kept well clear from the infected areas, and that our servants also stay to the house. They may have their cooking requirements placed by the gate to be collected. Salim, who is as you know,

Rule Of Thumb

a survivor of the smallpox and only a little scared, will be your negotiator.' Nighma nodded, dutifully, with eyes downcast, so as not to show too much of the independent spirit that lurked there. She had grown into an unruffled sort of woman. Any catastrophic occurrence was a mere jolt to her. She knew the ways of the poor and of the rich.

The village was beside a fly infested swamp and as Alex approached on the pony, and Vishwa on a camel, a column of smoke ascended on the still air. 'They are already burning their dead,' observed Vishwa grimly and urged his reluctant camel forward. Alex's pony was also uneager to resume the journey and dug his little black hooves into the dust of the road way and tightened his leg muscles, so Alex dismounted and led him into the village a few hundred yards away. As they entered they were greeted by the not so sick, who swarmed out of their ramshackle homes, eager for the food and medicines they hoped their visitors had brought.

One of the elders told them that they had for days been on a low diet of a little pounded dholl and a drop of oil, which was shamefully insufficient as the nights were bitterly cold. Those that did not shake with the fever, shook from the chill air that drifted over the swampland and permeated the walls of their homes.

To the left of their homes of cowdung plaster and bamboo slats, with grasses or reeds to cover the roofs, stood a small hamlet, where the entire population had been wiped out by famine and disease. It was the funeral pyres of those people Alex and Vishwa had noticed on their way into the village.

Both the village and hamlet stood only a mile away from the palatial dwelling of the opulent and tyrannical Taraporvala, who wined and dined and made love to a succession of women, who committed murder through want, cheated through poverty, and still waxed fat under the eyes of a gracious God.

'It is the same old story,' said Alex sadly, 'but told in a different tongue. The torment that every beggar feels throughout the world. We who have travelled know the look of the hungry and oppressed. The times when the old harvest has been finished and the new crops have not yet ripened.' They did not hope for help from their neighbour Taraporvala, the magnitude of his wealth had stunned them into dumb acceptance long ago. The lot of the women was to till half-barren plots of land, and the men to dig deep into the water logged gem pits near the swamp.

With the people depleted now, it seemed to Alex and Vishwa, that the best of all the dwellings must be improved on by scavenging from the worst.

The little streamlet that fed the swamp must be diverted from its course to come into the village, down a rocky ravine with pools and shallows, and then to join the original seepage from the swampland. This way they could get rid of the myriad flies which bred in the swamp because it immediately began to dry out. They would have fresh water in the village, the rocky ravine, the old bed of the stream, perhaps before some earthquake, would receive the water as before and join the water seepage from the swamp.

To the villagers it all sounded impossible, but Alex dogged them all on, knowing that it was the best course for these people and it did not need an engineer to know that they would be only restoring what had been there before.

They worked steadily for one month and the stream was then diverted. Some stood at the beginning and some stood by the ravine, and some stood where it joined the seepage from the swampland. They stood quite still and quiet at first and then the murmur of their voices arose to a cry of triumph as the stream of water hit the first of the ravine stones. The stones broke the stream of water, as it plunged downwards, splitting it into little riverlets, and in some places gathering into tiny pools, then dropping over craggy ledges and making falls of water no taller than a child of eight or nine. Then further pools and further falls until it joined the swamp seepage, which during the following days was to become only a steady trickle.

As things got better in the village, Vishwa, to Alex's horror, fell ill. For three days Vishwa writhed in torment, the flesh seeming to melt from his bones. Alex sat beside him constantly, watching his body shrink and wither, helpless to do anything to save him. On the third day, as the pale light of morning crept up the sky to herald the day, Vishwa struggled to rise from his bed. Alex took hold of him gently, urging him to lie still, but Vishwa's eyes stared out towards the door space, where the soft rays of light lit the earthen floor. In Alex's arms the poor frame stiffened, the throat muscles tightened, and Vishwa's head snapped back against Alex's shoulder. He shook him tentatively and called his name but there was no response.

Alex stood up and walked to the door. The fatigue of weeks of effort washed over him as he let others lift Vishwa Nath and bear him away. The little children stood around in the village, whispering amongst themselves, 'Tiger Dee is weeping for his friend and ours.'

In his heart Alex knew that he not only wept for Vishwa, but for his family, whom he must now tell of his death. He wept also for his own loneliness, for Dorinda, for Nighma, his own home and familiar things. He said his farewells reluctantly, taking the camel back to the Nath family, who fell upon him like children, wailing in their sorrow, tearing at their clothes as they protested their need of him. He stayed with the family for two days, until they were able to bury the body Alex had brought to them, wrapped in cloth on the back of their camel. He admired their garden plots and praised their children and grandchildren and made known to them that he would expect them to take up the challenge of life that Vishwa Nath had now dispensed with. And while he did this the longing to be with his own family grew like a pain in him.

When he arrived on the back of his pony at the house in the country he found his servants there and Dorinda, but Nighma and Salim were at the old house in the city.

The servants were quick to impart to him the news that Nighma had brought many of the sick children in the city harbour into the old house and made the whole of the ground floor into wards. She had methodically separated the worse cases from the better cases and recruited suitable women to nurse them.

When the following day, Alex arrived at the old house, many of the almost well children ran out to greet him, 'Tiger Dee,' they ran to him putting up their arms to him and swinging around his neck. At the commotion, Nighma came into the yard, and the children fell back from him, wide-eyed. What would Tiger Dee say at having his place of business turned into a hospital?

What could he say to that warm and admirable person who was a free woman and his wife? Nighma had always been intent on the furtherance of human interests and had become immensely popular as a result. Nothing was ever too much trouble for her, no request for help was ever turned down.

Too late Alex was to learn that she, in her generosity, had sacrificed all. Even as the last of the fevers abated Nighma herself became ill.

Her end came quite suddenly, leaving Alex besides himself with grief. The journey to the gem village and previous disappointments, had not prepared him for her nerve-shattering loss. For many hours he sat alone in the room where she had died, idly contemplating his own death. He threw open a window that opened out onto the inner court-yard and gazed down on the hard ground below, but he thought of Dorinda, still in the new house, and withdrew into the gloom of the room. He lit the lamps with a shakey hand and watched the beetles and moths, which had flown in through the unnetted window space. Frantically they flew against the lit lamps, then whirred away into the darker areas of the room, then back again. As Alex watched them, Salim came into the room. 'See, Salim, we are like these insects! We reach out for all that is bright and good, and we are burned and chastised!'

Salim laid his hand on Alex's shoulder, 'It is time to see your child. Go to her. Forget this house for the time being. The past is gone, the future beckons. Your child needs you. All will be well.'

'When the last of the children leave here I will go to my own,' said Alex. 'I will keep faith with Nighma's promise.'

It was almost another month before the old house stood, quiet, and disinfected within and without, the shutters thrown back to let in the light, the fine mesh window frames well secure against the flies. The daily hubbub washed around the house, and against the high-walled yard and echoed in the mosaic floored portals, but it did not enter by the heavy iron bolted door. The rooms were silent and undisturbed, but a new ghost haunted there. She flitted softly through the rooms, a fraction of a second before Alex, leaving an emptiness on the air, and in his heart.

CHAPTER SEVENTEEN

The day of June 8th 1856 dawned calm and bright, and as Dorinda Anne Deane lay under the mosquito netting, watching her sleeping ayah, Ruksana, in a bed by the door, a plan came into her head. Today she would take a journey into the city. She lay quiet, going over the way in her mind, smiling softly, as she thought of her adventure before her. That day her ayah's friend would come to visit her and Dorinda knew that they would be so busy putting the rest of mankind to rights that they would not miss her for a few hours.

She had, a few months before, taken the road into the forest where large tracts had been denuded of the more mature trees and only scrubby trees and whippy saplings were growing. She had been quite safe but it was nearly two hours before she had been missed. The gardener had told Salim he had seen her take the back road to the forest and Salim had appeared with a very cross look on his face, but by that time she had become a little scared herself. She had told Salim that she had seen such wonderful birds and flowers and trees that it was a shame that they should not be seen more often and by more people. She was so enthusiastic that Salim was soon smiling and promised he would not tell her father if she promised not to go there unaccompanied again.

Ruksana stirred, and getting out of bed started to wash and then dress herself. She began to gather Dorinda's clothes together. 'I will dress myself, thank you,' said Dorinda, and with a quick bound was out of bed and dragging off her nightclothes. 'You will wash first, Missie!' ordered Ruksana.

'Oh, very well,' answered Dorinda, impatiently, 'but I never know when I am clean! I heard someone say the other day, when you took me to the market with you, "Black skin is a curse."' 'Missie, that is a wicked thing to say!' cried Ruksana, pushing her as she pulled down Dorinda's petticoat.

'I did not say it! I tell of it! But I can see that it is, for however much I wash, which is often, I never shine rosy like father, and I never blaze golden like my mother did. I should very much like to have hair as golden as the sunlight and skin as pale as a jasmine blossom.'

'And you would very likely die of the sunlight, your skin burned to a cinder because of its paleness,' replied Ruksana briskly. 'Now come along, finish off your dressing. Where are your shoes, and don't forget to brush your hair.' She bounced out of the room to see about Dorinda's breakfast.

Dorinda found her shoes and brushed her hair, but she took her time about it, leisurely going over in her mind what she would do when she had made sure that Ruksana's friend had arrived. 'I will ask if I may go into the garden to the tree house and take the tiny cups and saucers and my best doll, Clarinda. I will ask for some fruit and nuts and little rice cakes and they will think I am giving Clarinda a party. They will be pleased to be rid of me whilst they talk of the people they know.' Smiling she went down to her breakfast.

She was particularly careful to stay close to her ayah all that morning. Getting under the feet would make her absence in the afternoon more pleasant. She thought of sharing her secret with the one-legged punkah boy, but he was a very truthful boy and if anyone asked him where she was he would be sure to tell them, she reasoned with herself.

Later that day Ruksana's friend arrived. Shortly afterwards Dorinda went out into the garden with Clarinda, her best doll, and a small wicker picnic basket packed with fruit and nuts and cakes which she had begged from her ayah. They were such delicate little cakes that Ayah had for her friends that, once in the tree house, Dorinda ate them all delightedly. Then she set out the tea cups and saucers and plates on the lacey cloth and sat her doll to preside over the proceedings. She scattered a few nuts on the plates, and left her a banana. It would not do for Clarinda to think that she was greedy. Ruksana had told her that when doll owners sleep, they come alive and have adventures till morning. She had not seen this, but Ruksana swore on her ancestors that it was true, and better be safe than sorry.

After looking around for a moment Dorinda blew Clarinda a kiss and then scuttled down into the garden. The gardener was by the gates attending to the green sola tree, so there was nothing she could do but retrace her steps into the shelter of the shrubbery, climb the white wall that surrounded the house and then climb down the other side. She felt quite confident climbing the garden side although it was of six feet in height, but when she came to the top and clambered over the drop on the other side was ten feet or more. It was smoother on the outside also, with less deep footholds and towards the bottom she lost her footing and fell backwards onto the dusty roadway. 'Oh, dear!' she squeaked, rubbing herself as she rolled over and scrambled to her feet. She tested her legs and arms, and she seemed to be alright, so she dusted down her clothes and then set off along the river road to the city.

Once out of the welcome trees in the garden and on the outer perimeter of the wall, the sunlight beat down on her uncovered head like a blow. It was too late to go back for the protection of her white hat with its puggeree of pink muslin, Ruksana or her friend would be bound to see her. She stood there, feet wide apart, shielding her eyes from the glare. Then she took off her pink cotton pinafore and tied it by the waist ribbons over her head and neck. Then clad in this strange headgear she proceeded to the city, that place of fascination where her father had taken her on only a few occasions, less than Salim or Ruksana. She was soon away from the house and joined a wider road which still ran alongside the river. For some minutes she watched an adjutant bird picking up tidbits from the shoreline and the fringes of tall, plumed reeds in their bed of rich mud. Other small birds and mammals searched for food there also and Dorinda edged nearer and pulled one of the reeds out of its bamboo-like base. The pale, fluffy plume wafted gently as she shook it slowly from side to side, and skipped on her way carrying it before her, a symbol of her new found freedom. Further along the road, the river ran over a few stones and boulders, making a chuckling sound that made Dorinda want to laugh and shout out loud. She moved the reed punkah to and fro, drafting tiny currents of air into her nostrils. A few paces away was a wooden landing stage with inviting broad planks, just right for hopping over and waving a reed, banner fashion, above the head. This she proceeded to do, executing fancy little steps every now and again. The planks had plenty of bounce in them and as she jigged, the water rippled unevenly between them with the force of movement and sent up a curious pungency from the rotting vegetation that had been caught round the staging poles.

Further along the road another smaller river joined the glassy amber flood, and on this a bargee poled along a merchant who had in his hand a book in which he appeared to be writing. He was so engrossed in his accounts that he did not see Dorinda, which was fortunate for her, for he was a friend of her father's. As he poled along the bargee sang a wailing song. A song of hard work and poor pay and no doubt he had plenty to wail about, but Dorinda thought him a splendid figure and clasped her fingers delightedly around her reed wand, as the boat slowly moved towards the harbour shimmering in the middle distance.

Around the next corner she came across a group of workmen breaking up stones and filling in the potholes. As she drew level with them all but one stood up, glad of a chance to straighten their backs, and wipe their perspiring

Rule Of Thumb

foreheads with their dust-powdered arms. As she picked her way she came face to face with the man who had not risen to his feet. He was crouched low, his tattered loincloth draped between thin thighs, his feet bare, and his long boney toes gnarled and scarred white by the countless flying chippings. His eyes as she looked into them were half-lidded and watchful, the hand which held the hammer poised and ready to strike the stone beneath. Dorinda spoke to him in the tongue her mother had taught her but he did not answer, nor did the other men. They regarded her with cast-iron insolence, noting her dusky skin and European clothing. Then the crouched man spat, with great deliberation, only an inch from her slippers. Instantly, she recoiled, her smile frozen in her cheeks, and the blood surged through her body with a great uneasiness. The crouched man moved slightly and let her pass by him. She sprang over the pile of stones like a young doe and ran quickly onwards the sound of the men laughing following her. She replied to them with her own defiant shrieks. She could be brave now they were well behind her, but somewhere along the road she had lost her reed banner!

On the main roadway there were more people, bullock carts, and vendors, all making their way into the city, and Dorinda felt less identifiable until she came to the three storied barracks. She looked anxiously towards the building hoping that no one who knew her would emerge and so take her prematurely home. A Sepoy stood at the gate, rigid, his eyes staring straight before him. But he was not as immobile as she thought, for when she came close he startled her by moving his position. A little shudder ran down her spine and her pace quickened but no voice called to her and she hastened on, weaving her way amongst the people who were now crowding the road, not one of whom gave her a second glance.

Soon she came to the place of a silver worker, of whom her father had spoken of often. She recognised him as the same by his crippled legs for he had to be carried there each day by two of his sons. His only canopy was an ancient magnolia tree, and under its shade his long, skilled fingers, tooled the intricate patterns, and fabulous beasts, and exotic flowers. They seemed to spring almost effortlessly from his tools and his facile originality was greatly admired by his employer who had become rich from the finished products, which were sold to the resident English and on the Asian markets.

Amongst the crowd around him were a group of ryots from a neighbouring area. The last monsoon had been bad, turning what had been a fertile valley into a dust bowl. They were full of anguish, and had come to Mother Ganga, thinking they had failed in their spiritual duties, and hoping for redemption. No one could guess the extent of the torment in their hearts as they thought of the despair and the disintegration of their families, least of all Dorinda who followed them as they walked onwards, their wind-whipped, sun-scorched, expressionless faces turned towards the walls of the city.

Dorinda's attention was soon diverted from this sad group by the presence of a heavily ladened camel and its driver. Colourful and clean, they were in direct contrast to the farmers and drew her, tingling with curiosity, to their side. On close inspection, the camel proved to have a bad-mannered grunt, and a foul breath, and the driver the cold and supercilious air of one who rides above the crowd. She lost interest in the both of them, and after giving the soft, creamy wool of the camel a final pat, which was responded to by a kicking back leg, hastily avoided, she wandered towards the broad ghats that led down to the river.

Among the varied crowd on the ghats, paced the little bare-footed thieves of the city. Bright faced youngsters, often orphaned and abandoned, not for them the endless war against the growing costs of life's necessities. All they needed was an expression of innocence to the face, a deftness of the hand, and if detected, a swiftness of the feet. Some of the harbour children were there also and Dorinda joined them at their play. For a little while they hopped up and down the ghats in the hot sunlight, playing touch, or making their pleasures from few resources, tossing miniature bamboo rafts into the swiftly churning flood, each cheering on their fragile crafts to win, and dancing with impatience at the laggards. Then suddenly the joy faded. A thin-limbed boy sidled up to Dorinda and poked her. 'You're not one of us!' he said almost angrily.

'No,' answered Dorinda calmly, 'but I know you. You live in the harbour. My mother nursed you through the smallpox and sometimes you come to my home with messages for father or Salim.'

The boy shrank back from her momentarily, but recovered and cried out to the others standing near, 'Here is Tiger Dee's cub come to visit us!' It was hardly a welcoming speech and Dorinda stepped out of the circle. He followed her, 'Come here cub and let us see you!' he demanded. He pushed his face close to Dorinda's. She could have counted the scars that pitted it if she had been so minded. With hands on hips he appraised her, from her pink pinafore head to her green slippered feet. The boy's father was a worker in the harbour warehouses and although he was only nine years old he could trade on street corners with all the aplomb of an experienced vendor. Her father had told her that, one day when he came to the house with a message. She could have admired him for that, but he now began to prod her towards the water and she could not swim! He began to pluck at the ribbons under her chin and

Rule Of Thumb

make grimaces at her. 'Let's capture the Tiger Dee's cub and take her to the temple of the children of Bod,' he shouted to the others. Dorinda's heart lurched. She remembered a conversation with her Ayah a few months before when she had told her that when parents prayed for a child to this God, and their prayers were answered, the child was then taken to the temple to serve there. Dorinda had said it was like giving a present and then taking it back! But Ruksana, her ayah, had said, 'No, it is a great honour for a prayer to be heard by the great God. It brings tremendous pleasure to the whole of the family.' Dorinda had her own ideas about that and now faced with the threat, was stung into action.

'I do not think I like your God – Bod,' she announced angrily, 'OR YOU!' she added to the boy before her. He put his face forward and jeered at her. Dorinda stretched out and seized his hair between fingers as brown as his own. He yelled and struggled. It was no fault of hers that the hair lacked firmness and remained in her hand. When the boy saw the lank strand, parted from his head with such suddenness, he began to howl, and turned to the others for sympathy. This they gave. They had no desire to annoy Tiger Dee by harming his child. They crowded round the boy, leaving Dorinda on the outside of a tight circle, with a dozen or so black hairs still trapped in her fingers. This sudden shutting out of their affairs, together with the fact that she had caused pain, unnerved Dorinda and she ran quickly up the ghats and on to the long walk. The pack of children turned, and seeing that she had made her escape, deemed it safe to cry vengeance and follow her, but it was a half-hearted attempt, and when she came to the end of the harbour wall she was alone. Breathing heavily she flopped down on the large, flat top-stones of the wall, and when she had recovered both breath and poise, looked down into the waters below.

The boats, tossed about in the sepia-coloured waves, sent a sour smell of refuse from their wakes which made Dorinda wrinkle up her sensitive nose and draw back. But it was an inquisitive nose, and the cry of a baby above the chant of singing brown-skinned men as they strained against the oars and sail mats made her once again peer down into the water. There were other sounds besides those from the baby, as older children called out as they played in the narrow confines of their water-borne homes. Suddenly, two of the smaller boats collided. There was a sharp, splintering sound, followed by frightened cries. Dorinda jumped on top of the wall, a few spars and baskets bobbed about in between the other boats, where life seemed to be continuing as before. For a moment Dorinda stood quite shocked by what she had seen, then galvanised into action she was running, homewards, longing for the comforting arms of anyone who would tell her the world she knew was still the same and had not changed.

Through the roadside markets she ran, her slippered feet sending up little puffs of dust over her legs. She wove her way through the crowd who gathered around the story-teller, who told tales of yesterday's hopes and tomorrow's dreams, crept hot-footed by the barracks where the sentry stood, unblinking in the sun. His thoughts were on other things! Half Batta – for being in the garrison, and Bayadére dancing girls, whose duty it was to dance before the Gods! On and on she ran, until her lungs seemed ready to burst. Finally, she came to the place where the road-menders had been at work, and slowed down. They had gone now, the large stones that had been there had been broken into small pieces and now filled in the hollows of the roadway. She looked at their work admiringly. She knew her father would be pleased. He was always complaining about the state of the road that passed their house when the rains came, and the dust turned to mud or was washed away, or churned into deep ruts by the waggons and buggies. A complete stone roadway would have been a wonderful improvement but Dorinda supposed that they would have to be content with the worst of the potholes being filled. 'I wonder,' said Dorinda to herself, 'if I brought some small stones from the river shallows every day, and filled all the small dust-holes, how long it would take me to have made a good road of my own?'

She was not to continue with her problem, as her musing was interrupted by the voice of Ruksana, calling as she looked up and down the roadway, searching in the pepper bushes and down in the ditches. 'Dor-in-da, Dor-in-da, Ba-bu, Babu!!'

'How like her!' said Dorinda peevishly. How stupidly like her!' But she started to run towards the voice and arrived hot, breathless and whining, just as Ruksana turned the corner.

Her ayah caught her up to her breast with passionate words of admonishment on her lips but was almost light-headed with relief as she hurried Dorinda up the dusty road, across the lemon scented garden and into the cool house where the air was heavy with the smell of spices. The adventure was over!

CHAPTER EIGHTEEN

That evening, when her father came home from the city Ruksana told him of Dorinda's escapade. 'It is not good, Sahib,' said the ayah, 'I do my very best for Dorinda, but she is wayward. She is restless. She longs to see things for herself. There will be more mischief if she is not allowed to find out about the things outside the garden walls,' she warned.

'I think you are right,' said Alex placatingly. 'I know that you take your duty to Dorinda seriously. There is no need to blame yourself. I will speak to her myself when the time is right.'

After supper Dorinda stood with her father besides the upper veranda window, where a small lamp gave out a sweet perfume with the flame, and there Alex spoke to her of her escapade.

'I hear you went with no one knowing to the city today.' Dorinda looked up into his face and said, 'Yes, father. I was lonely.'

'The house was full of people.'

'It was not enough! Ruksana's friend had come. I grow out of dolls. I am too young to listen to gossip!'

Her father hid a smile. 'Did you feel better when you had been to the city?'

'No, father, I was lonelier still. I did not understand them there.'

'Loneliness is a state of mind, Dorrie. If you have it, it is hard to cure.'

'When does it go then?'

'It is a mystery to me, Dorrie. A mystery!'

Dorinda looked out of the window, perplexed that the father she relied on did not know the answer. In the city, night had already settled, trapped in a medley of buildings but there in the countryside, the day was still dying, staining the sky with crimson. On the rim of the world tomorrow waited for all but the dead. On the edge of the river the last of the day's funeral pyres smouldered. The mourners walked to the brim of the flooded waters to float frail bamboo rafts but all Dorinda and her father could see from the high veranda were the lights fastened to them. A whole fleet of lights set out from the shore, to drift, to be suddenly extinguished, or to ride proudly down river. When the quick coming of night was complete, they watched the riding lights of the houseboats as they bobbed up and down on the water, starring the darkness with pale colours. Somewhere in that span of darkness, between the lights of the boats and the shore, the fragile crafts of the departed souls floated.

Dorinda stood close to her father, rubbing her dusky cheek against the pale tan of his hand, aware for the first time of his own loneliness, of the difference in people, their beliefs, the patterns of their daily lives, their daily deaths. It was punishment enough for her escapade to the city to find that her world was vulnerable. Alex realised this, and that Dorinda was a growing girl, with a mind to be fed with knowledge of her surroundings.

'Tomorrow you must come with me to the city, Dorinda,' Alex said casually.

'Oh, Papa!' Dorinda's hands flew to her face with joy. 'Oh, Papa.'

Alex smiled and touched her with one finger on her pert little nose. 'Now, off to bed with you. Ayah will be waiting and we don't want her to be cross with you again.'

'Oh, no, Papa! I will be especially kind to Ruksana! She will miss me when I go away all day with you.'

Alex shook his head gravely, 'I'm sure she won't,' he replied as he turned away to hide a little smile. 'In spite of the trouble you cause her, Ayah will have to go with us,' he whispered softly to himself as Dorinda ran happily towards her bedroom.

Every day Dorinda and her ayah, Ruksana, began to go with Alex and Salim to the city. At first everything that went on in the house and yard were of interest to Dorinda and she was content to stay there, but after a while she began to pester Ruksana about the city sights. Sometimes they did not go to the business house at all but made their own way into the city, spending the day as they wished.

Ruksana was delighted to be free of the white-walled prison, ensconced in the leafiness, away from the city noise. She was a gossipy woman and the city was life to her, and she was only too pleased to think of various ways of playing guide to Dorinda.

One day, just after Alex and Salim had set off for the city, her ayah said to Dorinda, 'Today, I will take you to the temple. You must be very good and quiet, and do exactly as I tell you. You mind?'

'I mind,' answered Dorinda, unconvincingly.

'May your face blacken and your limbs wither if you do anything to disgrace me,' said her ayah sternly.

'Do you take me for a fool?' murmured Dorinda stonily, with an air far beyond her years.

'You are many things, but never that!' said the ayah, as she dressed her in a native child's attire.

'Why do I have to dressed like this, I much prefer my own clothes,' protested Dorinda.

'So that you may not stick out like a boil on the bum!'

'OH, RUKSANA,' mocked Dorinda, raising her hands high and shaking them with the palms facing outwards.

Ruksana gave her a sharp slap on the arm. 'You make me mad. You go too far, Missie!'

'I'm sorry, Ayah. You are funny when you are in a dither.'

'I do not dither, Missie, I direct. Now, get dressed as I tell you and we will go at once. One more word, and you will spend your day alone in the garden house.' Dorinda was abnormally quiet for a full half hour, but after that they were well on their way to the city and her natural curiosity reasserted itself.

The way to the temple was through colourful bazaars, offering every allurement, and Ruksana bought a small trinket for Dorinda from one of the sellers. Although she was pleased to receive a gift, she was more concerned about the man himself, for his face was a waxy, greenish-brown colour, his eyes popping from his head in an alarming manner. 'That poor man, ayah,' said Dorinda, 'he looks like he had been in the river for a week.'

'What nonsense you talk, child,' replied Ruksana, hurrying her into a side street and stopping at the stall of the flower seller. They stood for some moments admiring the garlands and then Ruksana chose and paid the seller. 'Here you are, Dorinda,' said the Ayah placing the garland in her arms. She looked at the rose-coloured oleander blossoms tied with silvery thread and sighed. She wished her ayah had bought a garland of Jacaranda bells in splendid blue.

'Come along, you may carry the flowers to the temple if you wish,' said the ayah munificently.

'It is very hot,' replied Dorinda, acutely aware now that the trinket had been the prior bribe for her co-operation. 'I'll put it on my head and swing my arms about for a breeze. Let's walk in the shade of the shops.'

'You irksome child. Can you not do one simple thing!' spat Ruksana, and snatched the garland from her. She placed it over her own arm with a surly pout to her lips and looked down on Dorinda with a glaring eye.

Dorinda was too much impressed by her surroundings than to heed the pique of Ruksana and as they came into an open space Dorinda looked up into the pale lemon glare, produced by the excessive heat. Even the monkeys in the Niim trees looked sluggish, as they sat in the light boughs, their arms about each other and their babies. Down one of the side streets Dorinda saw something which amused her very much, and she left Ruksana's side to take a closer look.

'Come and see, Ruksana. Come and see!' she whispered back to her excitedly. 'This man is picking a fellow's brains!'

'You really can be quite stupid at times! The man is having his ears cleaned out!'

'Can't he do it by himself? I can clean out my ears. I cannot be as stupid as you say.'

'Perhaps not,' agreed Ruksana. 'But we must hurry. We shall be late. We waste too much time.'

She dragged her away down yet another street, where Dorinda's sharp eyes caught sight of a pious man, his tilka mark and Vishu fork, its prongs of white cow-dung ash illuminating his serene forehead. 'How cool and rested he looks,' said Dorinda enviously, wiping her perspiring brow with the back of her hand. 'Are we nearly there?'

'We are here,' said Ruksana, thankfully. They turned into another alleyway and there was the entrance to the temple steps.

It was cool between the high shading walls and the stones were close and comforting, but once inside the temple courtyard the sun beat down onto the stones making them quite unbearable to a tender skin. It was a very old temple. The flagstones were cracked and chipped deeply in places and the niches were empty of statues, but there was one, the most important. That was filled with the presence of the God Kali, the bloodthirsty one!

Ruksana made her offering and said her prayer, while Dorinda hung close to her skirts, conscious of being in the presence of something about which she knew nothing. She was glad when her ayah moved backwards from the offering place, and they moved out into the main courtyard.

There they witnessed a farmer having a goat sacrificially killed. The bleatings of others drowned the clash of the brass gongs.

'Now, Missie, what do you think of that!' asked Ruksana pompously.

'It seemed very theatrical, and quite repulsive,' declared Dorinda. Ruksana immediately clapped a restraining palm over her mouth and hissed, 'Be quiet! You disobedient girl. You have respect.' She gave her a little poke in

the back.
'Please, Ayah, let us go before the other goat loses his life.'
Ruksana stood there, torn between her desire to linger and her knowledge that Dorinda was as strong-willed as she was. 'It would not do if I was to make a fuss,' cried Dorinda stamping her foot, making her way out of the temple. Her ayah followed, but once outside the temple in the cool shade of the narrow alley she took hold of Dorinda and shook her by the shoulder. 'You mother's curse! I will not take you anywhere again!'
Dorinda smiled sweetly and said, 'Wasn't it funny when the black goat made water all over the Devadasi's foot?'
'You bad child! Wait while I tell your father. He will never let you out of the house again!'
Dorinda laughed. She knew it was just an empty threat. Ayah liked her own freedom and pleasures too much to jeopardize it by having to stay every day in the old house when the glorious riot of colour and noise washed the walls. Many mornings saw them walking together, down the long, shaded street which led directly to a colourful market. Sometimes they went to a stall where food was prepared, with a great clatter of pots and pans, and several spicey aromas floated over the booths in a delicious cloud. Ruksana always found the preparation of food fascinating, but more so if she was not providing the clatter and clutter herself, and Dorinda spent many hours in the presence of those cooks, listening to tales of culinary successes. She knew who made the tastiest sauces and where the best peppers could be grown and the superiority of Arabian dates for date syrups.
Some days they would go down to the harbour. Dorinda enjoyed that and always found something amusing or interesting. Several of the houses in the narrow streets on the way there had little shops at the front, and in them, trying to look unconcerned, were the shopkeepers. Their wares were always of the one kind. One would sell silk, one oil, one perfume, one fruit, one hashish, one ghee, and so on, each trying desperately to make a living.
One of the little shops was run by a distant relative of Ruksana's and they always called there for a gossip and some small item of silk, either thread or a yard or two of silken material.
On one particular day, Ruksana came to Dorinda in great excitement. 'Today we will go down to the river. We will call for some silk on the way back for a new dress for you. There is a woman whose husband has died and she is to commit Suttee.'
'I won't go,' wailed Dorinda, agonised.
'Yes, you will! You want your silk don't you?'

Rule Of Thumb

'I don't want to see a poor woman burned alive!'

'She is not poor, she is quite wealthy. It is a blessing to all who see her,' Ruksana told her with great reverence and awe in her voice.

'Very well, I will go with you, but I will not look,' said Dorinda, her forehead puckered up into an anxious frown.

There was a murmur of excitement on the shore of the river as Ruksana and Dorinda drew near to the place where the woman was to be burned with her husband. There was the heavy fragrance of the sal trees in the air, and the red and lilac of the bougainvillea made a cardinal backdrop for the scene. All around the funeral pyre, which contained the body of the dead husband lay garlands of flowers, some trodden down by the succession of people who had come to witness and be blessed by the widow. Dorinda moved her position in the crowd of watchers. Her legs ached and there was a tight sensation in her chest and her heart was beating in her ears. She clenched her hands tightly, the nails biting into her palms as she thought of the deed she was soon to witness. Would the woman never come!

There was a stir from among the casaurine trees and the palm and out of them came a colourful band of people. Happy and joyful the woman in the front, dressed as a bride in a red sari and veil, and all her jewels, bangles, necklaces, ear-rings, toe-rings, noserings, and finger-rings. She stooped gracefully, and took off her foot jewellery, then her bracelets, and necklaces, then all of her rings, and finally the jewels from her hair, and gave them back into the crowd. With elegant grace she allowed her 'executioner' to assist her upon the pyre, and laying down amongst the many scented garlands delivered herself into the hands of her Gods.

Dorinda hid her face in the folds of Ruksana's veil and stopped her ears to the sound of the wails of the bereaved and the final blessing which issued from the dying widow's throat, rising, as a dried leaf whisper into the curling rancid smoke of the flames.

'There,' said Ruksana, looking down on Dorinda with a satisfied air, 'wasn't that the most unselfish and loving act you ever saw in your life?'

Dorinda pulled away and said, 'Can we get the silk now?'

'You have no respect! No respect at all, Missie!' returned Ruksana sharply, giving her a little shake.

'I can't see anything loving about doing something that hurts so much,' said Dorinda surlily.

'The widow is now blessed, and beyond the contempt of the world,' Ruksana declared with cryptic conviction.

Dorinda moved away into the shadows of the trees where the greenish-

Rule Of Thumb

yellow petals of the mango blossoms littered the ground. She kicked her feet through them, wishing she was grown-up enough to wear her hair in a glossy chignon on the nape of her neck and have jewellery scattered about her person, and a silken sari of bluest blue, and a husband, who if he died, would love her enough not to want her to throw herself on his funeral pyre.

'Come along, dreamer,' Ruksana was now briskly walking on ahead of her. 'Come . . .' she beckoned to Dorinda, 'always you are dreaming. Come along, I'll get your sari silk now.'

'You'd better!' muttered Dorinda darkly to herself and the petal shedding trees as she sped under them.

Ruksana had a family relationship with the silk seller and it was better to deal with a friend or relative in business, no matter how tenuous that relationship might be. They found Abdul, as always, in his little shop, sitting cross-legged on a raised dias, his back resting against several bales of silk. He smiled broadly as they appeared at the front of the booth, and stood, shakily, for their entrance.

'Come, come,' he called in greeting and Dorinda ran to him and gave him both her hands, for he was a man in whose company she was as much at home as in the company of Salim. Ruksana made her greetings too. Polite, stilted and very much in command. She was there to buy!

'We would like a length of silk, Abdul. Pale pink, if you have it.'

He shuffled to his bales, giving sidelong glances at Dorinda, who looked bored and disinterested. He checked the bales off one by one, orange, gold, white, red, blue and black. Ruksana threw up her arms an explosive breath popping from her pouty lips. 'No, no!! We must have pink for my baby here!' She tried to draw Dorinda close to her, but Dorinda wriggled away petulantly. 'I am not a baby! I do not like pink. I have never liked pink. When I am older, I shall wear nothing that is pink, not ever!'

'She is hot and tired,' explained Ruksana. 'We went to see the Sutee. There was a crush.'

'You didn't take her, did you?' Abdul asked incredulously.

'Of course! Why not?'

'You know why not! It is forbidden!'

'Forbidden? Forbidden?' ground out Ruksana. 'And by what? A conquering nation who know nothing of our ways and care little for our feelings on the matter. They come, with their orders, and make demands on others, whose ancestral bones have whitened here for a thousand years. How can they know what is best for us?'

Abdul poured out glasses of weak cordial and they all sipped in silence for a few moments. Then Ruksana hissed in Abdul's ear, 'It is good for her to know what goes on in other quarters of the town. She is older than some children who watched!'

'Yes, yes. But I cannot think that it was right for her!'

Dorinda, who was gazing fondly at a bale of blue silk, looked up and said, 'I think they made a show of bad taste. It is not good to make light of such a matter. I think the widow very foolish to die in such a way. To what purpose can one die in such a way?'

'She is blessed,' repeated Ruksana.

'Why?' asked Dorinda, doggedly.

Ruksana drew in her breath and sipped her cordial down to the last drop. She put down the glass, carefully, on a small table.

'She is blessed because she has escaped from the life left to her. The contempt of all who see the widow. If her husband dies before her, it is she who has brought ill-luck upon him. But, if she dies first, then she is a wife without equal. Faithful, beautiful in nature, and a mother beyond compare!'

'Even if she has been a flighty, ugly, and childless whore?' asked Dorinda, lifting the end of the blue silk and letting it float on the air. Ruksana then grew very flustered, and slapped Dorinda hard across her cheek, not because of what she had said but because it was an echo of something she had said herself some months before. She had said it to her friend in the kitchen of the new house, about a woman they both knew.

Abdul smothered a smile in the folds of his sleeve. He knew Ruksana's gossipy tongue too well to question the child's authorship to such a statement. He walked over to the blue silk, and began to show more of the material to Dorinda. Dorinda ran her finger along the edge. 'I love the gold and silver stars and the broad, gold border.' She floated the thin material upwards, then downwards in a wave motion. 'See how it shines. A river of gold.'

'A river of gold!' Ruksana scoffed. 'How she talks, our baby!' Abdul put his head on one side and said, 'She is a baby no longer, Ruksana. She is a young lady who knows her own mind, I think.'

'Well, I think, such a bad girl, deserves not to have a new dress!'

'You promised!' said Dorinda, with a stamp of her foot.

'I'm sure your father won't think so either when I tell him you said a naughty word in company.'

'I'm sure you won't tell him, for if you do, I shall tell him of the horrid sight of the burning widow, and you know what father will think about that!'

Abdul looked patiently on, amongst his bales of silk. He needed a sale, but the moderations of his expectations of life, had guaranteed no severe disappointments. Today, tomorrow, some day, sometime, another customer would come to him and require something other than pink silk! Ruksana drew Dorinda to the doorway, and adjusting her own veil, stepped out into the street. She felt tense and was beginning to have doubts as to the wisdom of such an outing. 'I will be hushed about the word, if you will say nothing about the widow.'

'Oh yes,' replied Dorinda, agreeably. 'But I will not be hushed about the blue silk with the gold border and the silver and blue stars.'

Abdul laughed out loud. 'Be careful, Ruksana. I think the tiger cub may have a claw in her little paw.'

'I know it well!' she replied tartly. 'I feel its scratches daily.'

CHAPTER NINETEEN

The clouds in the heat hung, as yellow as lemons. The air pulsated with dryness. The vultures stood on the temple rooftops like so many broken umbrellas. Flies droned solemnly along the open spaces. From the yard gateway Dorinda watched a woman coming towards her. She had a broad parting to her lank, and greasy hair, and went unveiled. As she came closer Dorinda noticed that her pale and flaccid lips were pulled over sparse and decaying teeth. Her furtive manner and stumbling gait drew Dorinda out of the confines of the yard, and she continued to watch her as she hurried down the roadway. As she came abreast of another woman coming up the dusty road, she slipped something into the other woman's hand. A fleeting but significant glance passed between them, and each them hurried on their respective ways. To Dorinda, that glance was enough to indicate that something nefarious was taking place, and she ran into the house to tell Ruksana of what she had seen.

'What do you think of that, Ruksana?' Dorinda asked as she finished her tale.

'What do I think of it? Why, nothing! What silliness to be making a mystery out of such a thing as a lottery ticket, or a packet of herbs, or some such thing,' Ruksana said putting down her sewing and going over to the window. 'Hurry into the courtyard and bring in your dolls and books. The rain is coming!' They both ran out together and gathered up Dorinda's dolls and paints and books, just as the first drops of rain began to fall.

From the second storey window, Dorinda looked down the roadway, as the quick, pattering, raindrops gathered into lively streamlets, that hid themselves in cavernous places made by the drought. In no time at all the whole of the region seemed to be on the move, as over-hanging sandcliffs fell into the river beds, and roads sank or rose in accordance with the force of water beneath them.

Ruksana ushered Dorinda out of her parent's room and on to the third storey where the nursery and her own room was. From there Dorinda could see the rain sweeping across the inner courtyard, showering from the rooftops, sending the birds to seek shelter under eaves and ledges. There was nothing for them to do but to wait until the rains subsided. Afterwards there would be a feast of insects caught in the catastrophic downpour. Up on the third floor Dorinda, safe in her Noah's Ark of a nursery, played with the dolls and read her books. Once in a while she would say, 'I wish papa was here. He would know what to do.'

'And what, oh light of my life, can your papa do about the rains? Can he hold up the clouds? Can he stem the floods? Soon the weather will improve and then we will go back to our real home. Meanwhile help me to choose the ribbons for the dresses your father wishes me to make for you.'

Dorinda chose, then changed her mind, and chose again. She trailed about the rooms on the third floor, her tiny feet scarcely making a sound, as she hungered for the sound of her father in the yard below.

The minutes ticked by, the clock on the wall of the nursery, chimed the half-hour of seven. Dorinda, relaxing on a chaise lounge, thinking about her bedtime story, heard muffled sounds from the outer yard as the great gates swung open and her father and several other men, with carts and horses and camels, came into the enclosure.

'Papa, Papa, Papa!' she squealed joyfully, flying to the door of the room. Before Ruksana could stay her, she was scurrying down the innumerable stairs to the ground floor. 'Papa, Papa!' she cried out breathlessly as she ran out into the porch and then into the yard.

All she could see from the lights of the house and the yard, were hurrying, bulky shadows, unpacking and toting wares into the storehouse. She ran amongst them, fearless of camels and horses alike, searching for her father. Suddenly, he was there in the doorway. His arms were about her, his face buried in her hair as he held her close. He swung her upward onto his shoulder and carried her into the house. Ruksana met him stoney-faced. He smelled to her of sweat, and beasts, spices, and skins, and other men! She pulled a face as he put Dorinda down on the floor.

'He needs a bath,' she said to Dorinda. 'Come away to your room.'

To Dorinda, who had spent tedious days in Ruksana's company, her father smelled of security, dependability, prosperity, and strength, and she felt happy as she went to her own quarters and then to bed. But even there, laid in her frilled, white silk nightgown, between lace edged sheets of fine cotton, with embroidered cambric pillows to her head, her dreams were troubled. Something was amiss. Young as she was, there was an undercurrent about her, and she knew it as surely as if she were wholly part of it. She tossed, and turned, and became hot, and cooled in her restless sleep. Ruksana watched over her with an anxious eye. If she were to become ill, or die even, it could mean the end of her position in the household. She may even be blamed. Taking Dorinda to the city had perhaps been a bad idea after all!

It was morning. The rain had stopped and the sun was shining with its customary heat and Dorinda was soon babbling out to her father the fact that no pink silk could be had from Abdul's shop.

'But, father,' Dorinda went on, 'Abdul had the most beautiful blue silk. Could I have a blue dress, father, one with gold and silver stars and a gold border?' He looked down with amused eyes into Dorinda's innocent face. 'That sounds very fine, indeed, but don't you think it is just a little too old for you?'

'Perhaps it is, father, but then I will grow to it. Pink is young for me, don't you agree?'

'Yes, I agree,' said her father with a smile.

'There then, that is settled!' Dorinda clasped her hands together triumphantly. 'Since I shall never get younger, only older, the blue silk is for me!'

'Then you will get it yourself, Missie,' declared Ruksana who had been watching the proceedings with an annoyed expression on her face. 'I refuse to have anything more to do with the business of this silk, and what is more, Missie . . .' Here Alex broke in sternly, 'That will do, Ruksana. Kindly remember you are a paid servant in my house, if well-beloved. Salim will make the purchase, you can make the dress. I expect to hear no more on the matter! Is that understood?' Ruksana stood chastened and subdued.

When Salim entered the shop of Abdul the silk-seller he was sitting cross-legged on the dais in his shop, the glow from the lamp casting irregular shadows upon the wall. As Salim made the customary greeting, Abdul rose shakily to his feet. 'I know what you have come for,' he said with a smile, as he opened the bale of blue silk. Salim laughed. 'That Dorinda knows how to get what she wants. She does not wheedle, but speaks straight out with a bright face. No one could mistake her wishes. Ruksana is in a fit of rage. She always dressed the child in pink. She says it is because her mother always dressed her so, and called her little Lotus! Secretly, it is Ruksana herself who loves the colour, and much of the silk bought finds itself in Ruksana's clothespress.'

'I knew it!' said Abdul. 'She is a strange one! A scold and a gossip on one hand, a faithful servant to the British on the other, and yet so bound up in her own religious fervours. It is a great mystery to me that she still

Rule Of Thumb

comes here.'

Salim smiled, for he knew about Abdul, although he had not much religious fervour he was an unequalled raconteur, and could relate a third-hand story with such conviction as to make the hearer believe it was his own first-hand experience. 'There is unrest in the air,' observed Salim. 'Have you heard, perhaps, a whisper on the matter? One that might affect those of us who live and work with her Majesty's subjects?'

Abdul finished wrapping up the silk and looked at Salim. There was a grave look in his eyes as he stroked his scrawny neck.

'Well . . .' he said hesitantly, 'there are many rumours, but one would have to have been touched by the angels of Al Kader to be expert in the way of God.'

'What has God to do with the affairs of state?' asked Salim taking up the silk in his arms after placing the money for it on the counter.

'How should a poor creature such as I know the tides of Nations,' sighed Abdul.

'You old crow!' answered Salim fondly. 'You know they sit, like the vultures upon the trees around the fireworshippers temple, waiting, preening, trying to make themselves less ugly. I know it too. I know they only await the chance to hop down into the ordered lifestyles of the British here. After the kill, they will scavenge and turn to quarrel with each other. I know it will come, but where? And when?' Abdul shrugged his shoulder up above his ears.

'You must wait and see, like the rest of us, my friend. There is nothing to be gained by worrying without just cause. There has been unrest here before. It is no stranger to us! There have always been religious and political tensions here. Hindu against Moslem, who eat the sacred cow and reject images. The caste system. Moslem against Hindu who eat pig, and is capable of the highest philosophical flights of adoration through trees and rocks. Then, there is a Brahmin, who is against both, and will eat nothing that has been made with eggs – with life itself, and always insists that the wife and children eat after the husband.'

'You have forgotten those who degrade their bodies in order to exult their souls,' said Salim. 'But, the time is coming when a new struggle must begin. I feel it in my bones!'

'That is rheumatism!' laughed Abdul walking shakily to the door.

The streets were almost empty of people as Salim made his way back to the place of business. He had a heaviness in his heart and a strange disquiet in his mind, as he gave the silk over to Ruksana to put into the buggie. Half an hour afterwards Salim, Dorinda and her ayah and Alex were on their way to the country house.

Along the way, on the outskirts of the city, the homeless were cooking their evening meals, and settling down for the night. Sat amongst burnished brass pots two women baked flat, unleavened chapatis over a small cowdung fire, while a few feet away, five more women, their saris drawn across their faces, sat huddled together for warmth. Dorinda begged her father to stop and give them a few alms. 'Papa, please give them something, they look so ill.'

Alex got down from the buggie and took a handful of coins out of his pocket. He put them into the hands of a wizened, old woman, and she accepted the money without comment, into clawed fingers. As they touched Alex's fingers briefly, they were deathly cold, and raspy as a chicken leg scales. Alex wondered how she would fare in the screaming monsoon winds that lashed the rain down from the forests and swept the small, young animals into the riverlets and the ditches. She would be found some morning, he was sure, her stick-like limbs, rigid in death. He knew it was believed by Hindus that whoever died by the Ganges, achieved Nirvana, and avoided being reborn into the sinful world and guessed that these women, strung along the roadside, were here on a last pilgrimage, awaiting, with patient tenacity, the end of life and the final release from the wheel of reincarnation. Alex withdrew, hoping these women would gain their release without much sorrow, but Ruksana said bitterly to him, 'You gave them too much! Such women deserve what they are getting now. They have earned it from a past life!'

'I cannot believe that, Ruksana. What about the innocent little children maimed by their relatives for the purpose of professional begging?' She did not reply. She was still in a cross mood about the silk. Dorinda quickly changed the subject by asking her father if she and Ruksana could go to the harbour the day after, because she had heard that several wives from England were about to arrive and she would like to see them in their pretty gowns before they were whisked away into the mountains or just behind closed doors.

'I don't know if it is a good idea for you to leave the house every day, as you have been wont to do of late. I will consider it. Ask me in the morning.'

Ruksana turned over the silk on her lap with an impatient sound as the buggie turned into the drive of their home.

The following morning Alex was not to be cajoled into letting Dorinda and Ruksana leave even their country home, and Dorinda had to occupy herself as best she could, playing indoors, having long discussions with the punkah boy, and playing with Clarinda her brown-eyed doll. The punkah boy was very pleased to have someone to talk to him of the city, for he had lived there once, and so Dorinda told him of several sights she had seen there recently. 'Ask me what I saw somewhere – anywhere,' she said making a game of it all.

'What did you see when you went to the temple?'

'I saw a goat killed. Another watered all over the Devadasis foot.' They giggled together over that! 'I expect it was frightened when it saw the guts of the other goat in the bowl. I saw two fat priests swilling palm wine, in the corner of the courtyard, behind an idol. And I saw a beautiful woman, with a skin the colour of honey and a jewel flashing in her nose. Her eyes shone beetle-bright in her face, the upper lids were silvered and outlined with kohl.'

'What did you see in the harbour?' asked the punkah boy.

'We saw coolies loading and unloading the boats with all manner of things. And stalls of fruits and vegetables, and vendors, shouting out to one another and their customers. You never heard such a din!'

'I bet I have!' said the punkah boy. 'I've heard Ruksana and the servants. She has a tongue on her when she is in a wax!'

'I saw a holy man with a matted mop of hair. Not unlike your own . . .,' she added pertly. The boy pretended to strike out at her. 'He was quite naked, but for the smallest of loincloths, and his body was covered with symbols of white, yellow and red. Some people were bathing in the river but they had only gone to make a quick pilgrimage and were in and out of the water and into their clean clothes and laughing and chattering the moment they left the ghats. Ruksana said it was like Catholics at confession – a clean slate for the following week's irreverences.' The punkah boy laughed.

'I once knew a Catholic priest. He came from France, but he fell sick very soon and then went back to the vineyards of his country. He was always talking about his homeland.'

'He was like father then. He is forever speaking to me of England, and of his friend there. His name is Ambrose Cunliffe and he lives in the North of England at a manor farm. They have not met for many years but they still write quite often. I think he is not rich, like father, but quite comfortable. Father says he is a good man and respected, and he thinks highly of him. He has a wife, who, father says is extravagant, and a sore trial to him. She has a daughter a few years older than myself. Neither of them take an interest in the farm or the running of the house.'

'She will be like the lady of Banbury Cross with rings on her fingers and toes,' said the punkah boy, who had always shared the books Dorinda's

Rule Of Thumb

father had sent from England every year.

'And gems in her hair and gold studs in her nose, I shouldn't wonder!' broke in Ruksana who had been listening to them. She sent the boy on a small errand to another of the servants, and sent Dorinda out into the garden with a tiny plate of cakes and a cordial glass. Dorinda went into the bamboo-slatted summerhouse and throwing herself down on the wicker couch she placed the cakes and cordial on the little table before it. 'If father knew how bored and miserable I am here,' she muttered to herself as she began to nibble the cakes. Later she sipped the cordial, staring glassily into the distance, as she thought of adventurers she might have been having if she had not been there. While she was musing, Ruksana appeared at the doorway. 'So here you are. I have brought my work-basket. Why don't you read aloud to me whilst I put new ribbons on your sunbonnets. I can't think what you do with them to get them so worn.' 'I tie them in knots, then I have to nibble them with my teeth because you cut my nails so short!' said Dorinda crossly.

'Of course I cut your nails short. We don't want you looking like a monkey!'

'Monkeys can't read,' said Dorinda, taking up the ribbons from the workbasket.

'I know one who can,' replied Ruksana, shortly, as she took up the cotton and began to thread a needle. 'Why don't you read those old newspapers your father put in the old trunk over there. You might find a puzzle or a riddle-me-ree.'

Dorinda ran to the trunk in the corner eagerly and lifted the hinged lid. She took out the papers and spread them about on the floor. 'There are some here about Florence Nightingale at Scutari. There is a picture here of the Napoleonic Wars. I don't want to read about that. Why are men always fighting?'

'Because, when they are not doing that, they are making too many babies!' answered Ruksana, snipping off her threads, and placing the bonnet beside her.

'Now,' said Ruksana, 'if you will clear up these papers I will go into the house and instruct the servants about their duties, and here, you put this sunbonnet on your head, and bring my workbasket whilst I take in the plate and glass.'

'Boss, boss, boss,' said Dorinda as Ruksana proceeded in front of her. 'There is no one like her for ordering others about. Father says she could make a science of it! I don't know what he meant, but I'm sure she would be good at it!' She entered the house where she could her Ruksana's voice

Rule Of Thumb

penetrating to the kitchen, where doors began to slam and pots and pans began to rattle.

Dorinda had been wandering about the house for some time when Ruksana appeared and said, 'Let us go and see if we can see your father and Salim coming.'

'What, now!' cried Dorinda, snatching up her bonnet, and flying out of the door and into the garden. 'What bliss! Free at last!' she thought to herself, but she had reckoned without Ruksana.

'Here, Missie, hold my hand. I don't want you darting off the road and into the bushes to look for the nests of birds or other wild and rebellious creatures.' Dorinda did as she was bidden. They walked leisurely through the garden, admiring the gardener's handiwork. They walked down the dusty road to the end where it joined the river road, and sat on the top of some boulders placed there by the road menders. Boredom turned to fatigue for the day was sultry and clouds were gathering high in the sky above, boiling together, and darkening at the underside with a thin layer of a slate-grey colour. Somewhere, upcountry, there would soon be a rain storm but in the city they would have to wait for a day or two before the refreshing and invigorating wetness would lash down, in sparkling spears, and the thunder roll from hill to hill and reverberate from tower to tower.

A little way from them, on the main road, a family had made camp, with a strip of hessian slung between to low shrubs for shade and a collection of dried out camel and cow dung for fuel. They had with them a few goats, which threatened to wreck the newly erected shelter, chewing at the leaves within their reach. A young man with black hair, glossy with oil, came up to the goats and slipped a rope over their heads, and led them away and tethered them to a sturdy tree trunk. Dorinda saw a woman come out of the shelter and begin to cook chapatis. She was tall and slim and wore a sari and a jewel in her nose, and several bangles of silvery metal on her arms and ankles. 'She must be very rich,' whispered Dorinda to Ruksana, but she answered lazily,

'A woman would have to be very poor indeed not to have a small piece of jewellery, a toe-ring or a drop-ring to the ear.'

Dorinda looked at Ruksana with interest. 'Am I poor Ruksana? I have no jewellery but the little trinket you bought me on the way to the temple, and I have put that round Clarinda's neck. I thought she looked pleased to have it.'

Ruksana looked at her sharply, and said, 'Hush! Is that the buggie I hear approaching?'

Rule Of Thumb

'It is! It is!' she cried jumping up at once and waving her arms about until the buggie came to a halt. She was up besides her father in an instant and watched as her ayah approached more sedately. Her shoulders and head were swathed in a blossom-pink veil which imparted a warm glow to her mongolian features. She was definitely not pretty, Dorinda decided, and not young either. She felt a sudden rush of sympathy for her, and as she sat down besides her, Dorinda reached up and gave her a resounding kiss on her cheek. Ruksana put her hand up to the place and smiled a broad smile, giving, Dorinda thought, a wonderful lift to her ugliness.

'Now what was all that about, are you hatching something?' said her father.

'Not at all father. Ayah is so good to me, and I know sometimes I seem ungrateful.'

'It is no news to me that Ayah is good to you, Firefly, and for the next few days she must be better still. I have to go on business in the foothills tomorrow, and I will be away for a few days and nights. So I want you to be a good girl and not annoy Salim by quibbling about going to the city, and be very kind to ayah.'

'I would be extra specially good if you would take me with you!'

'I must say no, Dorinda. Where I am going is too far and the journey is not one for a young girl. It is over rough terrain, and on horseback.'

'If Salim is not to go with you, can I go to the city with him?'

'No indeed! There is much rumour in the city of insurgents. It would be best for you to stay here, in case of disturbances in city markets and on streets. Perhaps Ruksana will make a start on your blue dress. That will keep you both busy!'

'Well, if I am to be denied all outside pleasures, dressmaking will have to do. Will you do that Ruksana? I will take out all the dressing tacks, and thread all your needles.'

'I'll make sure that you do, Missie. It is time you learned to sew yourself. We will make a dress for Clarinda. I will show you how to make the seams.'

'Oh, a dress for Clarinda!' Dorinda clapped her hands together. 'What will it be like?'

Ruksana laughed at her enthusiasm. 'Well it will have to be fairly simple because the material is so embroidered already, but the borders of gold will be at the sleeve edges and the hem. The sleeves I will gather into small pleats and garter below the elbow with gold cord. The neck I will blend with a blue and silver beaded collar.'

'How lovely! Will Clarinda have a beaded collar too?'

'No, she has the trinket I bought you at the temple.'
'Yes,' agreed Dorinda, it will look very pretty against the blue.'
'You make it all sound very grand,' said Alex. 'I shan't know my girl and her dolly when I return.'
The buggie turned into the drive and while Salim took the horse and vehicle to the stables, the others went into the house.
'Come and help me to pack, Firefly,' said Alex to Dorinda as Ruksana made her way to the kitchen.

CHAPTER TWENTY

The following day Alex set off early on his journey. Salim took the buggie to the business house in the city, and Ruksana, contrary to Alex's wishes, dressed Dorinda in an old sari type gown, and they both set off to walk into the city. The purpose of Dorinda's nurse was to buy the beaded collar for the new dress. Dorinda was delighted with the idea, especially as it was spiced with the fact that what they were doing was of utmost secrecy.

They had told the servants that they were going to visit a bungalow on the edge of the forest. That in itself on any other day would have filled Dorinda with delight and expectations. She felt especially good as she ran merrily along the road towards the city, Ruksana striding purposefully along besides her, and it seemed in no time at all that the sounds of the busy city burst upon their ears.

It was certainly not a day to go searching for frogs invading the ditches, or for stopping the sweet-seller, used to hawking his goods from village to village. Urgency was the code word for the day, and Dorinda felt the excitement surge through her as they made their way to the covered bazaars. There, one man, large and colourfully dressed, was shouting at two coolies, giving orders to them with a very mean tongue. They appeared quite frightened of him and Dorinda tried to draw her ayah in another direction, out of the way of him. To her dismay, Ruksana ploughed majestically through the litter of packages the two coolies were stacking, and headed straight for the man's booth.

As soon as the man saw Ruksana his scowl reversed itself into a huge buttery smile, which Dorinda found somewhat repulsive, but which Ruksana responded to with much fluttering of hands and fussing about with clothes and hair. Dorinda looked from one to the other in amazement. The man's temper had flown away as swift as a bird, and Ruksana looked almost handsome as he escorted her into his office, a tiny cramped place, with not much room for more than five standing people at the most. Dorinda stood by the doorway, looking at the collection of labels and ribbons in boxes, and the large carboys of perfume and empty phials under the bench-like desk.

After a few moments of exchanging trivial pleasantries, Ruksana said to Dorinda, 'Go and see if you can find any Arabian dates in the bazaars, and come back and tell me when you have!'

Dorinda, at any other time would have made a face at such a request, but she was glad to get away from the dark office, and out into the clamour of the booths and bazaars. Almost at once she found a stall selling dates, but she was sensitive to the fact that Ruksana wanted to be alone with the perfume seller, so she wandered about nearby, trying not to draw attention to herself, in case she was thought to be a thief. As she gazed about, looking at all the colourful things, she thought she caught a glimpse of Salim. Her heart began to beat quickly, and she returned to the office, eager to enter the dim confines. At the doorway of the booth she almost collided with a tall, thin, dark man, who gave her a broad smile as she squeaked her fright and let him pass into the office before her. He wore a turban of green cloth, a sign that he had made the pilgrimage to Mecca, but carried a pistol in the sash around his waist. He spoke no word to Ruksana or the perfume seller as he entered the little room but held out his arm and rubbed three fingers together under the nose of the fat man. Dorinda had been a trader's daughter long enough to know that the mime indicated 'money'. The fat man began to fluster, his podgey fingers trembling over the contents on his desk. Ruksana's face took on a troubled air, but the thin man, still smiled a broad and tooth-filled smile.

'I have it somewhere,' the perfume seller hedged.

'Here is where it should be,' the thin man replied without blinking.

'Yes. Yes. I have it,' the fat man was groping desperately amongst the papers on his desk. Dorinda noticed he was sweating profusely.

'There is a stall just outside selling Arabian dates. Shall I go and buy some? Shall I?'

The spell was broken. The charged atmosphere shattered into a thousand tinkling pieces. 'What a child!' Ruksana chided playfully. 'Children are always thinking of food and small pleasures!'

'But you asked me to see, Ayah. You asked me!'

'Yes, yes, Babu. You shall have your dates. Here is a coin. Run along now and get some!'

Dorinda looked at the thin man who blocked her way as she took the coin, but he immediately stepped aside and began to laugh outright. Dorinda began to laugh too, and the hard tight feeling in her throat melted away, but

Rule Of Thumb

she hurried quickly out of the office.

After she had bought the dates, she wandered amongst the stalls nearby, listening to the twittering and laughing of the very young children who ran about the merchandise in a fever of excitement. This was their playground until the stall holders became tired of them and chased them out of the cool, ringing, shade of the bazaar, or from under the colourful awnings into the hot, white, sunshine of the open streets.

Suddenly, Ruksana appeared. She seemed quite jolly and festive as she took Dorinda by the hand and led her towards a shop where she could purchase silver thread and a collar for the new dress. Dorinda noticed that she carried a small article in the fold of her veil, and recognised it as being one of the phials from the fat man's booth. She had no doubt that he had given it to her as a present, but Ruksana said nothing of the gift as they purchased the collar and thread and then made their way homewards.

Dorinda loved the markets, and dawdled in the presence of Fakirs devoted to contemplation, seated upon little wooden chairs, spiked with vicious looking nails. They sat as easily as if they had been resting their skinny fleshed buttocks upon cushions of satin. It was a sight that never failed to fascinate her.

By now it was almost noon, and Ruksana drew Dorinda into the shade of a grove of trees where a food-seller was advertising his wares in the best way he knew, by tantalising aromas that tickled the nostrils and the palate, and drifted upon the warm air in a current of pure pleasure. Ruksana bought *luchi*, a light puffed pancake with mushroom curry, and scalding pepper-water, for herself, and fried banana fritters and *mohonobhoy*, a sweetmeat made of semolina cooked with sugar and milk and served with spices and raisins for Dorinda.

It was pleasant under the shade of the trees, counting the pots of water hung from the trees for the relief of thirsty wayfarers, trying to teach the Mynah birds to talk, listening to the fledgling tailor-birds, as they pushed one another about in their nests. The food was good too, but Ruksana had begun to be impatient, urging Dorinda to eat up the last of the fritters as they walked away from the grove. 'We must hurry if we are to make a start on your dress today,' urged her ayah, as they hurried home.

The new dress was not to be started. When they arrived home the buggie was at the door and inside Salim was walking the floor in a very agitated manner. 'You know you were asked to stay in the house,' Salim shouted at Ruksana as they entered the porch.

'Psshaw,' puffed Ruksana, quickly on the defensive. 'You men are like frightened chickens! Chittering your heads off at every strange sound. Nothing happened to us. We are all of one piece! We had an enjoyable time and you quite spoil things by your fears.'

'You know that I fear then?' Salim said scathingly. 'And what is this?' He pounced on the perfume phial with the air of a jealous husband. 'Have we not enough perfumes in our own yard that you must go spending money with others!'

'It was a gift,' Ruksana blurted out. She hated anyone to think she wasted money.

'From whom!' demanded Salim angrily.

'From Jamal! Although it is none of your business!'

'Jamal! Have you lost your senses woman? Do you not hear the talk in the bazaars?'

'I have two ears also. I hear, but I do not speak of such things. There are always rumours about the successful.'

'It is his success which is in doubt,' growled Salim. 'I warn you, Ruksana, if you cast your lot with the ilk of him, beware, for at the last your ambitions may outweigh your loyalties!'

Dorinda looked on dumbfounded. She had never hear Salim talk so hard and fierce to anyone, let alone one of their own household. It left her strangely perturbed for the rest of the day, but the following day Salim insisted that Ruksana and Dorinda accompany him to the business house. Dorinda was delighted. Ruksana meekly agreed to go to the house but said, 'The blue dress will have to wait again. There is too much for me to do at the other house.'

When Dorinda went out into the yard in the middle of the morning there were quite a few camels and their drivers in the yard packing and unpacking merchandise, and Dorinda made her way to one camel in particular. He was one well known to her for his protruding teeth, deep yellow in colour, and his much scarred underlip. He also had soft and velvety, brown eyes, which belied the stubborn nature of the beast. He took Dorinda's offering of food as he sat in a patient attitude, waiting for the driver to pack an assortment of rolls and baggages about his body. Dorinda knew that the camel would not move off with the pack until he had been cursed in a most virulent manner by his driver. Then he would waggle his ears, vibrate his hump and arise with an air of the greatest condescension. He would then soft-foot away, out of the yard, and into the dust of the road beyond, without so much as a spit or a grunt. She was awaiting the advent of this spectacle, when a stranger came into the yard.

Rule Of Thumb

He was very dark of skin, and was wearing trousers of a Turkish cut, and a shabby, green velvet waistcoat, which was carelessly laced across his ribby chest. On his feet, by contrast, he wore the most beautifully tooled boots Dorinda had ever seen. Ruksana came into the yard at that moment and flashed an indignant look towards the man as she went to speak to him. Dorinda looked on, wondering what her ayah could have in common with such a man. Suddenly, the man seemed angry and jerked his thumb in the direction of the street, as if he were imparting some instruction, and Ruksana stood nervously before him as if shielding him from view. As he seemed more angry, Ruksana became more agitated and plucked at his baggy trousers as if urging him to leave. He gave her a penetrating look and left the yard with quick, elastic steps, while Ruksana almost ran into the house.

Soon afterwards, Ruksana made the excuse to Salim that she must go out to the bazaar for some sweetmeats and a new pair of shoes for Dorinda, to go with the new dress she was soon to make for her. On this pretext, Dorinda must go too. Salim hardly looked up from his desk. He had more than enough to do with Alex away, without having to keep an eye out for Ruksana and Dorinda.

Dorinda, for herself, liked new shoes as well as the next child, but sensibly refrained from discussing her own desires and meekly followed Ruksana out into the street. They had scarcely got out of the yard when they met a man they knew who was very talkative, and who began chattering away at a rapid pace, his long, narrow hands accompanying his flow of words, his head nodding from side to side, as Ruksana asked him questions in return. It seemed to Dorinda, looking on, that her ayah had a formidable number of cousins for so the man deemed to be, starting each sentence with the word.

As the man left them, he touched his nose, which Dorinda knew to be a sign of secrecy between grown-ups, so she did not press Ruksana to explain their conversation, but concentrated on the new shoes. Ruksana bought the sweetmeats, and some ribbons, but began to dither about the shoes. The gold and silver shoes were too grand. The blue shoes were not the right hue, beige was too pale, and whoever heard of green slippers with a blue dress? Black, on the other hand Ruksana avowed was never out of place! Dorinda disagreed. 'Black is black, not a colour at all! Why can't I have white slippers or white boots even, like the European ladies.'

'If black is not a colour, is white?'

'Well,' said Dorinda, 'I know that there is a great difference in lies. Black ones are very bad and inexcusable, white ones are just excuses to cover up the real truth!'

Ruksana clapped one hand over Dorinda's lips, and snapped the fingers of the other hand, calling out the words SATH SHASHTHI – Goddess of children!! – to ward off evil.

'Why did you do that?' asked Dorinda, pulling away into a corner of the booth.

'Be still. One does not spit into the rain!'

'One must not speak in riddles if one is to be understood,' countered Dorinda.

'The child is very forceful. She is thoroughly spoiled,' Ruksana said smiling at the bazaar keeper who fawned upon her in a manner Dorinda found overbearing. Whilst Ruksana looked through the many shoes Dorinda found time to look at him. He seemed very rich, from the contents of his booth, and after a few moments he took a gold snuff-box from the pocket of his tunic. He gave it a couple of taps on the lid before opening it and taking a hearty pinch from the contents. His eyes watered, his nose twitched and eventually he erupted into an enormous sneeze. To Dorinda's horror a stream of green slime, streaked with snuff particles, poured from his left nostril. Ruksana, saw and looked away, still searching for footwear, serviceable, yet not altogether utility. Dorinda watched the man produce a scrap of cloth and wipe his face clean with a hasty movement. She found him less endearing than before when he tried to tickle her under the chin. 'I think, Ayah, that we must look elsewhere for my shoes,' she whimpered complainingly. Ruksana agreed. As they left the booth, the owner bowed several times, spreading his hands wide as they entered the street.

'Why did you tell that man that I was spoiled?' asked Dorinda sulkily.

'Well, you are! A new dress and new shoes. You do not need either!'

'I'm not getting either!' Dorinda declared petulantly.

'You will, if you can be patient! Oh, greetings, wife of Ramjam Singh, and greetings to you, mother of Bishu Chandra. Such a crowd in the markets today.'

'Have you heard? Someone has cut down my wild plum trees. Those that bordered my plot. I couldn't believe it. A nightingale used to sing there regularly. I never heard the like. Who could have done such a thing?'

'Who could not have done such a thing in these terrible days,' answered Ruksana, piously looking down at her feet, and pulling her veil about her face. Dorinda screwed up her face and hoped she looked agonised enough to warrant some attention.

'Is the child having a fit,' asked the mother of Bishu Chandra.

'I expect she wants to pass water and doesn't like to say so,' said the wife of Ramjam Singh.

'They speak about me as if I am behind a glass,' thought Dorinda darkly to herself.

'Did you hear that Jamal's brother is stricken by a cobra bite?' asked the wife of Ramjam Singh.

Ruksana's face snapped up into full view. 'How? When?'

'Early this morning. He went out to attend to the bamboo beds and the mango saplings, they had almost been washed away in a flood of water the other day. He had taken some bean curds, in a pot, for his breakfast, and put it down beside the thorn hedge. How was he to know that they shaded a den of cobras!'

'It is an omen!' declared Ruksana. 'I must go to Jamal at once.' She bid hurried farewells to her friends, and swept Dorinda along besides her. All thought of shoes were now forgotten.

The booth of Jamal was closed and shuttered, and Jamal, who had always brought many smiles to Ruksana's usually surly mouth, was nowhere to be found.

'We will go and ask Potiram Banerji. He is a friend of Jamal's and will know where he is,' said Ruksana confidently, as Dorinda skipped along besides her. Soon they were walking through the banana orchard that led to Potiram Banerji's house. They walked past the grove where one could pick bitter oranges in January from around a neglected shrine, past the rice barn and the custard-apple tree, and then they were in the Banerji's dusty yard. His wife was there in the outer yard, her glass bangles sliding up and down her thin brown arms as she pounded the dal in a wooden vessel. Her ancient mother was sitting besides a clay oven, slicing dried bamboo into incredibly small sticks for the fire. Nearby, curds lay in an earthen pot, together with a basket of baked rice ready for grinding for sweet rice cakes. It was a domestic scene repeated a million times throughout the country, with one exception. This domestic scene was as a play, acted out with consummate skill, fear in the breast controlling every motion of limb with well-ordered precision.

Less than an hour before Banerji had returned home covered in slime, saying that he had been looking for wild yams, when he had disturbed a nest of bees and to escape from them he had been forced to wade into the silted up pond besides the remnants of the temple. Ruksana knew the temple well. A low-lying land, full of water sinks and filled with wide-eyed lotus flowers, and fringed with wild fig trees, and the occasional mulberry.

His all-seeing wife had seen guilt in his eyes and blood on certain parts of him that was not his, and Ruksana found him stripped to the waist, head over a bucket, water flying in every direction. She brought him a clout across his back that would have felled a lesser man. He stood up puffing, his eyes shifty. 'What do you know of Jamal and his brother?' she asked agitatedly.

'I . . .? I, know nothing!' he wailed unconvincingly, as he patted himself dry slowly, letting his naked skin soak in the heat of the sun.

'Nothing? Nothing?' Ruksana shrilled hysterically. 'You! His friend! You know nothing?'

'Be quiet!' said Banerji's wife fiercely. 'Do you want our neighbour to know our business?'

'Yes, I do,' cried Ruksana recklessly. 'I want them to know of a man who wades into a slime-pit and then washes only his upper body on his return.'

'That is easily explained. I walked through the paddy-field field on my way back and washed most of the slime off me.'

'You have murdered Jamal! I know it! You have killed him and put his body in one of the temple sinks!'

A scream that had been hidden in the dark of his wife's fears broke loose and went ricocheting around the courtyard. 'You may well scream, wife of Potiram Banerji, mother of dead infants. Be glad that they live not to see their father's shame,' cried Ruksana, as she swept out of the yard with Dorinda in tow, who trembled from both excitement and terror. A hundred questions crowded her eager lips but something in Ruksana's manner made her be still for the time being. They walked along the dusty road covered with a pall of silence.

Then they were in an ancient courtyard. The air of neglect about the place struck Dorinda forcibly, until they walked through another archway, and there faced an enormous statue of bronze set in a niche, on an elaborately painted plinth. Ruksana did not speak but put out a hand to stay Dorinda, and pointed to a ledge of stone in a significant manner, where she expected Dorinda to sit. She then walked towards the statue, her offerings at the ready. She bound up the sweetmeats she had bought with the new ribbons, and added a sprig of blue linseed flowers before placing it before the statue. Dorinda felt restless and confused by the actions of her ayah. She felt that the visit to the shrine was something to do with the disappearance of Jamal. She herself did not like him, but she did not wish him hurt or dead, although she felt nothing at his presumed loss. She let her vision wander to the carvings around her where a sculptured frieze of figures danced along in obscene revelry. She did not recognise the sexual overtones, she thought them amusing, and would have laughed outright, but she caught sight of Ruksana's

Rule Of Thumb

face, and had no desire to get in her bad books!

At last Ruksana rose from her knees, held out a hand to Dorinda, and drew her out into the open air. Dorinda wondered why Ruksana had come to say her prayers here. Why had she not gone amongst the chanting devotees of Shiva, with wailing conches and the frenzied Devadasis' dances? Why had she not gone secretly, in curtained palanquin, or even in a Doolie, drawn by a loinclothed coolie? That was the usual behaviour of grief-stricken persons.

They walked down the pathway, listening to the scuff of their shoes in the thick, red dust, and the whisper of the breeze in the leaves of the bamboo thickets. They made their way along a rocky outcrop, and there in a hidden dip, a fish-hawk sat in the topmost branches of a solitary tree. Under the tree sat an old man, his hair and beard grizzled with age and neglect. Ruksana dropped a coin into the man's bowl to console him in his sorrows, the fishhawk flew away towards the river.

'There is another kindness in my favour for my next life,' remarked Ruksana piously.

'I do not think it kind,' retorted Dorinda crossly, 'to give alms in this world in the hope one might fare better in the next! I think that is a sly way to gain merit. Surely, one unselfish act is worth a million rupees in the eyes of the Almighty?'

Ruksana pulled up sharp, halted in mid-stride, the jewel on her brow quivering with the emotions going on in the head beneath. She shook Dorinda by the arm. 'You have too much to say for a child of your age. It will do you no good! You have no respect!'

They walked along in silence until they came to the suburbs, where many of the Europeans lived. Their houses had well tended gardens with tamarind and lemon trees, and luxuriant growths of creepers over tree, trellis and archway. They were fond of this type of garden where deep fragrant shadows protected delicate skins from the burning rays of summer, sheltered them from the slanting rains of monsoon showers, or under the heavy leaved arbours they could sit, moisturised, whilst the dry tindery breezes winnowed through the open garden, spiralling the dead bamboo leaves up into the sky.

They turned a corner and the hot air from the narrower streets of the city smote their nostrils. Ruksana continued to pull Dorinda along after her with a determined air. Dorinda thought grimly that if they walked much further, they would both need new shoes, for the ones they were wearing would be quite worn out. But she said nothing. She was thirsty, she wished she had a coin to buy water from the carrier with his goat-skin water bag slung on his back. In his hand he carried an enamelled brass cup of uncertain age and cleanliness to serve the portions of water. Hung precariously on his arm was a small bowl of coins held by a worn and fragile chain. Dorinda decided that it might be better to be thirsty for a while than chance a refusal of a coin from her ayah, as she was still wrapped in her vengeful thoughts. Then she stopped and brought Dorinda closer.

'This will not do. I will make better progress alone. Do you know your way to our home from here? There the servants will take care of you.'

'But . . .' started Dorinda uncertainly.

'But me not! I know you know the way well enough by road. I will tell you a quick, safe way, to the main road, avoiding the city.' She knelt down in front of Dorinda and spoke low, and hurriedly to her, her lips within an inch of her face. 'Listen carefully! Go down this lane, that leads past the old Indigo Factory. By the old gates there is a large clump of bamboo, and a lone tree, where the cranes roost. Behind that is a little stream. Follow the stream, it leads to a neglected temple pool. At the far edge of the pool there is a flight of stairs that leads into a small but dense grove. Do not be afraid. The path is well marked but narrow. Do nothing you should not do. Do not take a stick to the ant-hills there or collect bright beetles, or go after butterflies on the way. Keep your eyes ever on the path for it leads to a broken wall with an archway. Go through the arch-way and you will be but three tree lengths from the main road. Now – Juldi – Juldi. Hurry, hurry!'

Ruksana stood up and gave Dorinda a little push in the right direction and she set off. She felt perplexed at her ayah's behaviour, and was near to tears as she went down the lane to the factory, but she soon forgot her resentment at being sent home alone, when she saw the cranes up in the dark luxuriant foliage of the tree and the sparkling waters of the stream. She was still thirsty, and she went down to the stream and taking a broad leaf, made a little cup as her father had taught her, and drank her fill. Then, she thought, all this water, and my feet are hot and swollen and Ruksana said nothing of bathing feet in the stream. She took off her shoes and dabbled her feet in the cool pleasantness. It had been a tiring day. A tiresome day! She splashed her feet in the refreshing flow. The cranes nearby stirred and flapped their great wings, and a few downy feathers drifted onto the water. It was quiet. Why no one was there puzzled her. Such a treasure of a place!

A sudden chill swept through her. There was no reason for it but fear made her jump up and put on her shoes, and before the second was fastened, she was running along the path. As she ran along, stumbling and tripping and jumping, now and again over old exposed roots and debris, she tried to keep her eyes on the scarcely visible pathway. She could not help thinking

Rule Of Thumb

of her ayah and her assignment. Where could she have gone? And for what purpose? Her father would be angry if he thought she had even left the house. Salim would be angry too, because he had been left in charge, and it would seem to father that he was at least unreliable. But it was all that Ruksana's fault. Her and Jamal!

A young man leapt out of the undergrowth a few paces in front of her. She screamed. He laughed, 'Daughter of Tiger Dee. What brings you to the old temple of Kali.'

'I am going home. Ruksana sent me home. She is looking for Jamal, the perfume seller.'

'Jamal Thakrun? That dingy dog! What does she want with the likes of him?'

'I don't know,' said Dorinda, remembering her ayah's need for secrecy. 'I expect she wants to buy perfume. Father told us to remain at the house while he was away, but Ruksana wanted some sweetmeats and ribbons. The sweetmeats and ribbons she made as an offering in one of the temples. Then she said she would get me new shoes, but she did not. She could not make up her mind the whole morning.'

'You have had a bad time of it, little one. Never mind, here is the wall.' He helped her through the archway. 'You are nearly home.'

'Who shall I say has been so kind to me?' asked Dorinda.

'I am the son of Tempi Lahl. My father knows your respected father well.'

'I shall ask father to send a packet of herbs for your mother's cookpot and a bundle of cinnamon for yourself.'

'Alas, my mother's cook-pot has grown cold. My father and his three sons must shift for themselves.'

'Then I will ask father to send two packets of herbs, and four bundles of cinnamon,' said Dorinda. 'Father says a home without a wife and a mother makes for a jaded palate!'

Waving to the young man Dorinda began to run towards home with loping steps. She felt more settled than she had all day, as she ran into the driveway. She called out to the punkah boy who was hopping along, taking food to the gardener, in a little packet wrapped in a white napkin, and hung on his wrist by a ribbon.

'Here, let me take that,' said Dorinda reaching out her hand.

'Why you here?' asked the boy surlily. 'You go to city on father's business. This is my business,' he flicked the parcel away from her grasping hand.

'It's alright . . . He can still give you a puff of his cigar.'

Rule Of Thumb

'You know! You know everything!'

'Well, I know that!' replied Dorinda with conviction. 'What I don't know is if I shall get anything to eat myself! Ruksana prepared luncheon down at the city house and then sent me home here. She is in a funny mood!'

'Anyone who can come from city alone can find way to kitchen to make own food,' observed the punkah boy.

'That is just what I will do. I shall have all I like best with no one to tell me not to eat too much of that or too little of this.'

'You must not forget to say grace,' reminded the punkah boy.

'No, I will say grace, but I shall leave off the cloth and eat with my fingers.'

'You must wash your hands well,' remarked the punkah boy. 'You know Ruksana would not allow you to eat without that!'

'I really do not know why I bother about my own safety when I have so many watch-dogs,' Dorinda exploded pettishly.

'Ruksana told in the kitchen that your head was far in advance of your body, and that to be so was a disadvantage in one with a wayward nature, such as yours.'

'Wayward? How am I wayward? I am obedient in all things.'

The punkah boy rested on his crutch and looked wistfully into her face. 'I do not know what it is to run with the wind against my face. I would be obedient forever for that one wish.'

Dorinda fell silent for a moment and then she said, 'Take the gardener his food, then come into the kitchen and we will eat a meal together.'

When the boy returned to the kitchen he found Dorinda and one of the servants busy preparing vegetables and rice. He watched the servant expertly slicing up cucumber and onions, and frying sweet, spiced rice, hopping round on his crutch like a brown bird, chirruping, laughing, and teasing Dorinda, who was labouriously mashing dates for the filling of sweet pancakes. The meal proved a happy affair. The giggling of the woman servant at the boy's antics lightened her heart but when the boy left to carry out his duties, gloom once more settled over her.

She went up to the bedrooms and looked at the blue silk. She stepped inside the wardrobes and tried to peep through the tiny key holes. She played hop-skip-and jump, along the corridor. She looked out of the window towards the city to see if Ruksana and Salim were coming home. The day dragged on with leadened minutes. Boredom was alleviated by the servants preparing her supper and saying Ruksana would come home soon. Dorinda went to the summerhouse to look for a puzzle in the old newspapers there. She spread the papers around on the tables and chairs. She found nothing and the daylight was fading. She felt annoyed, and left the papers just where they were. 'Someone will put them away,' she thought angrily to herself. 'They always do.'

She went back into the house. The servants were talking in whispers to one another, but they stopped when Dorinda appeared. She hunt about the kitchen until eight o'clock and still Salim and Ruksana had not come home. Worn out with indolence and anxiety she went to her bedroom and got ready for bed.

It seemed strange to be alone in her room at bedtime. She put Clarinda in her own bed, then crept into Ruksana's bed by the door. She slipped into the hollow of the mattress and pulled the cool sheets over her head. 'What a surprise for ayah when she comes home and turns back the sheets,' she thought as she drifted off into a deep and dreamless sleep.

CHAPTER TWENTY-ONE

At two o'clock in the morning Dorinda was awoken by a piercing shriek. She turned over in Ruksana's bed wondering what she had heard. She folded back the sheets and lay on her back, looking up at the ceiling where a strange flickering pink light rested. Then, another shriek burst on her ears, closely followed by another, and then it seemed the whole house was shaken by sound and she was wide awake. Jumping out of the bed, not waiting to put on her slippers, she ran to the bedroom door, and after peering cautiously outside, tip-toed out onto the landing.

Down in the hallway, two men were setting the draperies alight. 'STOP! STOP!' cried Dorinda, and instantly regretted her action. Their faces stared up at her through the thin grey smoke of the torches they carried, and as one, they began to move towards the staircase. As they came towards the stairs a burning tapestry dropped pieces onto them. They struck the burning pieces away from each other, and stamped the charred remains into the rug at the foot of the stairs. It halted them for only a few seconds, but in those seconds Dorinda saw Salim appear in the hallway. Brandishing a ceremonial sword, he made for the two men, shouting unintelligible words. As he lunged at them, a draft of air, caught at the curtains, and the flames from the flimsy drapery fanned upwards with a roar, forcing the men up the stairs.

Dorinda fled back inside her bedroom, and trembling locked the door which was at the head of the stairs. Then she went to the inner connecting door, which led to her father's room, and opening it quietly, looked in. Ruksana was stood before the long mirror, the blue silk draped about her body and shoulders. The silver and gold embroidery lightened up her skin, which was like that of a purple grape with a delicate powdery bloom on it. In her densely plaited hair she had placed the emerald which Srinivasan had given Dorinda's mother on her wedding to Alex. The green stone in its gold cage flashed in the light against Ruksana's brow, like a third eye. Dorinda stood in her white lawn nightgown transfixed by her ayah's composure. The noise, the shrieks, the smell of smoke, the atmosphere of mayhem. Yet here, her ayah behaving as if all was normal. As she saw Dorinda's reflection in the mirror she turned.

'Why are you not in your room?'

'There are wild men in our house. They are burning our things!'

'You are dreaming child. Go back to bed!'

She turned impatiently to the door and swept out onto the landing just as a man came to the head of the stairs closely followed by Salim who was now flailing about his head with a long knife. The man was struck in the chest and fell with a gurgle to the floor of the landing. Salim then turned his attention to Dorinda who had run to him, whilst Ruksana had returned to her father's room.

'Go downstairs into the garden and hide where you can, Firefly. Quickly, quickly!' he urged her. Dorinda hesitated as Ruksana came out of the bedroom again still dressed loosely in the blue silk, and wearing the emerald in her hair, the gem flashing against the dark of her forehead. With a roar Salim hurled himself towards her, the sword upraised. Ruksana drew back with a piercing cry, 'Salim! No! Not me! Not me!'

Salim did not heed her but advanced. The blade was on high as she turned and ran along the corridor, but Salim was after her. Dorinda saw Salim raise the weapon high above his head, and stood at the head of the stairs as if turned to stone. She heard the swish of the blade as it came down with a scything movement. She saw Ruksana's head take off and go skimming bloodily along the floor to come to rest under the dainty legs of a gilt-painted chair. A scream froze on her lips as she turned and leapt down the stairs two at a time. At the bottom of the stairs lay two dead men, at the top she knew there lay another. Fear lent speed to her feet now and she ran down the fire charred passage to the kitchen door which stood open and fled outside into the enclosing shrubbery. There was a smell of burning and flames sprang briskly all along the edge of the house roof. The glow illuminated the lawns of the garden for Dorinda's terrified gaze, disclosing there a scene of all the gross horrors of systematic slaughter. Half-fainting she made her way across the garden, when she saw a man with a long torch in his hand start out from the fire-illuminated house. He went to the summer house but did not go inside. He peered in, and the light of his torch rested on something white, and fluttering, in a corner, which he thought was one of the servants. It was the sheets of newspaper left there that afternoon by Dorinda, wafting in the disturbed air. He threw the torch into the little bamboo house. It was ablaze in seconds. Dorinda saw the man back away from the fierce flames, and head for the driveway at a fast pace. She eased herself back towards the north wall that overlooked a rocky terrace some twenty feet below. At that moment she would have gladly welcomed extinction from such a height, but too exhausted to climb, she flung herself sobbing against the rough surface of the stones.

The house was quiet now, she could hear no shouts or screams, only the crackle of flames and the falling of plaster and rafters. As she turned her gaze towards the smoke palled ruin that had once been her home, a dark shape lurched from the nearby shrubbery and staggering forward, took hold of her, and drew her back into the bushes. There was a smokey smell to his clothes, his voice gurgled in his throat, and his arms and chest were wet to her resisting hands, but she hesitated only for a moment as the terrifying truth dawned on her and merciful darkness swirled into her brain as she lapsed into unconsciousness.

It was morning before she stirred in the close, glossy greenery of the shrubs around her. As she stretched her cramped limbs, the branches about and under her scratched at her, pawing her like living creatures, jolting her memory of the night before. She closed her eyes tightly, whimpering, trying to shut out the remembrance, but the smell of burnt wood and the sound of voices in the garden made her open her eyes again. There was a heaviness across her arm and chest and as she turned her head she saw the blood soaked body of Salim. He lay besides her, his limbs covered with innumerable cuts, one arm, in death, still laid protectively over her and in the fingers, Srinivasan's emerald. Suddenly, arrows of light pierced the murky dark of their hiding place, and Dorinda screamed and screamed as a brown face came into view.

When Alex Deane returned home two days later it was to find that Salim was dead and Ruksana supposed dead, as were the servants. Even the little punkah boy had been savagely butchered. Dorinda had been taken to the hamlet of Vishu Nath, by his elder sons, who had found her alive when they had searched the ruins of the burned out house.

A week had gone by and Dorinda was still too stunned by the violence she had survived to want anything but to be left alone. She could tell her father nothing of the incident and Alex wisely let the matter rest and concentrated on arrangements to live in the old house in the city permanently.

After a few days with the Nath family they moved back into the business house. The yard doors stood open again for trade. Friends were eager to resume relations and offer sympathy and support. Old adversaries were eager to denounce for fear of being blamed. Some melted into the background as silently as they had come, leaving doubt in the minds of others. Some just

Rule Of Thumb

stood by respectful and in awe of this lean, and angry man.

Srinivasan came hot-foot to Alex's side when he heard that Abdals, (Persian fanatics who think to kill a person of another religion merit, and if slain in the attempt are themselves accounted martyrs) had killed Alex's servants and left his house in utter ruin.

His account was quite different. Alex was popular. He was a fair trader with all castes and creeds, but he was a British subject. To Srinivasan's mind, the killing of his servants was nothing but a warning to other less-loved Europeans. How better to sow the seed of terror in others? To dispense with others less worthy may make the crime seem less heinous on the surface but how best to unnerve those who had relied on their services!

Alex listened politely. Dorinda was silent on the subject. Her brain was numbed by her terrors, her lively movements slowed, her face unsmiling, her eyes shaded with wariness.

Already Alex was missing Salim, who had been his mentor for so many years. Why Dorinda did not speak of her ayah, Ruksana, he could not tell. As time passed he thought that all she had seen and heard would be remembered and told, but even he in his darkest dreams could not picture the horror she had felt at seeing her beloved Salim attacking her ayah with such violence. The sight of her decapitated head, and later his bloodstained body was something she felt she could not share with anyone.

On their third day, Alex was sat in his office, his lean cheeks buried in his hands, thinking over the events of the past days. On thinking back further over the years he had to admit that his life had been filled with more than the unconsidered trifles of life, although up to now, the natives had generally kept peace with him. Perhaps, he thought, he must conclude that the attack on his home was not personal but a sign of a more disseminated unrest.

Finally, Alex began to pen a letter to his friend Ambrose Cunliffe, at Hinchley, in England, telling him of their experience.

'I see breakers ahead, dear friend, and I fear for my frail craft. Can you offer me a safe harbour for my girl, Dorinda? I will flee myself, when my affairs be ship-shape. She is an obedient child, but has been in the company of too many clever persons. She has picked up some of their ways of speech but she is not given to affectation. She has a brain and can use it. I hope to hear from you within the three month. May your God be with you in all things, Your affectionate and true friend, Alexander Deane.'

The letter duly completed and sealed, Alex tapped his fingers gently with it and pondered. Was it the right thing to do? What would his little girl think of the idea of going to England? Perhaps she would not want to go!

She would have to go. The burden of responsibility for a motherless child of a mixed marriage was too much for him, and should terror stalk again perhaps even her dusky skin would not save her.

He placed the letter in the rack and went heavily to bed. The following day Srinivasan came early to the house. He was dressed expensively, and beamed a friendly smile on Alex. He was the only man who would have dared to do so, after all Alex's trouble, but Srinivasan was a man of endless smiles. Cruelty or kindness were all expressed by an expansive show of teeth. Ever since Alex had bought Nighma's freedom from him a tentative friendship had sprung up between them. They had transacted deals of business, hunted together, and on rarer occasions, dined with Europeans. When Jo-Jo had taken a position of body guard to him, Alex had begun to feel more comfortable in his company. Jo-Jo was Alex's friend. There was no question behind his loyalty.

'What brings you here so early?' asked Alex wearily. 'Have you more news of disruption?'

'I hear that Jamal Thakrun's body has been found in a temple sink. His brother, bitten by a cobra, is almost dead, his wife and seven children wail for him day by day, but there is no purpose to it. He will die, there is nothing more sure. Potiram Banerji has left his childless wife. He has disappeared, no one knows why, or where. Neighbours tell of Ruksana's visit to the Banerji home. Today is the day they sift through the ruins of your home. There are sure to be bodies charred in the ruins, perhaps Banerji's will be amongst them.'

'Perhaps Ruksana's will be amongst them. I dread the fact, but she appears to be nowhere else.'

'Let me take Dorinda in my home. Just until this matter is settled. It would please us all to have her.'

'I do not doubt it, and especially you!' Alex exclaimed with a wry smile. 'The child of an ex-slave in your home would, no doubt, amuse you!! You old raven!!'

'I am not sleek enough or black enough for a raven,' laughed Srinivasan, pouting out his cheeks, puffing up his chest, and patting his pot-belly.

'No, bull-frog is a more apt term,' replied Alex turning as Dorinda came into the room. 'Here is my Firefly now. Ask her for yourself if she would like to stay with you.'

Dorinda fell silent for a moment and then said softly, 'If you want me to go, Papa, I will. But only for a little while. And I have need of new clothes.'

'I will see to them myself. She shall have the best. Such a brave girl. Such

Rule Of Thumb

an experience. You must tell me of it, sometime, when you are more settled.'

'I will tell you of it now!' she declared clearly, 'It was all very terrible and unheroic.'

Srinivasan rocked back on his heels as if he had been hit with a battering ram, and then burst into a roar of laughter.

'You have a gem here, Alex, a perfect gem. She will have a tart tongue in her head before she is much older.'

Alex hastened to excuse her. 'She has been too much in the company of adults. She requires the company of children of her own age.'

Srinivasan patted Alex on the shoulder. 'In three weeks I will return her to you. By then she will be tired of our company.'

'Very well, I agree, it might be best under the circumstances, Dorinda. There is much we do not know about what happened. Will you go with Srinivasan and Jo-Jo?'

'If I am to have new clothes, I may as well have a new home. But only for a little while, Papa, I could not bear to leave you for long!'

They left the premises. Alex returned to his office where the letter to Ambrose Cunliffe lay, waiting to be put into the hands of a captain of a fast ship bound for England.

As Srinivasan and Jo-Jo took Dorinda to the bazaars for her new clothes, they both noticed how well informed she was about prices, colours, textures, and style.

'Children of your own age! Your father does not know it but you were born old!' said Srinivasan to Dorinda as she cast aside clothes she thought too expensive or too cheap, too elaborate or too plain. Trousers, tunics and sleeveless waistcoats, lawn dresses and organza hats, and a selection of shoes and slippers, were soon piled into the buggie. When they were travelling to Srinivasan's house Dorinda said to him, 'What did you mean when you said I was born old?'

'You have an old soul!'

An old soul! What a stupid man! I shall be glad when my three weeks with HIM are over! thought Dorinda to herself. But her next thought was, How ungrateful I am when he has bought all these clothes for me to wear, just because he knows my father and once owned my mother. I wonder if he is sad mother is dead? I will ask him one day. When I am in his house. Not here in the street, father would not think that proper. He may be glad she is dead! THAT would be worse!

'Where will I stay?' asked Dorinda of her host. 'And with whom.'

'We have just the place for you. In the garden we have a summerhouse which you may call your own, for the whole of your stay,' said Srinivasan, beaming majestically down into Dorinda's face. 'You will have servants to wait upon you and you will sleep there but the gardens are open to you also, and the reception rooms of my own house. You may speak with my women when they are with me, but their quarters . . . I regret, I must request you not to enter there.' Dorinda made no comment. She was already well-versed in the partialities of eastern gentlemen and rich eastern gentlemen in particular.

When Dorinda saw the summerhouse which was to be her home, she was filled with wonder. She had thought it would be one of wood, gilded, no doubt, but nothing like the miniature temple of white stone before which she was ushered.

'Now, Dorinda,' said Jo-Jo, 'what do you think of that?'

'I think it is very elegant,' answered Dorinda, much in awe of the delicate tracery work in the apertures and the colourful mosaic panels depicting flowers and birds. 'It is a fairytale home, all icing and gingerbread and jujubes!'

Srinivasan laughed out loud. 'No, no, no, you cannot eat your house! It will not melt on your tongue like a festival sweet-meat. Bite that and your pretty white teeth will fall out onto the grass.' Dorinda smiled and her little white teeth flashed beguilingly in her bright face, as Srinivasan said, 'Come, come. See inside.' She stepped over the wide white marble threshold and onto the blue and gold tiled floor. The spacious airiness was cool and inviting. Thick rugs on the tiles were of a colourful wool which hushed every footfall. There was an array of small pieces of furniture, each displaying the nacreous gleam of inlay. In the main room a pierced metal burner hung on chains from an ornate brass stand. The air from the window drafted a thin, grey, aromatic smoke from the burner around the room and off into the surrounding chambers. A servant came into the room adding sticks of incense to the brazier to keep away from the inner rooms the numerous insects which invaded the garden.

'Now,' said her host, 'I will show you my own house.'

'It is a very beautiful house,' observed Dorinda, as she was led from one glorious room to another. 'You must be glad to be so rich and powerful.'

'I am indeed,' Srinivasan said. 'It is good to feel power over others.'

'It is very bad for the others!' Dorinda observed, looking up at him with an unwavering gaze.

'You have a lot of your mother in you, but you have your father's unflattering tongue.'

'You are quite wrong, sir. Salim always said, and I deem him right, that each person was himself or herself alone. Salim . . .' her voice trembled at his name and she burst into tears.

'Cry, cry, Firefly,' said Srinivasan softly, 'before your heart drowns in its sorrows.'

As Dorinda looked up at him she saw two wet streaks on his cheeks. His tears surprised her and she went quickly to his side, putting her small hand on the purple and green silken sleeve of his coat. He covered her hand with a plump palm and patted it gently. Dorinda withdrew and straightened her hair and ribbons about her face. 'I seldom cry,' she announced seriously. 'Ayah used to say it was a fault in me.' His face melted into a huge smile as he said, 'Let us go out into the courtyard, we can see the terrapins and the lotus flowers on the pool.' He held out his hand and she took it, her small fingers clutching the damp flesh, and together they went along the white walled corridor and out into the garden. The sun was hot, the air heavy with the scent of blossoms, and Dorinda breathed deep and appreciatively. There were a few flowers scattered around the pool, but the ground was concrete hard, and as they walked round the cool waters, a boy came running towards them, gurgling and waving his arms high over his head. 'This is one of my sons,' said Srinivasan.

'Have you many?' Dorinda asked innocently.

'I have nineteen sons and also fourteen daughters.' Dorinda put her hands over her mouth in amazement. 'Were they all gifted to you?'

'Gifted? Why, my sweet child! Gifted? Would you think this one here a gift?'

Dorinda noted the pallor of the boy's cheeks. He was different from other boys she had seen. 'Are you sick?' she asked.

'He has not been outside for a long time. He is better now. Is that not so?' he asked the boy. Their relationship seemed strained and Dorinda crept to the side of the pond and looked into the hearts of the lotus flowers that grew there. The boy had taken up a stand at the end of the pond away from his father and Dorinda and sank into a mood of melancholy dejection. Dorinda suddenly remembered that Ruksana had once discussed with her friend a child of Srinivasan's who was given to uncontrollable fits of rage, followed by almost inconsolable weeping without a known cause.

'Is that the boy who troubles you with his temper?' asked Dorinda.

'That is he! A devil child! a pixie, I think your father once called him. I do not know for that, but he sours my days. I wish I had never met his mother, with her alluring embraces and her jewelled arms!'

'I do not know that word "alluring",' said Dorinda, sitting back on her heels and looking intently up into Srinivasan's face. 'I know the natives lure birds and fish into their nets. Is alluring a sort of net? A trap?'

'A trap! You have it, Dorinda. A trap. A jewelled trap, with jaws of steel!'

Dorinda could not understand this flow of speech and lost interest, her eyes wandering around the quiet garden. The boy had gone over to the colonnaded portico and sat, his head in his hands, his thoughts caught, once more, in the shifting folds of mental twilight. The extreme loneliness of the place struck Dorinda, and she began to long for the bustle of the business yard and the high road outside. 'I don't know how I shall pass the next few weeks here,' she remarked demurely to Srinivasan.

'We shall find something to amuse you,' he remarked tonelessly, as he looked at his son who now sat, motionless, in the deep shadow of the porch, staring out towards the inner courtyard gate where the guard stood, impervious to all except his duty.

Dorinda saw him, sad, and untouched by the scene around him. He did not see the trees, stark shadows, washed with sunlight, along the walks, or the shimmering waves of blossoms, that flashed and faded, as colours through a stained glass door. The scents of the garden that engulfed Dorinda with a silent joy, passed by him un-noticed. She sorrowed for him, but she was not articulate about him, and passed into the little house allotted to her without comment, her dark reflective eyes downcast.

CHAPTER TWENTY-TWO

To Dorinda's surprise the three weeks stay with Srinivasan passed with ease. There were many people under his roof, each with their own part to play in life, and Dorinda, in the main, found them good company. But at last her father returned her to her own home.

She was pleased to be back but was perturbed to see that her father had done nothing to make the house more habitable. She remarked upon this on the first day, but her father said nothing. A few days after he said casually, 'There is little use in making ourselves too comfortable here. Soon we will be leaving for England to stay with my old friend Ambrose Cunliffe. At least,' he hastened to add, 'You will be going, and I shall follow after as soon as my business here is completed.'

Dorinda's heart sank deep inside her. She felt quite ill and swayed on her feet. Her father was much alarmed and quickly told her that it was best for both of them to go from India as soon as possible. 'Just think, I can show England to you at last! No more a story to be told at bedtime! You will like it there, Firefly.'

'I like it nowhere where you are not!'

'That is very commendable, my dearest, but quite impractical and so like a woman!'

Dorinda knew, from past experience, that when her father spoke of her as a woman, it meant she was to be burdened by something far beyond her years. She remained silent, but could not still the churning of her emotions as she thought of England, so alien and so far away.

The days passed slowly as both she and her father waited for a letter from Ambrose – her father hoping for a favourable response, and Dorinda dreading the expected communication.

Eventually the letter from Ambrose Cunliffe arrived, full of the quick sympathy and kindliness that Dorinda was later to find was the hallmark of his personality.

Too soon, it seemed to Dorinda, the day for her departure dawned. It was

Rule Of Thumb

'goodbye' to the tongueless bells that hung in the inner courtyard, to the silent fountain and the ancient tortoise, the yard with the clutter of wooden-wheeled buttock carts, the matting-wrapped packages, the spice boxes and the spirit soaked kegs. 'Goodbye', to the high gate, shutting good in and evil out, to the old house with white walls and green and orange shutters. 'Goodbye' to her father, with his kind eyes and gentle kisses, to her dead mother, Salim and Ruksana, and all her friends past and present. 'Goodbye' to India, land of her birth and her awakening.

Alex Deane stood a long time in the harbour watching the ship bearing away his heart and his hopes to England. A great empty space lay in his ribs, cold as an ice cap mist and yet the few tears that ran from his eyes were like a hot acid on his cheeks.

He walked along the water's edge and onto the shoreline and stood alone amongst the dying garlands of the flowers of the dead. Vague disturbing ideas churned in his head as he thought of Dorinda, now so irretrievably set upon a long and tedious journey. It was true English children arrived from England regularly, having enjoyed their voyage over the ocean, but that gave him small consolation. He strode on, careless of his direction, his eyes blind to the world, and then, in the dim tunnel of his despair he saw a light. The kind eyes and smiling lips of Ambrose Cunliffe, flashed upon his inner eye, like a balm-filled vision. His turmoil quieted, and he became aware once more, of his surroundings.

Before him was an oblong pyre of logs, ready to receive the next corpse which lay nearby, swathed in white linen and secured with fibrous ropes. As he looked another corpse was brought to the place. This body was swathed in red, a happy sign that she had died before her husband. They set her down gently at the edge of the water, to allow the thin, pale lemon coloured feet, to be blessed for the last time with holy water. The water was thick with offerings, and sleek flanked girls in the shallows, who climbed out and sat on the ghats, gossiping, as if they had forgotten the lonely shape below, bathing her dead feet.

'How strange, this life of mine, has been,' Alex thought miserably. 'Am I always to be confronted by death and departure on every side? Is there to be no joy in my remaining years?'

His melancholy gaze rested upon the corpse burner's assistant, chopping wood until he was almost dropping with fatigue. The corpse burner beside him, lifted up a piece of the wood and brought it down heavily upon a dead man's skull, in order that his soul could escape from the worn out garment of his body. People with thin skulls did not require this service, their skulls burst asunder in the heat of the fire.

A naked Saddhu approached a pyre and dipping his claw-like hand into it, scooped out a handful of fine, grey ash, and began to dust it liberally about his person. Although the act faintly disgusted Alex, the thought struck him that he had just committed a more strange and cruel gesture, the sending away of his only child to what could be the end of the earth, for all she knew!

Alex mentally crucified himself without mercy, while he watched others mourn their dear departed, with garlands of thrown flowers, and bowls of rancid ghee.

Then to the water's edge came a man, alive! Alex turned to watch the crude litter on which his bearers carried him. Some attempts had been made at decoration, and they were altogether a merry party. Alex felt he must find out their purpose in being there, and as he approached he called out, 'Why are you come to this spot, when your charge still lives?' They became serious at once, and guarded, until one of them recognised him. He called the others close, 'It is Tiger Dee. He would know why we are here!' He turned a betel-plug once or twice in his mouth with a fiery tongue before he went on, 'Shall we tell him?' 'Yes, yes!' they assented, cavorting about once more, agile as fleas. 'We are the offspring of mixed caste.'

This told Alex all. He knew now that they were garbage and sewer workers, subjected to the utmost contempt by others of a higher caste. Their very shadows were enough to pollute others. Only the dead were uncaring of their presence. The Dead and Alex, who cried, his arms outstretched, 'Take heart, brothers, one day there must come a man who will raise you. He will protect and honour you, and your families. But until then, consider this, that if it were not for you, others would be buttock high in their own filth.'

When the man on the litter heard this, he jumped up, took off the garland from round his neck and threw it over Alex's head and neck. Then, dressed only in a loincloth he capered along the shore, sprang into cart-wheels, and ran on the spot, until the rest of his friends were helpless in their glee.

Alex joined in their laughter. The gloom in his heart was for the moment dispersed. The proverb was true, but it was reversible. In the midst of death, there could be life.

It was a November afternoon. Deep in the shadows of the houses hard faced young thieves, hurried furtively along the streets on quests of their own. Alex watched the white bullocks with gold and white garlands about their necks as they sat chewing nonchalantly in the sunlight. A black and stinking male goat being led on a rope to the temple for an offering, suddenly broke loose. He grabbed at vegetables on a nearby stall and then with a wicked toss of his horns, cleared a way for himself down the centre of the street.

Alex felt a strange affinity with that goat, wrestling with a new life after the old had gone. He elbowed his way through the gathering laughing crowd, as the goat was hotly pursued. He turned away searching in the crowd, his brows knitting together, hardly hearing the laughter and shrieks of the people still dashing frantically after the goat was loathe to surrender without a last ebullient struggle. Shouts and squeals of anger and pain and fear filled the air as at last he was cornered and caught. The jostling melée smothered the poor creature's bleating protests and bore it triumphantly to the temple courts. Alex decided that this day was not for him. The great outdoors called him. A region of dense forest just a few miles away from the city and with numerous wild creatures seemed an ideal place to go.

He was tired of the grind of the city. He missed Salim. He now had a manager to attend to his affairs of business and he could afford to take a break amongst rural pleasures and leave behind the pressures of social and business obligations.

He felt cheered by his decision and half an hour later was jauntily swinging his cane as he went to make arrangements for his excursion into his paradise.

It was difficult to make arrangements just then, there was still a feeling of unrest. Soldiers were prominent everywhere. On all sides there were native skirmishes, and quarrelling amongst families of note. There was a general feeling that the East India Company was soon to be replaced by a stronger and more regal bond.

All this washed over Alex without so much as a ruffle. He had never laid any great claim to patriotism. He found it difficult to assess himself as an Englishman but no longer looked upon it as a fault in himself.

He set off into the hills and was away for several weeks but came back renewed in health and spirits, eager to resume his ties with both native and foreign people.

On his return, Srinivasan was his first visitor. His life behind the white walls of his house had become strangely uneventful since Alex had gone away. They renewed their friendship with enthusiasm, much to the disgust of Shantilal who was jealous of their comradeship and took no pains to hide the fact. The opinions of women were never taken seriously in the Srinivasan household and he and Alex continued to enjoy hunting, riding, and business ventures as before.

CHAPTER TWENTY-THREE

Dorinda Anne Deane, stood on the deck of the ship, taking her to England. Before her lay a country unknown to her, behind her, and far away was all she knew and loved best, her father, and India.

A few miles in front of the ship lay the docks. Their image, in a wispy mist, lent an ethereal beauty to the scene and she felt a brief raising of her spirits, as the ship sailed onwards towards her goal.

She did not know that the India she had left was now in the throes of rebellion and unrest, and if she had it was debatable if the fact would have overshadowed her present thoughts which were not for the India she had left, but her concern as to whether she would like her new friends or, more important, whether they would like her!

As the docks hoved into sight Mrs Holiband joined her on deck. She had shared her cabin with Dorinda for the whole of the journey. She was a woman widowed some eighteen months before in a native skirmish and was returning to England with a bitterness in her which had not made the journey too comfortable for Dorinda. She was always dressed entirely in black. Leathers, laces, ribbons and feathers also, and wore steel jewellery. This jewellery, flashing at throat and waist and in her hair, together with her black garb, helped to create an impression of a formidable guardian, armed to the teeth. Although over the weeks Dorinda had adapted herself to all the miseries of sea travel and the indigestibility of the food without a tear, Mrs Holiband's sharp and doubled edged tongue could raise a pebble of anxiety in her throat that no amount of swallowing could down. It is little wonder then, that she looked upon the shores of England with something akin to joy, as the time for their parting drew closer. She stood there, teeth chattering with cold and nervous tension. 'Good Heavens, child!' said Mrs Holiband fretfully, 'Don't tell me you now have the fever!'

'I have nothing of the sort,' Dorinda retorted fiercely. 'It is cold! I should have put on my shawl. I will go and get it.'

'Then do hurry, we are to disembark soon. I want you with me when we do!'

Dorinda fled along the deck to the cabin. Most of their trunks were packed but her shawl was laid over the back of a chair. 'At least it's not raining,' she said to herself as she drew the shawl around her tightly as she went back on deck. Mrs Holiband was speaking to another woman, and Dorinda did not feel obliged to go and stand with them, and leaned idly over the rail watching the coastline coming nearer. It was a little disappointing and her anxiety grew, as the ship entered the harbour and the buildings took on solid shape. The sunlight, half-absorbed by the dingy hues of the stonework, gleamed so faintly, as to only serve to deepen the effect of the shadows. Yet, under the side of the ship the water was so transparent as to permit the sight to penetrate the greeny depths to many feet.

At last the ship docked. Every spy-glass was trained upon the arrivals. Gaily dressed women and spruce family men, hovered around the disembarking points, and were in direct contrast to the barefooted and ragged clothed girls and boys who earned a penny or two by carrying bags and bundles, or giving directions to the nearest carriage stand or hostelry.

Then to her delight she heard someone say, 'Dorinda Deane.' She looked about her and there was Ambrose Cunliffe. She was not altogether prepared for the solid yeoman who gathered her up into his arms and planted an explosive kiss on her forehead. She struggled a little, and pushed back from him all the better to take him in, whilst he beamed on her with a smile as welcoming as any she had ever seen in the whole of her life. His hair was grey at the temples and his back was ramrod straight. As they were taking stock of each other Mrs Holiband came by, but swept past them with a haughty look on her face. She took hold of the arm of a well-dressed man who had come to meet her, and turning neither to right or left passed out of their vision.

'I did thank her for looking after me,' said Dorinda, by way of conversation to Ambrose.

'I'm sure you did,' my pet,' Ambrose replied, taking note of her luggage.

'She is a very hard woman to get along with,' offered Dorinda, 'but, she has had a good deal of trouble. First her little boy died of the fever, and then her husband was killed in a fight with a native.'

'I expect time will soften that shell of self-pity in the poor, dear. We all have our troubles. You have had many yourself as young as you are.'

'I have indeed, and I must say, that if Mrs Holiband had the starch washed out of her, she could lay claim to beauty.'

Ambrose laughed and shook his head. 'You have a pretty way of speaking, my lamb. Your father told me of that!'

Ambrose was delighted with Alex's daughter. He had half-expected her to be incorrigibly wild and godless from living with foreigners, but here she was, full of young liveliness, and, he had to admit, a dusky skinned loveliness he found quite enchanting. As he looked down at her he felt entirely pleased with this new addition to his various household. 'Ah!' exclaimed Ambrose looking about him, 'here is Nicholas Tandy, my coach driver.' 'Call me Nick,' said that person, with a lopsided smile. 'Everybody does!'

Dorinda shook his offered hand gravely. 'I hope I shall be pleased to meet you.'

'I hope so too! If you are a friend of the squire here, we shall have no cause to quarrel!' He took hold of her leather bound trunks and began to throw them at the back and on the top of the carriage with much vigour and abandon. He moved with the easy grace of one used to labour and seemed well able to manage all the luggage Dorinda had brought with her. Ambrose helped to tie the ropes binding the luggage secure and then helped Dorinda inside, and then got in besides her. Nick Tandy got up in the driving seat, and away the two horses went, rattle and slide, out of the dockyard area and into the main street.

'It's worse than being at sea again,' said Dorinda as the carriage swayed and rattled over the cobblestones.

'You'll soon get used to it, Dorrie, never fear.'

Dorinda made a wry face that made him laugh out loud, but it was not long before they came to crowded streets, and she began to lose her uneasy feelings and looked eagerly out of the windows at the pageant going on at both sides of the carriage. The roadway was so congested that they could hardly make pace, and she was not bored for an instant. The buildings shone now in the strong sunlight. Bottle-glass windows, winked along the sidewalks, there were oyster booths and hawkers of saloop and fresh herbs and flowers. There were also hawkers of mournful ballads, fortunes, and music sheets. 'It is just like at home,' said Dorinda with amazement. 'All these sellers of things along the main road, how they shout and scream,' she went on covering her ears, but only for a moment, as she was afraid of missing a single word.

Ambrose looked down amused at his young charge, 'You will find your new home very quiet compared with all this,' he laughed as the carriage was brought almost to a halt by a tangle of vehicles. This gave Dorinda an opportunity to see into the side lanes and alleys which they were passing, and she was very alarmed at what she saw there. It was very different from the noble houses which lined the main thoroughfare. The alley courts and back streets with which the buildings were honeycombed were unpaved and filthy with rotting garbage and litter, and open drains from which nauseous odours rose, lay at the doors of the overcrowded tenements. Dorinda put a finger and thumb to her nose and made a grimace. 'Quite bad,' agreed Ambrose seriously. 'There is much illness here, among the children of the poorer classes. I have been told that even some of the rivers are little better than open sewers and that birds flying low over them can actually be overcome by the fumes and fall dead into them.'

'People who are rich should see that things are made better!' said Dorinda with conviction.

'Oh, my dear, sooner said than done!'

'Just look at that man over there, the one in the satin coat, with silver buttons and buckles on his shoes. How proud he looks! See the woman besides him? She has hardly a rag to her name! She begs alms but he looks above her.'

'I am afraid,' said Ambrose steadily, 'members of the lower classes find little sympathy amongst persons of fashion.'

The carriage moved slowly along till they came close to an orator who immediately took Dorinda's attention. To her he was a fascination. He had a moustache and beard which seemed to explode over his lower face in a riot of bristle. As he raised his fist in the air and brought it down with a thump into the palm of the other, Ambrose put down one of the windows the better to hear what the man said. 'I shall work all my life if need be for the abolition of . . .', and here the orator's gravelly voice was drowned by the raucous shouts of the various carters who had drawn up to listen to him, and the whistles and boos of the occupants of several carriages, that had like theirs been stranded in the melee. The man, however, was not to be deterred. He would abolish something, and these sentiments were, in general, meant to excite the gathering towards the speaker, but instead it sparked off a searing indignation against the laws of the land. For several minutes he was hard pressed to keep down the babble of voices which interrupted his speech.

Suddenly Dorinda felt stricken and alone. Her father had spoken of England as being a green land, filled with flowers and farms, and tiny villages with steep cobbled streets and thatched or red tiled roofs, and here she was enmeshed in city streets filled with as much noise and squalor as those she had left behind her. She felt a lump come into her throat and her eyes moistened. Ashamed, she buried her face in the folds of her cashmere shawl, which still smelled faintly of the frangipani of which her mother had been so fond. She gulped in drafts of stale air through the window-space and tried to quell the lurching sickness in her stomach. Ambrose moved towards her and putting his arm about her shoulders said coaxingly, 'Come, Dorrie. You have not smiled at me this last hour.' The exaggeration of his remark drew her out of her misery, and she raised up her head only to find that before the carriage was an open road, and in a few minutes they were wheeling into an Inn Yard. Nick Tandy jumped down and opened the door of the carriage, and unfolded the collapsible leather steps. He held out a hand to Dorinda and imitating the voice and manners of a fop begged Dorinda to do him the favour of partaking of a morsel of refreshment in company of Ambrose, whilst he himself sought out an apothecary for the purchase of a phial of oil of cloves, for the hollow tooth which troubled him greatly. Dorinda was more impressed by the hollow tooth than by his foppish manners. It was the first time she had come in contact with anyone with a cavity actually on show, for Nick opened his mouth widely and pointed to the offending molar and then creased his face into a lopsided grin. Ambrose gave Nick a coin and said, 'If you can get rid of the tooth, do so. We have a long way to go for your face to be so out of shape and so painful, and I know you like your vitals. How will you eat?'

'To tell the truth, I already feel as odd as a left boot. I'll be rid of it at once if I get the chance. If not, it's cloves and whisky all the way.'

As he set off, Ambrose ushered Dorinda into the hostelry. She gazed at the cold meats, cheeses, pasties and pies, and several sorts of pickles laid out on a sideboard. Ambrose made an order for her and himself and they sat down. The whole tavern was something she had not dreamed of in her wildest fancies. Her eyes glowed as she looked around her. Spode dishes, delph ware, pewter tankards, snuffers and snuffer trays, sugar bowls and sugar sifters and tongs, horse brasses, horn spoons, velvet curtains, heavy rugs, wooden landsettles and benches and chairs, and a large table at which they were seated, polished by time and beeswax until it shone as water and reflected all that stood upon it. All delighted her. 'How happy everything is here! How everything shines and twinkles.' Ambrose nodded as he helped her to meats and side dishes. She ate only a little being too full with emotion, but was comforted by the pleasant companionship of Ambrose, and later Nick, who joined them to eat sparingly of the crumbliest of bread and cheeses, followed by hot spiced ale for the aching tooth. The meal finished, Nick was dosed by Ambrose with the oil of cloves, and then he plugged the cavity of the tooth with a pellet of new bread. Nick made a great pantomime of it, laying back on the landsettle and kicking up his heels in the air, and bringing forth from Dorinda a tremulous laugh. The tooth business over, they all three went out to the stables where the horses had been rested, fed lightly, and watered.

In the stables, the straw littered floor rustled under their feet, and the blackened beams of the building hung low over their heads, but the place was clean and tidy. The leather buckets for oats and water were neatly stacked, the heavy rugs, smelling strongly of horse, flung over the wooden frame of one of the empty stalls. The horses were led out into the yard and the carriage was got ready for the next stage of the journey. Whilst they waited Dorinda looked round the yard. There was a large waterbutt, and a wooden bucket bound by a crown of iron, and a long chain which was attached to a water trough, against which leaned a rosy-cheeked boy. He was lazily polishing a horse brass and gave Dorinda a sly look as she smiled timidly at him, but then he turned away and sniggered behind his hand. A passing box-man cuffed at the boy's ears and said gruffly, 'Manners!'

The boy deftly avoided the full blow, but it was Dorinda who felt guilty, as Ambrose handed her up into the carriage.

'People will not always be kind to you,' whispered Ambrose as he sat down beside her, and took hold of her small hand with firm fingers. He must have seen the flash of dismay pass through her as she looked up at him with solemn eyes, for he bleated on in an agony of embarrassment. 'It is because you are a stranger. Nothing more! You are not like them.'

Dorinda looked carefully out at the pale coloured faces about the carriage, and then looked up at Ambrose. 'They are not like me,' she announced gravely. Ambrose threw an arm about her shoulders and said heartily, 'They are not like either of us, Dorrie. I think we shall do very well together.'

Dorinda laughed too, shaking her head until her warm, brown hair fell over her face, ashamed that Ambrose might see the tears that were brimming in her eyes.

As soon as the carriage was well on the way, Dorinda became more cheerful. The countryside was green, there were flowers and birds, and the sun shone down with a gentle heat that was new to her. The little lanes with many a rut and jolt soon became a game, as to who would fall about the seats first. Each night the carriage bowled into the yard of a Coaching Inn, where for one shilling a head and eight pence a night for stall, hay and oats and water for the horses, they were entertained, fed and rested most royally.

Every night as Dorinda said her prayers, Ambrose, who shared a room with her, heard her say, 'And please God that we arrive safe at Hinchley Manor, before ill befalls us. Amen.' But each morning would see her running happily hither and thither about the inn or yard taking in all that she could of her surroundings.

And each day brought the end of their journey nearer.

CHAPTER TWENTY-FOUR

For a long time on the last day of the journey to Hinchley, the horses clung to the rough roads with unrelieved monotony, then with a sweep of the dirt road, the carriage was bowling through open moorland country. Cotton blobs flecked the boglands with woolly heads and the first thin haze of the purple red of the bilberry bushes, tinted the knolls and rises. Lower down the hills birch trees with silver barks and pale green leaves fluttering, took up little stands in woodlands, where grew clumps of bluebells, willowherb and foxglove. Lower down still, in the meadows, working and riding horses rolled from side to side on the lush grass, kicking up their hooves. Young foals stood upright, their flanks touched by buttercups, and fescue, their feet amongst all-heal and daisies. Groups of small cottages with stone-flagged, or crumpled moss-green roofs, or new golden thatch, hedged the curves of the hills, or crouched defensively under their shadows.

Then, towards evening, came a long stretch of desolate country, where masses of heath and heather, skirted the roadway, and tawny coloured peat water flashed down flagged spillways, and under millstone grit culverts.

In the distance a rounded hill pushed its shoulder into the sky. To the right, on the skyline the keep of a long ruined castle ceased raggedly in mid air, a silent watcher over the scene below.

When the carriage drew to a rumbling halt outside the Elizabethan building of the Cockpit Inn at Lynwych Village it was almost twilight.

Nick peered in at the carriage window, his blurred face still swollen from his bad tooth. Ambrose got down from the carriage to inspect Nick and shook his head. 'Lewis the blacksmith will take that offending article out of your mouth in the wink of an eye,' he declared. 'Go and see if he is in the Cockpit. I warrant it will cost you no more than a jug of ale for its removal!'

'I think I must be doing that Squire,' Nick replied as he rubbed his tender cheek. 'I think this tooth of mine will be chewing for me no more! And this head on me feels like a rotten apple. It does so!'

'I have been losing my teeth since I was six years old. They fall out one at

Rule Of Thumb

a time so that I have not had any inconvenience as regards to eating. My ayah told me that was the way of "first teeth" it was the teeth of adults that caused many problems.'

'Will you listen to that, Squire!' said Nick looking admiringly at Dorinda's teeth. 'You keep your tooths as long as you can, little lady. There is no pleasure in the exquisite pain of toothache, or a gappy smile! You are a lucky girl to have such a gleam in your face. Like starlight!'

His conversation was brought to an end by Ambrose who urged him to get along to the Cockpit Inn snug where he was sure to find the blacksmith willing to act as dentist to him.

Ambrose then sat in the driving seat and Dorinda was left alone in the carriage. She knew by the rocking that the road was rough and stoney in parts, and the hedges high on either side made the carriage even dimmer. As Dorinda craned her head over and lay her face flat against the window she could see in the distance the lights of a house. She was impatient to see Hinchley Manor now, and all the people she had been told lived there.

She whispered their names over to herself in the darkness. There was Sabetha the housekeeper, and Janet Marie the deaf maid, Irene who was stepdaughter to Ambrose, and Ralph who was nephew to Ambrose. Dorinda had been most anxious to know about the wife of Ambrose. He had said nothing about her and Dorinda's enquiries had only revealed that the subject was painful to him. Ambrose had told her that Ralph's father, a stern brusque man, had squandered all but a trifle of his own money, and the entire fortune belonging to his wife, who was sister to Ambrose, and had been dead for some years. After a prolonged bout of drinking and gambling Ralph's father had taken up a pistol and shot himself through the head. Ralph had come with all speed to Hinchley and was as sullen as a sixteen year old boy can be, after losing contact with the world he knew. Dorinda thought, on reflection, they were not altogether a happy crowd of people to be staying with, but resolved to settle as best she could. She was browsing hard on being happy, when her thoughts were disturbed by the carriage wheels rumbling onto cobblestones and then jerking to a halt. Dorinda's heart lurched as she heard Ambrose jump down and then the sound of his footsteps as he came to the carriage door. He opened the door with a flourish, and called jovially into the interior, 'Come and meet your new family, Dorinda Anne Deane!'

Dorinda stepped down carefully, adjusted her dress and shawl, retied her bonnet strings, and then allowed Ambrose to usher her across smooth flagstones, and then into an entrance porch, and finally into a spacious hall where, it seemed to Dorinda, a host of people waited with bated breath for her arrival.

'Well, here we are, at last! Journey's end,' cried Ambrose cheerfully. Ralph, who had been leaning against the large white marble fireplace, crossed over to Dorinda at once, and taking hold of her hand shook it gravely without one word. Ambrose beckoned Irene next and Dorinda dropped a small curtesy before Irene, overawed by her beauty. She was as beautiful as any of Srinivasan's ladies, even though her hair was as golden as the sun and her eyes as blue as a linseed flower, and her skin as pearl pink as a newly opened Persian rose. Irene bobbed her head just a little way and said cryptically, 'Welcome to the haunted Grange!'

Sabetha, the housekeeper shushed her and said, 'Don't you go filling the child's head with nonsense.'

Dorinda smiled, 'I am not in the least put out. I lived all my life in a haunted house. Our business house that is. I am well acquainted about the facts of demons and ghosts.'

Ralph burst out laughing. 'Well there, Miss Irene, I expect your little joke will be the cause of a loss of sleep to you this night!'

Sabetha, cook, comforter, and zealous supporter in family troubles stepped forward and gently taking off Dorinda's shawl, led her to a seat by the fire. 'Sit here, my dear, Janet Marie will fetch you and Mister Ambrose some jemmy-broth, this very minute.' This Janet Marie did, in blue bowls with alphabet borders, full to the brim with goodness.

While Ambrose and Dorinda ate, they related many of the sights they had seen on the way from London, and the saga of the rotted tooth brought forth quick sympathy for Nick's discomfort. Dorinda looked round the smiling faces and decided that they were her friends, and Hinchley was her home, at least for the present, until her father joined her in England.

The logs of wood settled in the iron-barred gate basket with a slurring sound, and the fine grey ash came riddling through the bars almost to her feet as she sat on the little white-wood chair that Ambrose had arranged to be specially made for her. Ralph had put the poker into the fire a little while before and now he took it out and inspected the hot metal with satisfaction. 'Stand up, Dorinda Anne,' he requested mysteriously, and her heart froze for an instant, as she wondered what Ralph was about to do, but he held out his free hand to her and said, 'Don't be afraid.' He went to the chair she had vacated and with the hot poker burned a letter 'D' into the curved backrest of the chair. The pungent smell of burning wood filled the room, rising an old terror in her mind, but as she looked around the room again, it spoke of other things, of meadows and woods, and days of summer warmth, and acts of unparalleled kindness. He worked on the chair for half an hour or so, using the heated poker like crayon and enclosing the letter in a wreath of oak leaves and acorns. When the chair appeared finished, Dorinda clapped her hands with delight. 'You are so kind,' she said embracing him shyly.

'It is not quite finished. Tomorrow I will finish it by making the lines deeper. Then it will have to be washed and dried several times, and lastly given several coats of varnish.'

Dorinda was further impressed. 'You would do this for me!'

'Have we not sent to the far ends of the earth for you!'

'You have indeed! It was well worth the awful journey. I must write to my father tomorrow and tell him of my arrival here, and how well I have been received.'

Ralph looked down into her shining, brown eyes, and turning to the others said, 'This little brown bird sings a sweet song.'

'Amen to that!' said Sabetha, 'but little birds need their nests! Come chicky, Sabetha will show you to your bedroom.'

Dorinda obediently followed her after bidding all goodnight.

'You must say your prayers tonight, child, for your safe arrival here,' said Sabetha as she climbed the stairs. Dorinda looked aghast, and cried out, 'I quite forgot to say my prayers to Boroon the sea-god. It was he who gave me a safe journey over the ocean.'

Sabetha looked solemnly at Dorinda in the light of the oil-lamp.

'Well, chickie, I dare say that now you are English, that heathen god, will not be listening to you. A prayer to Gentle Jesus may be more proper and acceptable under the circumstances.'

'I will pray to both. If Boroon is listening, it would be a pity to offend him. I'm sure Gentle Jesus will understand.'

'I am sure,' said Sabetha, with a shake of her head, 'that I know nothing of the life you have led in that terrible wild place, with its foreign Gods. But, if they have helped to bring you safely to us, then I give also my thanks to them, and hope I may never offend them in my ignorance.'

'Everyone here is so kind to me I would not be surprised if I should suddenly find that I was drowned at sea, and now I reside in heaven.'

'Why, bless you child! What a thought! Heaven indeed!' said Sabetha opening the bedroom door. 'Here we are, now your nightgown is laid out and there is fresh water in the ewer and soap and towels. You are big enough to get yourself to bed whilst I go and put lamps in the other rooms. I will come back and tuck you in.'

Long before Sabetha returned Dorinda had said her prayers and climbed, unwashed and half-dressed, into the soft downy bed and fallen into a deep and restful sleep.

CHAPTER TWENTY-FIVE

It was high summer and harvest time was near when in August 1858 Dorinda sat on a rustic stile besides Irene, overlooking the coppice near Hinchley Manor. 'Just look at all that golden corn,' said Dorinda, touching Irene's sleeve. 'How the people of India would like to see it. Look how it bends and sways. So full, so heavy.' Irene smiled and took more flowers from the sheaf on her lap, to arrange them in the bouquet she was making for the hall table.

'What are those pretty blue flowers?' asked Dorinda touching them.

'Those are cornflowers. The red ones are poppies.'

'I have seen poppies in India, but they were white and yellow, not red. They were opium poppies. Men make a mark on the pod and a sticky resin comes out and then it is dried and made up into little packages to sell in the cities. People smoke it. It is supposed to make those who smoke it forget their troubles.'

'It sounds revolting!' said Irene making a face as she shuddered delicately. 'No wonder your father sent you here.'

'There were a lot of good things in India,' Dorinda went on defensively. 'We have lovely fruits and flowers, and such a variety of animals. Fruit bats and monkeys, camels and elephants, and funny ones like wart-hogs and crocodiles or alligators. The streams and rivers were full of interesting types of fish.'

'I have seen a camel and an elephant. I did not think either of them beautiful,' said Irene grandly, picking up her flowers, and gently sliding down the stile. Dorinda jumped down besides her and they began to walk along the edge of the coppice where the ewes and lambs lay, away from the sultry heat of the open field. In the sky above them hovered one of a pair of kestrel hawks. They made their nest in the ruins of Castle Mount and terrorised the chickens, moorhens, and small life in the neighbourhood with their mauraudings. They watched the hawk slowly circling the coppice before it hovered for a moment and then stooped down into the field beyond. Then it soared upwards and away, the long tail of a small creature in its grip,

Rule Of Thumb

dangling against the background of blue sky.

Ralph emerged from the coppice with a long handled slasher in one hand, five dead weasels hanging from a pole over his shoulder, and one of the otter hounds yelling up at them. Ambrose followed behind with a ferret muzzled on a line, for a hole in his pocket had taught him long ago that it was not the best place to carry home a young ferret. Dorinda ran towards Ralph eager to see the chestnut and creamy-white fur of the weasels they were compelled to kill. Dorinda touched their little carcasses tenderly.

'Five hawk dinners there, Dorrie,' said Ralph.

'Oh, dear! God goes to so much trouble to make those lovely animals and they end up as something else's dinner?'

'Not always! Everything is either carnivore or herbivore. Carnivores eat herbivores. We like herbivores too, so we kill to survive. You want your rabbit pie don't you? Mr Weasel will make short work of a rabbit.'

'Speaking of survival,' went on Dorinda, 'do you know what all the strong argument was about this morning?'

'That was Henry Froste and Uncle Ambrose. They are always in an argument about something!'

Ambrose turned at the sound of his name. 'What is it?' he asked coming to a stop and looking at them both quizzically.

'Dorinda wants to know what Henry Froste was doing at Hinchley this morning.'

'A small matter of policy. Nothing more!' replied Ambrose, smoothing back Dorinda's hair from her face before putting the ferret in her charge. He strode onwards, leaving Dorinda trailing behind him, the ferret tugging at the line.

'There was a good deal of harsh talk and table thumping for a small matter,' she observed to Ralph who was walking alongside.

Ralph made no reply but puckered up his lips into a whistle and so put an end to her questioning. They wandered on, silently, until they came to the house. There Janet Marie and Sabetha were airing the bedding, laying out the linen and covering the edge of the five acre with a snowy drift of sheets.

'If you want, you can put on a rough pinafore, and help me to clean out the ferrets.'

'How shall I do that? I have no experience with cleaning.'

'Then it's time you had,' said Ralph. 'Bring that little beggar in. Now,' said Ralph, once all the ferrets were back in their cotes, 'While I go and set box-traps in the barn, you go and ask Sabetha for a pail of hot water. Tell her to set the kettle on again too. And put on a rough pinafore.'

Rule Of Thumb

The kettle on the hob was not quite ready, so Dorinda put on a slip-on pinafore that came down to her ankles, and waited until the kettle was boiling and lifting its lid.

'That scallywag has taken no time in getting you to help with his work,' said Sabetha as she filled the pail with both hot and cold water.

'I don't mind at all. Ruksana and Salim . . .' she hesitated and then went on, 'they would not let me do anything that they considered menial. They used to say "What is the world coming to if the Master's daughter is burdened with the work he pays servants to carry out".'

'Well, I am sure they were quite right,' said Sabetha blandly.

'I am sure they were quite wrong, Sabetha. I found it most tiresome, and it left me ill-equipped when I have to fend for myself. I had to fend for myself when Salim cut off Ruksana's head, and then when he himself died I was filled with terror.'

'Dorinda Anne, you must not tell such fanciful tales. Thinking and doing are two different things.'

'I never thought once of seeing Ruksana without her head. She could be difficult. Hard one moment, laughing and making fun another. But in my heart, I did love her, Sabetha, and I do miss her, for all her faults.'

'Why did Salim want to kill your nurse then?'

'That no one knew. I always thought Salim was fond of her in his way, but several things had happened that had put him out of temper with her. There was unrest everywhere in the city and no one knew who their true friends were any more. When he killed her she had my mother's emerald in her hair and was wearing my length of blue and gold silk.'

'But, my darling child, that is not a killing offence!'

'Perhaps not here. I am glad of it. No one knows Salim killed Ruksana. They all thought the other men had killed everyone in the house except me. I did not tell them anything. Father was away when it happened. He had known Salim a long time and was very upset about his death. Was it bad of me not to tell him?'

'No, not at all,' said Sabetha, taking off the kettle from the fire and topping up the pail with hot water again. 'Now, can you carry that out to Ralph?'

'There is no need,' said Ralph who had come into the kitchen, 'I will carry the pail. Where have you been all this while?'

'Waiting for the kettle to boil,' said Sabetha evenly. 'Do you have soda, scrubber, soap and mop?'

'I have them already. Come along little skivvy,' he called to Dorinda. 'Let me see how you can make our Jacks and Jills comfortable.'

Rule Of Thumb

'Do you clean the cotes every week?' she asked.

'No, no!' laughed Ralph. 'I clean the cotes out regularly, but I scrub them out once in three months. After they are washed and dried I give each cote a lining of thick whitewash. Here take them one by one and put them in the compartments over there.'

Dorinda did as she was bidden. After that for about one hour it was wet, scrub, rinse, wipe and dry. Then came the time for whitewashing.

'Let me help. I can do that!' said Dorinda, full of enthusiasm.

They found they worked well together and it was not long before all the cotes were drying. In the evening they returned the cotes to the brick shelving. 'Now then lean the cotes well away from the wall so that the wet and refuse cannot lodge and give them footrot and foul fur.' This done he liberally scattered the floors of the cotes with fine sawdust which he had carried in from the woodyard. 'Nothing gets wasted here, does it Ralph?' said Dorinda. 'Everything is used for something.'

Ralph brought in the newly killed rats from the barn. The ferrets began to get very excited squealing and leaping around the cotes. 'Now don't you get all huffy,' he said to Dorinda. 'Give that little titch one. He looks fair starved.' She did as she was told, then said, 'How often do you feed them?'

'Every twenty-four hours so that they don't get fat and lazy. Sometimes, when they might be a bit poorly, they might get a bit of bread and milk and a spoonful or two of minced liver. We don't feed them just before hunting rabbits or rats, so don't you go feeling sorry for the little beggars!'

'Do they get poorly, sometimes?' asked Dorinda sympathetically.

'Oh, aye. One Jill ate up her own young litter. We had to dose her with buckthorn and then starved her for forty-eight hours.'

'Did that do her any good?' asked Dorinda.

'Well, she didn't get milk-fever, but she knows the Buckthorn bottle,' Ralph replied with a laugh.

Just then Dr Burr rode into the yard and hitching his horse besides the barn, went into the kitchen. 'He'll be after Sabetha's cooking,' said Ralph. 'You go in now. Take the pail with you!' he shouted, as she went running off. She turned and picking up the pail ran across the yard to the kitchen.

Dorinda had never seen Dr Burr before and Sabetha drew her out from under the kitchen sink where she was putting the pail away.'

'Here is our Dorinda, Dr Burr. All the way from India.'

'Are you a healthy child, Dorinda?' said Dr Burr, feeling her pulse.

'I have never been sick ill. I've been frightened ill, and bored to death ill, and on occasions, eaten too much ill.'

'And how would you describe sick ill?'

'High fever, chattering teeth, shaking limbs, spots, yellow eyes, green slime . . .'

'God in heaven! Where has the child been?'

'She appears to have been taken into the city by her nurse, though she lived in a respectable part of that city with her father who is, I believe, quite wealthy. She is, Dr Burr, quite a precocious child in some things.'

'I can well believe that myself,' said Dr Burr. 'Tell me, Dorinda, where is your nurse now?'

'That I do not know. My father's best friend cut off her head. She was wearing mother's emerald and my blue silk and he just took up a sword and cut off her head. It went spinning down the passage but I ran away into the garden where Salim found me and saved my life.'

'The saints preserve us!' exploded Dr Burr.

'My mother was a Saint,' broke in Dorinda innocently.

'Leave it, leave it, Doctor,' begged Sabetha, filling a bowl of broth from the pan on the fire and putting it on the table. 'I know it has been a hot day but it is good food. Now, sit you down. Dorinda, you go and tell Ralph to come in directly and get something to eat.'

Dorinda went obediently. She understood when adults had heard enough from children. Some day they would know the things she said were true! Then they would be the ones to look silly!

Doctor Burr dipped his oatcake into the stew and pressing his angular frame close to the table, made sure that not one drop of nourishment escaped his eager mouth.

'Do you want a mite more?' asked Sabetha. 'You looked clemmed to me!'

'I must admit, Sabetha, I eat badly. I have no good women to cook for me and I make do with a crust here and a pot of ale there.'

'You should get yourself a housekeeper. You treat your patients' troubles with care, why not yourself? I hear you go ten miles or so to see some of them. Your skills are widely known!'

'Ah, it is easy to be popular with folks who can afford to pay nothing!'

'Do I hear aright. Are your patients short-changing you?' gasped Sabetha.

'I never see a penny from some, but then they are poor and sometimes they die. If it is the man who dies, the family are like to end up in the Workhouse. How can I go dunning there?'

'Well, if that is the way of it, you must prise a guinea or two out of the pockets of the rich folk they work for from dawn to dusk. They can spare for the poor and needy the sum they gladly lay on the cut of a card!'

'You don't suffer much yourself, Sabetha.'

'Suffer? Oh, I suffer alright. But some get better of their own accord, while others potion and poultice till they are worn out.'

Dr Burr grinned all over his lean face. 'You're a tonic. You really are! You think then, some time in the future, I could live well and be a better doctor?'

'Well, you'd be a live one!' replied Sabetha with a hearty laugh. 'The first epidemic that you come across will carry you off with your poorest patients if you fail to fatten up those lean chops and thighs. You need strong thighs here for the winter snowdrifts and rutted roads. You know nothing yet. Wait till you witness a real squealer of a blizzard or a freeze up that lasts from Christmas to Easter! Put up your fees, dear man, to those who can pay, and see that you get it! That way alone will you survive many a cold night and dreary day!'

The following day Henry Froste came again to Hinchley. Dorinda was standing in the porchway as she saw him approaching and ran into the hallway. She disliked him on sight. His lips were thin, and resolute, and a sharp bridged, hooked nose, jutted out high between cold, blue eyes. Dorinda decided that he was a man of mean appearance, in spite of his lavish ways of dressing. He certainly cast over Hinchley a shadow far larger than a man of his size should. What could be the secret of his appearance here again?

She watched for the reaction of Sabetha, who frowned and drew in her lips whenever he appeared – and he was to make several visits during the next month. Sabetha disliked him for diverse reasons, the greater being the way in which he looked at Irene, the lesser the manner in which he thumped his riding crop on the brocaded chair in the hallway, for it not only raised the dust but it bespoke an authority she was loathe to let him have.

It puzzled Dorinda beyond endurance why he came, without welcome, so often, and she was determined to find out.

One day when he arrived and was talking with Ambrose in his study she hid behind the sofa in the drawing room where she knew they would take tea together when their business was over. Almost at once she regretted it. Space was limited. 'I must have grown lately,' she thought to herself, for she had hidden there before in playing hide-and-seek without much trouble. She wriggled herself almost flat and rested her head on her elbow, as Ambrose entered the room followed by Froste.

Ambrose rang the bell for tea to be brought in to them. The jangle of the bell fell unheeded on the deaf ears of Janet Marie, who, Dorinda knew, was alone in the kitchen. After a few minutes of waiting, Froste declared testily, 'I would not stand for such delay if I were master of the house.'

'Indeed,' Ambrose replied icily. The word was uttered with such emphasis as to be almost written on the hot, sultry, atmosphere of the afternoon. Ambrose crossed from the table to the fireplace and pulled the bell rope again, and a few moments later Sabetha came into the room. She bristled when she saw Froste, but Ambrose said, 'Tea, if you please, Sabetha.' She withdrew without speaking and several minutes later returned with the tea things on a tray, and began setting them out on the lace bordered tea cloth on the table.

All the while Ambrose and Froste had not spoken, but paced about the room, leant on the mantlepiece, struck poses, looked out of the window, and rustled sheaves of papers. Dorinda was sure she must be discovered, but Sabetha left quickly and made for the kitchen again.

Ambrose sat down and Froste sat on a chair opposite to him. Now they were facing each other they were out of Dorinda's line of vision. From where she lay she could hear the chink of the tea-things and then Froste remarked, 'Sabetha is an excellent cook.'

'Yes,' admitted Ambrose. 'She is a good woman. I do not know how we would fare without her.'

Dorinda crept nearer to the end of the settee and popping out her head could see Ambrose, sat back in his chair. He was clenching and unclenching his hand beneath the shadow of the tablecloth. She would have been glad to see him punch Froste on the nose, but instead he took a small box from his pocket and opening it, took out a large emerald, caged in gold filigree. He dangled it before Froste, on the thin gold chain. Froste cupped his hands under it as it hung glinting in the light from the window. 'That is the last of the debts.' Ambrose grated, as he let the emerald drop into Froste's outstretched palm.

'Many thanks, dear friend,' Froste replied with raised eyebrows. He got up from the table and took the pendant to the window where he began to examine it carefully. 'Pretty bauble!! Cost a pretty penny, I'll wager.'

'It has cost me my peace of mind.'

'Come! We made a bargain! You to pay your wife's debts, I to collect. Is that not so?' He put the emerald back in the box and ensconced it in his pocket. 'I regret,' he added sardonically, 'if these debts have taxed you sorely, as I feel they must have.' Ambrose pushed the pen and ink-horn towards Froste and gave him the receipt to sign.

After he had signed the receipt he fumbled with his cravat and made himself small in the high winged leather chair by the fire, like a pet that has taken a liberty, but it was only for an instant. In the next breath he was saying, 'If you feel obliged to sell Hinchley, I hope I will be the first to know. I will give you a good price, providing your cook-cum-housekeeper is included in the sale.'

'It will be a sad day for many if I were to consider selling Hinchley. I have many irons in the fire that I trust will see me through this thin patch,' said Ambrose as they walked out of the room.

'I am glad to hear that,' said Froste with a mirthless laugh, 'I charge you though, to take care when you extract them, less you are burned yet again.'

Dorinda, still hidden knew exactly what Froste would do in the hall, she had watched him with curiosity several times before.

He would pick up his hat from the hall table and standing in front of the gilt framed mirror would place the hat at a jaunty angle on his head. Then he would pick up his riding crop from the little brocaded chair, and putting the crop under his arm would adjust his cravat, then with a light step he would make for the door.

When Dorinda thought she had given him enough time to join Ambrose in the forecourt, she came out of her hiding place, with cramp in her knees and guilt in every fibre. She shakily made her way across the hall and through the kitchen into the cobbled yard.

Froste had gone, spurring his horse to a fast pace down the road that led to Fennyford Bridge and Lynwych.

Ambrose and Dorinda watched him go. She knew Ambrose was sad at heart but could not say anything to comfort him without laying herself open to criticism for her eavesdropping. She knew that to sell Hinchley was not the answer. Hinchley thought and breathed Cunliffe ways. Their joys, past and present permeated the mellow stonework and the much loved gardens and meadowlands. As if to echo her thoughts, Ambrose declared loudly and defiantly, to the diminishing speck on the road that was Henry Froste on horseback, 'Sell Hinchley? Never!'

'Sell Hinchley? Why must you do that?' queried Dorinda, looking innocently up into the worried face of Ambrose.

'Oh, I have had some expenses lately. I am running out of money.'

'Then you must pay in kind, as father used to do.'

'I have nothing to pay in kind with,' said Ambrose dolefully.

'Then you must use my mother's emerald. It sits in its box all day. I am too young to wear it. Use it. Let it make you smile again. I cannot bear it when you are unhappy.'

It was simply said and she did not expect it to bring forth such a warmth of feeling as it did. 'Bless you, Dorrie, and bless the day you came to us!' he hugged her up to his side and gave her a resounding kiss on her brow. 'It is an offer I shall never forget.'

'You will take my advice then?'

'Gladly, gladly!!' Ambrose was smiling now, his face creased into the kindly lines Dorinda loved best. They went back into the house together, Ambrose to collect all the papers and put them in a secret drawer in his desk, Dorinda to go into the kitchen where Sabetha and Irene were preparing the evening meal.

A few moments later Ralph came into the house and threw some letters onto the table. One was from Dorinda's father, much travel stained and dog-eared, having been carried by various people, from Captain to Carter to mail-coach for several weeks.

When Dorinda had struggled to read the letter she felt empty. There was nothing in it to indicate that her father would soon be on his way to England. It spoke of people she knew and exhorted her to try and fit in with Ambrose and his family, and to take her lessons seriously, and not to disgrace him by a wan face or bilious tempers. It finished with the request for her to keep a warm place in her heart for her father, so far away, who would be glad to hear from her as often as possible.

Ralph, noting her sad face and tremulous lips, took the letter from her. After reading it he threw it down on the table again. 'It looks like you will have to work hard to fill in the time twixt now and then.' Dorinda looked up at him. 'He will come,' she asserted. 'He promised!'

'I'm sure he will try,' retorted Ralph. He took hold of her hands and kissed them both and said, 'We must see to it that when he does come you are a young lady worthy of a rich nawab.' Irene snorted from the fire oven where she was banking the coals. 'Don't you go putting grand ideas in that head, there are enough there already!' she urged, but she turned and smiled, not unkindly, on Dorinda, who was indulging in a few tears. She wiped them hurriedly away and said to no one in particular, 'I will be strong for father's sake, as well as my own.'

'I'm sure you will,' assured Ralph, 'and . . .' he put his hand in his coat pocket and pulled out a pink sugar mouse, 'now you can be sweet as well!'

CHAPTER TWENTY-SIX

Far away, in India, Alexander Deane had been informed, from time to time, of men and women being mauled and children being carried off, by tigers in the foothills some miles outside the city. He had paid little or no attention to the reports. Tales were always being bandied about of great striped beasts or wild boars half the size of elephants. Cunning, wise, elephant tales were legendary. The cunning ganged up on unsuspecting villages in the night, trampling the inmates to a red smear. The wise elephant stories were feats of endurance or bravery on behalf of mahouts, or owners, or little children lost in the jungle. Most of the tales were the figments of an arrack fevered imagination or eccentric hallucinations induced by imprudent imbibing of some potent native drug. But one day Alex heard a tale which to all events appeared true.

Early in the year of 1859 Srinivasan came into the yard as he was sorting out a new batch of native work. Srinivasan looked very pleased as he rode into the yard seated upon a fine cinnamon coloured camel. He was dressed in an under-robe of dark green and blue silk embroidered down the front with seed pearls and pale green and blue beads. Over it he wore a hooded djellabah of cream wool of good quality. On his feet, placed on the camel's neck, he wore slippers of camel leather, dyed a bilious yellow, and upon his head a turban of yellow muslin, threaded with gold.

'You look very splendid,' said Alex going up to him. 'Where are you bound?'

'Here!' Srinivasan replied. 'I came to ask if you had heard of the new terror in the foothills. A tiger with yellow fangs and red eyes, much given to the tender flesh of pregnant females and little stumbling babies, which it is said to devour whole.'

'I have heard of some such tale,' agreed Alex, hastily avoiding the searching teeth of the camel. 'Is this tale like all the rest?'

'I think not, Alex. I have decided to make up a party of twenty men and boys. I have other business in those parts. If we do not sight and kill the beast, my time will not be wasted.'

'What business can you have in the foothills?' asked Alex boldly.

'I have heard of a gem pit there. I would see it for myself!'

'Perhaps that is an illusion also!'

'Are you willing to come with us?'

'Yes!' agreed Alex. 'I also would like to see this gem pit!'

'We start the day after tomorrow. I will dress in boots, and shirt and linen, as I expect you to do. I will also take a gun suitable to kill the fiercest tiger ever kitted!'

'It is a fair step. We must go well prepared.'

'All will be taken care of, Alex. Just present yourself at my house at six o'clock on Wednesday morning.'

Alex watched him turn the camel out of the yard and into the road. They waved farewell and Alex went into the house, eager to prepare for the journey.

Alex liked to hunt, but he loved the chase more than the kill. He loved the exhilaration of the countryside filled with sounds other than those that fell on his ears in the city, and he looked forward to Wednesday and a few days away from the toil of business.

Srinivasan, true to his word, had collected together a party of twenty men and boys and they set out for the terrorised village when the mountains were still shrouded in moving mists and seemed far away. Their way to the village where the attacks had taken place lay alongside a tract of forest on the one hand and a fairly sluggish river on the other. The sides of the river were stippled gold by the sun and a little further away, arrows of light pierced the murky dark of the tangle of jungle plants. Just before reaching the first clearing one of the boys went down to the river and found pug marks from the day before, in the mud at the edge of the water. It was obvious that this was where other animals came to slake their thirst, and if they were to make camp here they might catch more than a glimpse of prey and quarry. They made camp leisurely, but after two days became painfully conscious of the cause of their failure. Biting ants were on the move over the matted floor of the forest and the banks of the river and there was nothing to be done but break camp and trek out into the flatlands where they spent an exhausting day.

After a day in the flatlands they settled down for the night. The fire in the sun which had baked the earth was now gone and in its place was a still coldness, gnawing at tired muscles with a dull ache. Towards dawn a swift wetness came, that seeped into clothes and brought a chill to blistered skin and unease to the sleepers.

Rule Of Thumb

Alex stirred whilst the sky was still a deep, luminous lilac, overshadowed by thin orange wafers of fast changing cloud. He shivered with the cold as he emerged from the makeshift tent and looked out over an expanse of waving, tawny coloured grass, with only a few trees visible. He knew tigers frequently laid up in such places, and wondered if their quarry was out there, twitching his tail in a dawn slumber.

The camp suddenly erupted into life, and within the hour the sun was drying up the sweat as it ran from the pores, the salt from it stinging their bodies with a thousand smarts. Iridescent flies buzzed incessantly in the ears and punctured the skin as the whole party set off across the terrain, the boys using poles to beat the longer grasses, the horses being pressed forward gently.

Courage is to no purpose without intelligence, and Alex was well aware that to hunt a tiger an elephant mount was better than a horse, but Srinivasan insisted that the added danger gave spice to the adventure.

They travelled on through the countryside, noting a number of old temples to Kali, the villages near them abandoned. Once forsaken, the walls and roofs soon became desiccated and forlorn. Red and white ants ate away all trace of the shredded matting and banana fronded roofs, and the jungle moved in on the plantations, garden plots and well worn paths. Here and there frail vestiges of settlements remained covered by the thin tendrils of cucumber and shaded by castor oil or ju-jube tree. A fencing of thorn bushes crazily enclosing an ancient guava tree and rotting banana suckers, gourd shells, hard as teak, hung from the branches of the Palmyra tree (Fan Palm) mute evidence of the spirituous liquor once obtained from the sap.

No gem villages came to light. They debated whether or not to go on. Sunbeams filtered down through the canopy of greenery, casting a dim, smokey violet light, from which there came the vague chatter of monkeys, and the flashes of brilliance from the wings of some bird as it sought refuge in the leaves above their heads. On the fringes of a torpid river, covered with patches of thick green scum and dotted with the barky, log-like poses of alligators, they made camp. Taking care to skirt the green shallows of the water, and well armed with gun and a boy with a gong, they slaked the intolerable thirsts of their mounts, put up tents and fed themselves adequately and quickly, as the night descended around them with a damp and enveloping blackness.

Morning came. Birds began to stir, calling sleepily to each other, insects flitted, buzzed, and whirred, under their quivering canopy of leaves, snakes slithered from holes in the banks of the river and slid into the water. The alligators, blinked and gaped and got ready for the dawn assembly of drinkers.

Rule Of Thumb

The men in the camp began to stir as the first bar of lemony-green light showed between sky and earth. One boy stirred the fire to new life, added more fuel, and a column of smoke went spiralling upwards. Alex left his tent and went towards the larger tent of Srinivasan. There he found him relaxing on a rug, having his limbs massaged by a young native boy.

'What is this? Surely, you are not played out already?'

'I have such cramp in my arms and legs, Alex, I fear I have a fever on me!'

'I am sorry, indeed, to hear that,' replied Alex genuinely alarmed. 'Perhaps we should make for higher and more open ground where there is no miasma from swamps.'

Srinivasan agreed that they should make for a higher ridge, and Alex left him to check over the equipment, as he had found that native boys could be singularly lax in such matters. He found the head boy having a very satisfying scratch by the stout ropes and empty water bottles. Alex instructed him that the water bottles should be filled with cold water which had previously been boiled.

'Yes, verily, Sahib,' agreed the head boy, still sitting calmly.

'It will take time!' snapped Alex. 'Be about it!'

'I am gone, already, Sahib.'

'Aye, verily,' remarked Alex with a wry smile, and went to supervise the work himself.

The opal light of morning was already beginning to change, and Alex knew that in an hour or two the unrelieved sunlight would be beating down on their backs. He felt bored with the whole expedition, although he tried to conceal it by relating witty anecdotes, and showing to Srinivasan the indulgence and tenderness a sick child requires. At last they were on the move and heading for firmer ground. The sun gave out a fierce heat. Srinivasan's horse, puffed and panted as it carried its rider's huge bulk over the clutter of rocks and shrubs, whilst Alex examined the area around through his telescope.

'Would you care to cast an eye over the scene, Srinivasan?' said Alex, offering the instrument. 'We still have to catch that tiger!'

Srinivasan, speechless, waved aside the offered telescope, gracefully conceding Alex the honour.

Sometimes, the group had to make sideways excursions, like ship-tacking when they came to steep trails leading through fallen rocks and rubble. They approached these rocks cautiously as they were aware that vipers often made their homes in the dark crevices between the stones. It was cooler there on the ridge and they decided to stop and refresh themselves. They tethered the horses on short hobble and had only been there for a few minutes, when the horses began to sway and whicker in a state of alarm.

Alex leapt agilely onto an outcrop of rock and then, sinking into a ditch-like hollow, glanced upwards into the chilling glare of a magnificent tiger, whose head hung just above the rim of rocks. The beast sprang down towards Alex. The vague mass turned into a golden glory of claws, fangs, and steel-lined fur. With an incredible turn of speed, Srinivasan took up his rifle and fired, just as the foetid breath of the animal caught Alex full in the face. The beast fell on top of him without a further sound.

Alex lay there, his body distorted and mutilated. Odd thoughts went zinging through his head. There was a clatter besides him and on the rocks over him. He was hardly conscious of their presence, and had but a dim realization of pain as they hoisted him onto a litter and headed back for Srinivasan's house.

Two days later Alex was bedded in Srinivasan's home with genuine feelings of affection and hospitality, but by then a raging fever had clouded his senses and his heart was vibrating with an odd rapidity. On the third day his breathing became laboured. Srinivasan sat at the bedside chafing Alex's still hand. Shantilal kept her distance. She felt annoyed at this intrusion into their lives. She had heard with envy and surprise, Srinivasan's vow to Alex, to revenge his hurts. A vow given in the fervour of gaunt despair, as slow tears fell unregarded down his plump cheeks and into the folds of his embroidered tunic.

On the afternoon of the fourth day, in the room in which Alex lay, a silence suddenly fell. The feeling of relief to his watchers, deepened second by second as they realised that he was no longer struggling for breath. Then to their horror, blood rose up in his throat, and unable to pass the tightly clenched teeth and stretched lips, welled up in the nose and gushed out of his nostrils. The carmine flow was hurriedly wiped away by Jo-Jo's gentle fingers bearing cloths and sponges. Alex's last breath faltered in the blood soaked lungs and whispered dryly out into the perfumed room. A large and gaudy butterfly, until then unnoticed by the others began to flutter around the room, batting against the cool spaces of the window niche.

Then it was free, away into the garden, flittering amongst the heady scents of flowers, dipping over the moist air around the fountains, where a light breeze lifted the winged body and bore it aloft towards the lemon tinted sky where it was lost to sight.

Srinivasan dropped to his knees and raising both arms towards the window, gave a shuddering groan. Shantilal, who was used to him agonising over his acute indigestion, gave him a disapproving stare, and put his anguish down to too much mango pickle or the depravity of his own nature.

Suffering severely from wounded pride because of Srinivasan's friendship with Alex, she felt gratified by the sight of his still body upon the bed. Amiable forbearance had long since ceased to be her strong point. She hoped Srinivasan would now become more attentive to her, as she had never, as his first lady, been in the slightest degree deficient in attention towards him. She felt bitterly that she deserved better.

Srinivasan turned to her and said, 'Alex's daughter must not know how he suffered. Better to think his end was quick, beneath the weight of some fiery, untamed beast, than to portray a death without dignity.'

'How you do chatter on, dear heart,' said Shantilal, helping him to the doorway of the room. 'The child will feel nothing! She may scarcely remember him! She is thousands of miles away.'

'Ah, Shantilal, my dearest love,' he chided, 'distance is of no consequence in matters of feelings. I could guarantee that her father has never been further away from her than a breath's length. What are oceans and continents in the face of such regard?'

After the death of Alex things did not go well with Srinivasan. He received much censure as to the folly of the venture from both native and foreign factions.

Shantilal found that she had been pushed further away from Srinivasan, who brooded and moped about his house, and seemed to have no interest in every day affairs.

Shantilal peered into his room one day to find him laid upon his couch yet again and her temper overcame her. 'I am surprised to see you still distressed at the death of Tiger Dee. You have never been one to take criticism from others, why start now?'

Srinivasan did not answer, and seeing the expression of sadness in his eyes, she crossed the room, and sat besides him on the couch. She petulantly picked up a fan of curled feathers of scarlet, ensconced in the handle of a richly carved tusk of a wild boar. It had been a gift from Alex. She began to waft the air about his face, but he sighed heavily and pushed the waving plume away. She threw it down amongst the brightly coloured cushions, and withdrew a few paces into the room.

She knew his health was failing. His thoughts dwelt on death. He had taken pains making himself ready for it, and made plans for all who were dependent on him. Shantilal seated herself on two large cushions at his feet.

Rule Of Thumb

'I remember the first time Alex came here. You were so proud as you sat viewing him, toying with him. You were a man of substance and of power!'

Srinivasan stretched his hands before him, resting them lightly on his thighs and said, 'I remember well the time he came here. He was defiant yet fearful as he asked to buy the freedom of Nighma, that angel-woman. At first I despised him, but as I came to know him better I began to envy is popularity with others, and his happiness with Nighma, a woman who had never responded to me or my wealth. Then I came to admire him. He had grown fearless in his challenge to every day life. He spoke out for what was right and fair. He brushed aside the unalterable perversity of life with a kind word or a hearty laugh. My life became better for knowing him. Now he is dead, I feel as if all the snows of the mountains of the world, have been heaped upon me. It grieves me to wonder how Dorinda Anne will fare so far from here.'

'She is not my concern,' broke in Shantilal. 'You are my concern! I care for her as little, or less, than I care for the children of the harbour-side.'

'She was a beautiful child.'

'She was not! She was rather plain, although she had a graceful walk for one so young.'

'Ah, Shantilal, I think you saw only her face. To my idiot son she showed her heart. I was there and saw it too! It shone like an opal and burned as a ruby.'

Shantilal put her arms about herself and made herself small, her knees drawn up under her chin, and thought despairingly, 'The old fool! He is grown quite mad.' Srinivasan touched her with the toe of his shoe. 'You know the tiger skin is ready for lining. Have it made ready for Dorinda Anne. It must be lined with a heavy blue felting and a pleated frill all round. The claws must be gilded, and the teeth and fangs cleaned but not enamelled. The eyes must be chosen with care. Not too green and hard looking, nor too golden and mild. He must have an intelligent eye, as like to the real eye.'

'It is a pity you shot him!' Shantilal spat fiercely. 'You could then have sent the live beast to the child. Then, she could have seen him in all his magnificence!' He gave her a push and she fell forward on to her hands and face.

'We will let Dorinda Anne see that her father did not falter beneath the spring of a poor bundle of aged tripe!'

Shantilal rose to her feet. 'As you wish, my love,' she conceded meekly.

A few weeks later Srinivasan became very quiet and pensive. He called Shantilal to him and said in a hoarse whisper, 'All is made ready for my demise which draws close.' She drew away from him stricken with horror. He had spent weeks in preparation for the time he would no longer be there. It had become something of a game to her, and now, she could not face the realization that his death was imminent. She held him around the neck, his head resting in the fold of her arms. 'You must live on! You must! I will breathe life into you!' She attempted to kiss him upon the lips, but he pushed her away. 'Go, my last love. I grow cold.'

'I will give you warmth and breath.'

'No, Shantilal! This time you can not have your way. Be content. Not even the midday sun could warm away the cold in me. It is only habit that makes my heart jump in my ribs. Tell no one what I have said to you. I tell you, to warn you, for of all here, you are the least prepared for life without my presence.'

She left him then, her head bowed low with her unspoken sorrow.

In the early hours of the following day, Srinivasan, awoke in his soft bed and looked around him. 'Alex?' he queried. There was no sound. A chink of moving light, from the unglazed window, alighted on the colourful glazed tiles of the floor and walls of the room. He felt fevered and restless, but he closed his eyes once more and tried to sleep. He stirred again, suddenly, and struggled to sit up. He had heard Alex Deane's voice! He knew that tone. Rich and warm, the voice floated in the dim, violet light, and then was gone in an instant.

'Alex! Alex!' he called throwing off the bed-covers and stepping down to the floor. He stood shakily for a moment before making for the door of the room. He opened it, and tottered, splay-legged out into the corridor. All was quiet. He gathered his remaining strength and tried to hurry along the passage to a further door, his white robe floating out behind him, his bare feet pattering along the cool tiles. 'Alex, Alex, wait for me! I am coming,' he cried out huskily.

Faithful Jo-Jo heard his cries. He went out into the corridor just as Srinivasan came abreast of the heavily carved door.

The door was shut and he beat upon it with weak, and open palms. As he did so his knees gave way, and he slid into a heap, his head resting on the carved tracery. Jo-Jo helped him up, and Srinivasan turned to him complainingly, 'I am shut out! I am shut out!' Jo-Jo picked up his limp frame in his thick muscular arms, and carried him back to the bedroom where Shantilal was waiting. Jo-Jo placed his master gently on the bed. The eyes that looked up were dark and dull. Shantilal, her face wet with recent tears, peeped at him nervously. Jo-Jo leaned over and pulled the folded back lids over the sightless orbs.

'What has happened?' asked Shantilal, simply, as a child might.

'He is no longer shut out,' replied Jo-Jo, bowing reverently to his late master's still form. He left the room quietly, and Shantilal watched him go.

Her face was as empty as her heart as she drove the slim blade of a knife up between her ribs.

Outside, the wheel of day, spun into the world of the living, with a blaze of orange fire.